XINDER RISES

A Tale of Dust and Dreams, 1

JJ HAWKEN

JERICO PRESS

Xinder Rises

Book One
A Tale of Dust and Dreams

Jerico Press
First Published in 2017
Copyright © JJ Hawken 2017

Xinder Rises is written in UK English.

Paperback ISBN-13: 978-1-910134-19-1

EBook ISBN-13: 978-1-910134-20-7

To Edward.

The best bro a brother could have.

DANNY, WEDNESDAY

anny's cupped hands cascaded cold water onto his face, the shock waking him. Wincing, he touched the mark, the nerve endings raw and fleshy. A quarter of an inch, perhaps, as neat as a red underline.

The blade!

Memories rushed in. Danny stared at the rouge on his fingers, then rubbed till it cleared.

It can't be. His initial reaction.

How come? His second.

Danny crashed into the wall, then righted himself and spewed into the toilet.

Why? Why me?

He heard the others downstairs, but their words died before his brain could register what they said. He tried to speak, but the sounds reverberated back, spiralling as though he were in a tunnel.

In the kitchen, the sink and table spun around the room, along with the outline of his sisters and Mrs Puddy.

Tinkling of glass? Raised voices?

Grabbing a jacket, he weaved his way to the door. He needed to breathe, to clear his head. He needed to run.

LUNA

With a tiny flash, Luna uncurled from her fiery, electric blue midriff known as an "infiniti". She stood up on two long, thread-like, spidery legs and looked out over a desolate landscape through large, ovate black eyes. A soft wind whipped around her.

Luna was an Animais; human-like in form with a delicate, smoky textured, silvery-grey outline that melted into the atmosphere around her.

She sniffed at the stale air as she remembered how, long ago, grasses, trees, and beasts filled the pink, green, and ochre-coloured landscapes of the planet of Genartus.

Carpeted in spiders, this area of Genartus was once known as the arachnid lands. A vast area of mixed terrains filled with spiders.

Animais had harvested spider webs in these lands from which dream powders, or dusts, had been made into dreams of love, kindness, and inventiveness. Dreams skillfully crafted for all living things.

These lands, though hostile to most and rarely visited

by other species, had been bountiful to Animais and beneficial to all living creatures, notably humans.

On this exact spot, an area had once been cleared and a tall, open-roofed structure had been hastily constructed. Its outer perimeter was like a giant wooden palisade, and from afar it looked liked a fortress. Its outer walls were high enough and thick enough to shield it from the lurking eyes and ears of even the tallest and craftiest of beasts.

A circular table made from one slice of the trunk of a pink-wooded mammoth tree filled the middle. Luna remembered how the Council of One Hundred had debated the fate of the worlds.

Like many young Animais, Luna had sat in the sky above the Council, invisible to all except other Animais. Nestled on the rim of her mother's own electrical midriff, her infiniti, Luna had bathed in the warm blue energy currents that splayed over her as she watched the drama unfold.

The humans and animals and trees had argued and raged before finally putting their differences to rest.

Luna recalled the desperate faces of the Founders of Genartus as they heard the charges against them. These five, four men and a lady, moulded by the irresistible energies of the universe, forged in birth from the collisions of sand and water and gas at the very beginning, were found to be guilty of corrupting all life.

The Founders had yearned for forgiveness, demanding an end to divination, begging them to find a way of destroying their immortality. They did not seek pity, just atonement for their part in the destruction. Tears had rolled down their cheeks, Luna remembered, as they accepted their punishment; all bar one.

That man was Xinder, from the planet of Halaria. Xinder, who threatened to freeze every human being on

Halaria if he was burned. Xinder, whose light blue eyes exuded a dark, menacing power, and who held a magic beyond that of others. Xinder, who felt his fate did not justify his actions.

Luna uncurled a long finger, turning the tip into a needle and then a pincer before dipping it into her fizzling infiniti, feeling the soothing mass of swirling energy within. The old memories were returning.

Xinder had delivered on his promise.

The moment flames had licked at his flesh, his spell cast all Halarian people into domed, crystal-like puddles. Devoid of form and starved of magic, Xinder had never been able to turn the Halarians back. Frozen in time, they still wait for his return.

Luna had watched the Frozen Lord, as he was now known, roaming his palace as a burnt spirit. Always looking, never giving up his futile search to find and restore his magic. A desperate hope burned from within his spirit-shell, although, as millennia after millennia wore on, she'd felt his vibrations move to frustration and thereon to anger.

Luna glided through the air like a ghost, her limbs floating on particles of air. She reached the top of the great stone and looked out over the wastelands.

Strange, she thought, how events had turned out. The world of Genartus in front of her was now devoid of life, while Halaria, not even visible as a pinprick in the sky, was starved of people. All the while, Earth had trudged on, oblivious to wars and the planets they had yet to discover.

Perhaps for this reason, Animais had become deeply associated with Earth. Nothing thrilled Luna more than to sneak away and watch humans dream. It thrilled her to see how they twisted and reacted, how the dusts seemed to give them hope and creativity, and fill their world with meaning.

And, now, as if out of the blue, the mysterious energies of the universe had awoken.

The inscription on the huge rock beside her had the instructions. Luna held her old, wiry arms out into the sky, feeling for vibrations. Trying to see if she could find *answers* for there was no point in denying these forces, these changes.

The fate of Animais, the destiny of animals, plant life, and every living being on Earth was now in the hands and minds of three humans under the protection of Mazeen the Great, the elder of the Founders.

When Luna gave the First Dream, these three would be named as the Sacrum. They would have seven days to fulfil their tasks and demonstrate the success of the current human race.

Fail, and all life on Earth would perish. A new epoch would begin.

DANNY

Danny ran across the courtyard to the track and cut down towards the river. He hurtled along animal tracks, weaved through long grass, leapt over fallen branches, jumped foxholes, and untangled brambles from his clothes as he ducked, crashed, and sped through thickets and bushes.

In the semi-darkness beneath the rusty canopy, he approached a huge round boulder three times his height. In his mind's eye he measured the distance and set off at a sprint. At the last moment, he sprang up and grasped hold of a stony outcrop just high enough to haul him to the top. He sat down and reached into his bag, drank from his water bottle, and swirled the liquid round his mouth.

Breathing hard, his heart thumping in his chest, Danny watched the sun rise like red-hot coals under the base of the vast black cloud jettisoned above.

It had happened, it had really happened, he thought, fingering the tiny nick on his chin. Why else would such a neat laceration be there? He recalled the moment as clearly as he could remember.

He'd been told he had to do something horrific, beyond imagination.

But why him, of all people?

He stared out over the valley, his eyes drawn to the candy shapes in the village of Sutton, perched just above the floodplain at the foot of the moors. He noticed the rugged, menacing, dark forest and jagged rocks that jutted out of the steep slopes like gnarled, angry faces. In contrast, manicured, cartoon-coloured, light and dark green stripes of the school playing fields lay on the valley floor.

Man's doing down below, he thought. *God's above.*

So many questions crowded his brain.

What if he didn't survive? What if he didn't find this stupid cave? Who was that woman?

That was unclear, but the ghost said it would be back and that's all he remembered from last night. It didn't mention a time, or a place, only that it would be back.

Danny cast his eye over the large weeping willows that marked the position of the meandering river. To him they guarded the village like sentries positioned at perfect intervals. Sutton looked stronger, and more important, than the old, monastic-looking school whose high, square tower rose high into the sky. It was, he thought, a perfect contrast to the river curving elegantly in front.

In the distance, the soaring cliffs of the moorlands protected the village like a shield. He could see how Sutton had fostered a sense of security with its toffee-coloured chunks of masonry and loophole arrow-slit holes. Balancing this were subtle lines of symmetry; the intricate round, rose window pixelated with stained glass resting above a meaty, carved oak door.

Right now, Danny thought, *he needed a shield of his own. But where would that come from?*

Alert to the sound of a twig snapping in the undergrowth he glanced behind him. Then, he looked to his right towards the sheer rock face that climbed high into the sky.

No eagles. No hawks or harriers circling or soaring like model aircraft.

He listened.

Strange.

An almost intolerable silence.

He flicked his wrist, glanced at the dial and sighed.

If he didn't hurry, he'd be late – again.

Standing up, he stretched his arms wide before sliding down the stone curvature and tumbling over and over until he collided with the thick trunk of a larch.

Danny brushed himself down, feeling a multitude of soon-to-be bruises birthing in the tissue under his skin.

Recklessly he ran, weaving a fresh path through the undergrowth towards the silver band of the river that cut through the red and yellow apron of autumn leaves towards the school.

GUDA

Guda sat alone, floating, watching planet Earth spinning, as it always did.

Every so often a tiny burst of light, invisible to any other creature flashed for a nano second. He mused that he was not the only Animais taking time from dream-giving to reflect upon the news Luna had given them.

Guda noted Earth's moon rising in the near distance against the endless expanse of space.

Twisting, as if his leg were made of rubber, he dabbled a slender foot in his infiniti, feeling the warmth from the blue electrical field in his middle, bathing it.

Was there still a need for inspirational, magical dreams? Demand for dreams that offered insight or inspired change or for dreams that elicited love and joy?

Guda cranked his small, round head, and stared at a distant star, as he replaced one leg in his infiniti with the other.

If dreams were nightmares, at least the Animais would still exist to knit and spin them? Their sole purpose as dream-givers could not end simply because there were no longer any joyful dreams. So long as *any dream* could be given, he reasoned, from *any* powder blended from *any* spider's web, surely the Animais would continue to have a purpose?

This, he realised was the choice.

He thought of the boy. The boy who knew nothing.

What had fate in mind for him, and for his sisters? Immediate death?

It was clear that Mazeen had failed in his task to nurture and train the Sacrum, if indeed these children were the Sacrum.

Even Luna could tell Mazeen was no longer the man he once was. The old man's sharp mind was but a shadow. Earth had drowned him in a wallowing pool of denial and apathy.

He'd tried to explain that it must be a mistake but Luna would not listen. She swept aside the doubters.

The words on the great stone could not be twisted. They were as clear to her as space was black. He'd visited the monolith to see the words for himself. The message was exactly as Luna said:

The three Sacrum of the human race live under the protection of Mazeen the Great on Earth.
They alone must receive the First Dream.

Surely, Mazeen was in the wrong place, caring for wrong people.

Guda noticed a pinprick of yellow light coming from a spot on the Moon's dark surface. The birthing of Animais, he realised, hatching from cocoons in caverns dotted around the universe. More Animais, to nurture, guide, and instruct in the art of dream-giving for the booming populations on Earth.

It made him reflect on what Luna had told them. Three Sacrum, selected to represent mankind's dominance of life on Earth, she'd said. With seven earth days to fulfil a series of tasks.

But the Sacrum were children! Absurd!

If they didn't die at the very first hurdle it would take them seven years, not seven days.

Guda reached into his infiniti with one hand and weighed up his last dream dusts from the planet of Genartus. Forty dreams, he estimated; more if he thinned them out. But did he really want to dilute such a precious cargo?

Guda remembered how dream powders, or dusts, had once lain in huge conical mounds, brought in to the magnificent chamber by every pair of animal or beast or Genartan tree that was leaving for Earth.

If these children were the measure of life on the planet, then perhaps Earth deserved its outcome.

Knowing that this could be the last time he knit and span the wonderful dreaming dusts of Genartus, Guda inverted through his infiniti to seek out dreamers for the very last time.

Danny sprinted along the towpath, over the bridge, and across the playing fields. As he neared the chapel steps, he wiped his brow with his cuff and brushed himself down as he caught his breath.

'You stink,' Olivia said, intercepting him and forcing him to the side. 'You can't go in there.'

Danny shook his head. 'Wasn't my fault. I fell over a couple of times. Might have landed in something.'

'Dan, go home and change. You're so embarrassing.'

Danny recoiled. 'No way. I want to know if Ani's in the team. It's unmissable.' He pulled up a sock for Olivia's benefit and, glancing at the tower clock, took off, slipping in moments before the oak door boomed shut.

He ran, head down, almost bent double, over the large flagstones until he found his row, squeezed in to his class position and sat down. Further along, he noticed Anika chatting to her friends, some turning off their phones. He caught her eye.

She frowned back, and mouthed something at him.

Was it about the team?

She jabbed a finger.

Or about him?

He smiled back, weakly.

For a brief moment, he experienced the intrusion of being watched, similar to the sensation he'd felt the previous night. His instinct was right. On the platform at the far end of the hall stood Mr Wynn-Garry, the headmaster, whose eyes were boring into him like lasers.

Danny's heart sank. Those who had even the tiniest scuffs, or tears, or buttons missing, were being entered into his dreaded green book. Maybe Olivia wasn't being petty, after all.

He gave himself a quick once-over. Appalling. He had about three seconds to get up, run, and sneak through the side entrance.

Instead, he grappled with his tie, drew up his socks, and dragged a hand roughly through his hair, removing the tendrils of a creeper, several strands of grass and a piece of bark. Before he could tidy himself further, a familiar voice boomed through the hall.

'Good morning, school,' it said. 'Please rise.'

As the pupils had done for twenty-five years, everyone stood up.

WYNN-GARRY

Mr Wynn-Garry patted the breast pocket of his coarse tweed suit and raised his thick eyebrows. Twenty-five years he'd been at the school, almost to the day. Twenty years as headmaster, and his performance every morning was almost the same now as it was then.

'Quiet ... please,' he said. *Isn't it strange*, he thought, *how noise levels always seem to rise as conversations rush to a conclusion?*

He removed his glasses from his round, ruddy nose and inspected the students.

'Thank you. Sit down.'

Two hundred and seventy-two pupils parked on the hard wooden benches lined up row upon row, the noise whispering into the safety of the huge, vaulted ceiling above. From weighty cross-beams, large chandelier lights dangled from thick, black metal chains, illuminating those below with a dim, almost church-like glow.

From their tall portraits on the sides, former headmasters eyed this generation of children sternly. While etched onto dark wooden panels running around the perimeter of the hall, the names of former scholars, captains, and musi-cians reminded the children of past glories.

Wynn-Garry stared out over the throng and cleared his throat.

'School dress!'

Danny felt a strong urge to disappear.

'I see some of you shaking,' Wynn-Garry said, smiling and staring around the room. 'And rightly so,' he contin-ued. 'There has been a marked deterioration since the beginning of the term. After leave, those who fail to comply with every part of the school uniform code will discover detention. Now, to show you what I'm talking about, no one is shaking more this morning than Sutton goalkeeper, Danny Delaux.'

A cheer went up. 'Delaux, please stand.'

Danny sat stone-still in disbelief.

Not again.

He felt a jab in his back and then another from the side.

'Come on, Danny. Up you get,' the headmaster prompted.

Danny regarded his worn shoes, and, taking a deep breath, rose from behind the frame of his friend Ryan Williams. Every single pair of eyes stared at him. Danny could hear girls giggling nearby. His face reddened, the heat of his blush growing by the second. He didn't dare look up.

'Danny, I hate to make an example of you,' Wynn-Garry continued, 'but this morning you have beaten your spec-tacular record of being a complete and utter shambles.'

Cautious laughter flittered around the hall.

'It is almost as if you fail to realise that a dress-code actually exists. In fact, you are almost the perfect example of how not to come to school.' He addressed the throng. 'Let us take a closer look at our specimen. Your shoes are filthy; you have no belt and, as a result, we can see rather colourful underwear. Your socks are around your ankles because there are no elastic garters to hold them up. These are torn to bits like everything else.'

Wynn-Garry paused as laughter pealed into the rafters. 'Your shirt has lost buttons, your tie is halfway across your chest and, I'm not sure how this happened, but you happen to be wearing the wrong coloured jersey! Please turn around, Delaux.' Danny shifted.

'Yes, just as I suspected,' Wynn-Garry continued. 'Blazer ripped and, of course, your hair is not only too long, but a decent imitation of a mop head.'

Danny feigned a smile while others pointed and grinned.

On Wynn-Garry's instruction, while hopelessly attempting to pull his attire together, he sat down and glanced up towards his sister, Olivia.

Her hard, cold stare drilled into him. He spotted her grinding her jaw. *Never a good sign.*

Wynn-Garry's tone softened as he smiled, showing his small, tea-stained teeth.

'Let this be a lesson to you all, but especially to you, Danny. Today, and today only, because you're part of our famous football team, you are excused. And this, of course, leads me on to the other, main item on this morning's agenda.'

With these words, the mood in the hall lightened, and the noise level increased. Along the row, nibbling her nails, Anika stared at the floor.

The headmaster raised an arm for quiet.

'Most of you are aware of the situation. As a small school, our selection for teams is limited and I regrettably endorsed that a girl could play in the boys' team. As you know, this team has gone on to great things to the tremendous credit of our school. However, I ... we, were found out.'

The headmaster pulled a letter from his breast pocket and waved it in the air.

'Let me interpret the relevant parts of this communication I received yesterday from the president of our Football Association.' He nudged his glasses onto the bridge of his nose and thumbed his way down the page.

'What they are saying, is this: if Anika Delaux has played in ten matches in a row this season, they are willing to be lenient. Well, anyone, has she?'

He spied a hand from the back.

'Yes. Sas Smith. Do you have the answer?'

'Ani's played in twelve, sir. Thirteen if you add the German touring team.'

'Thank you, Miss Smith.'

A buzz passed around the room.

'*It is our opinion,*' he read, '*that Sutton School has severely abused the goodwill of this league. However, not one opposition team member reported or noticed Miss Delaux's disguise until we received an anonymous letter.*'

A hissing noise developed and several heads turned to the right.

Mr Wynn-Garry continued, this time up a gear.

'*As this happened before the Under 14 Cup Final, and Miss Delaux has played in every round, we have decided to impart the following. Should Sutton School win, then with the full backing of the Football Association, Miss Delaux will be allowed to continue playing for Sutton School and the rules changed with immediate effect—*'

Cheers filled the air.

'*However,*' Wynn-Garry said, and he raised his hand for quiet, '*should Sutton lose,*' and here, his voice went so quiet that you could almost hear his forehead crease, *then it will be Miss Delaux's last game for Sutton school.*

Silence spread over the pupils as they listened to the headmaster.

Wynn-Garry picked Anika out of the assembly and spoke directly to her.

'So there we have it, Ani. I have spoken with the authorities to make sure we are clear. You will play in tomorrow's final against Newton, but with no disguise. Do you understand?'

She nodded.

'Good,' he said. 'Regardless of the outcome, this doesn't mean your sporting career is over,' he said. 'No, no, no. Not by any means. It would appear that your exploits on the field have been, "talent-spotted". After half term,' and here he slowed, a smile spreading over his face, 'you have been invited to join the national team's training squad.'

Gasps shot out from the assembly floor.

'Yes, indeed. It is a great honour that you've been picked to train with your country, the youngest player ever to be invited. Anika, we are extremely proud of you.'

Applause rallied and Wynn-Garry let it continue for its deserved time.

'There we have it, Ani. There is plenty for you to look forward to after half term even if it means you don't play for Sutton School.' He dramatically thumped the lectern, making the juniors in front of him jump. 'So, let's make sure that we jolly well do win and we change these silly rules forever!'

GUDA

Guda flashed out of his infiniti, landing in a huge cavern. He hovered in mid-air, extended his arms wide and switched, by thought alone, out of his invisible mode.

Suddenly, a flurry of activity appeared, like magic, in front of him. Animais were dashing here and there across the sky, blue flashes denoting the arrival of some and the departure of others.

He turned his wiry neck upward towards the roof of the cave, and found it packed with yellowy-brown cocoons. They sat in layer upon layer like the neat chambers of a beehive.

Walking through the air, he passed younger Animais, who turned or bowed their heads. Good to see the old signs of respect for the Animais Elders, he thought.

He noted a flash, and Guda realised an Animais had joined him.

'Juno,' Guda said, her fingers vibrating together so fast as to form words. 'I see you.'

'And I you, Guda,' she replied, her vibrations softer. 'You have come to see the birthing of the young Animais?'

'Indeed. By the look of their movement, their time is close,' he said, indicating lines of Animais perched in the air. 'See how many others crowd the chamber?'

'It has always been so,' Juno replied. 'They are our future. And what kind of future do we leave them?' her vibrations dimmed. 'Do you know who the Sacrum are?' she said.

'I am aware,' he responded, 'that they are young. But, of course, it is nature's will—'

'There!' cried a voice. 'Look! Their sun moves in line with the entrance, it is starting.'

A sudden flurry of activity began, with blue lights flashing everywhere. Guda and Juno were almost blinded as thousands of Animais flashed into the chamber, unfurling from their infinitis and changing into their visible forms as they did so.

The entire cavern buzzed with vibrations.

From the cocoons high above, one chamber wriggled and shook more violently than before. Then another, and, before long, multiple cocoons along the length of the huge ceiling rattled, cracked, and split exposing tiny Animais.

Then, the entire ceiling seemed to open up like popcorn and before long, the tiny, stick-like creatures flapped about like new-born chicks, clawing at the air as if swimming in a soup.

The onlookers, Animais of all shapes and sizes, vibrated words of love and encouragement.

'Fall! Jump into the light!' said a youthful, black Animais nearby.

More and more Animais appeared in the chamber. Vibrations increased.

Thousands of shells cracked apart, sections of their nests floating to the ground like loose strands of straw.

To the mock-horror of the crowd of Animais gathered

around, the tiny creatures began to fall, plummeting head over heels towards the rocky ground beneath them. A collective gasp shot out from the watching mass of Animais.

Guda noticed how Juno covered her black eyes.

As they fell from the dark roof into the bright sunlight, a sudden bolt of yellow light flashed in, enveloping the first hatchlings in circles of iridescent light, stopping them exactly where they were.

Then, as if a firework display had gone into overload, the remaining hatchlings tumbled through the air and into the light. As the energy bathed them these fledglings were now Animais. Borne of light and energy. Ready for a life of making dreams.

Guda too, vibrated his feelings, offering the newcomers strength, love, and a long life.

The energy of the creation of life, he mused. Such a beautiful thing.

He was about to flip into his infiniti when an idea of immense magnitude slipped neatly into his mind. Picking his way across the sky, he leaned into the jagged rock-edges of the huge cavern, out of sight.

This last Earth night, he'd taken Xinder, the Frozen Lord, to see the boy. Every time he thought of it, his legs rattled. Initially, he'd gone to ask the spirit what he thought about having children as Sacrum. After all, he thought, if anyone could remember and comprehend the tasks ahead, it was, he suspected, Xinder.

Guda recalled how he had flipped out of his infiniti onto the balcony of the ballroom of the old palace. He'd looked over the once bustling rock city of Halar, capital of Halaria, and its renowned stone formations. Even for an Animais, the dramatic cityscape, with its huge craggy buttes that soared into the air like icebergs, and the deep canyon that circumnavigated it, filled him with wonder. He remembered the cacophony of noise rising up from the narrow streets. How the rock faces above were perforated with neat, square holes of ancient dwellings. And further on he noted the fertile lands that bordered the wide, twisting river that snaked towards distant forests and the sea beyond.

Now, the only sounds were the echoes of the squawks of large birds, redundant from their past lives of flying people from one great rock to the next.

These birds inhabited roof tops and old cliff houses, their wide, messy nests formed from debris and branches plucked from the river.

Many of the city's house-caves were overrun with creepers. The diamond, ruby and emerald stones found naturally in the rock that once sparkled like a million candles in the moonlight, was dim and cracked. Forgotten and unloved.

And then there was the sprawling palace that stretched above the face of the canyon. The way it overlooked the ruddy, sandy-coloured rocks reminded him of a beast who had sucked the life out of the city below.

Although his flesh had long been destroyed, Xinder's spirit loomed large because he could never truly die. When Guda arrived in Halar, he had quickly picked out Xinder's low vibrations.

He stood next to him, invisible, and was surprised by Xinder's brusque, hostile, and bitter manner. And his endless questions.

Later, in return for information on the trials of the Sacrum, he'd shown Xinder the Animais' secret of their infiniti.

When Xinder realised what it meant, the former Founder's mood lifted. And when Guda had told Xinder about the three children who were Sacrum, the ghost had thundered that this was impossible.

To test the Animais, Xinder had demanded to go to the Sacrum to see the boy for himself. Not long after this, Xinder, the blind spirit, had faced the Sacrum the humans called Danny.

Guda needed to think. Turning invisible, he flashed his head through his *infiniti*, sending him in an instant to his favourite place several miles above the Earth.

As he hovered in space, he remembered how he'd watched the ghost, Xinder, with the boy in the night. Watched the ghost produce a knife and flick his chin. Watched how the ghost had marvelled at the spot of blood.

And all the while, the boy's eyes bulged. Disbelieving.

Xinder, he thought, had a kind strength ordinary ghosts did not possess. The way he could carry objects for a certain length of time, pull things, lacerate with his small knife.

But a thought had nestled into his mind and it had refused to budge. And now, as he floated alone above the blue and white orb below him, he thought about it deeply.

What if one of the Sacrum might somehow ally with Xinder?

Perhaps with this boy Danny?

Why did this idea sound so right and yet feel so horribly wrong? The more he thought it through, the more excited and more fearful he became until he realised he knew exactly what he had to do.

Guda felt his *infiniti* expanding as the enormity of his mission dawned upon him.

After eons, the *Animais*, the most lasting species created at the dawn of time, would no longer be neutral in the ways of the universes.

But it must be done, he thought, *for the benefit of all.*

2

FITZPATRICK, WEDNESDAY

Fitzpatrick watched Anika heading down the assembly row. As she neared he thrust out a leg, stopping her in her tracks. Shrugging, Anika promptly kicked his shin hard enough to hear a whimper.

'I only wanted to say congratulations,' he said, rubbing his leg.

'Yeah, right.' Anika sneered, looking down at him. Then, as if a thought had suddenly entered her mind, she whispered. 'Know what, Fitz, you fancy me, don't you?'

Fitzpatrick's nose seemed to expand sideways, a look of utter incredulity on his face. He reddened.

Ryan Williams flashed his friendly, toothy smile at her from the row in front.

'Ani, you are bloody hilarious,' he said, leaning in from the row behind him. 'If it's any help, I fancy you!'

She turned and winked. 'You like everyone,' she said, as she found herself whisked away by her fans.

Ryan turned to Fitzpatrick, his large eyes bulging with excitement. 'Kicked by a girl, Fitzy. Now, that shouldn't be painful for a big, tough boy like you?'

'You're asking for it, Williams,' Fitzpatrick spat.

'Fine,' Ryan replied, 'Anytime,' he whispered. 'Just you and me.'

DANNY

Danny draped an arm around his twin Anika. 'What was that about, with Fitzy?'

Anika ran her hands through her hair. 'Oh, nothing, usual jerk-stuff.' She smiled cheekily at her brother and sighed. 'Why does Fitzpatrick hate me so much?'

Danny rubbed his freckled nose and laughed. 'Because he's jealous of you. And because you booted him off the team.'

Anika shook her head. 'But he was always giving away fouls and kicking people ... and that was last year—'

'He's like an elephant who never forgets—'

'Well, it's ridiculous,' she complained, 'elephant or not.'

Danny grabbed his sister playfully by the waist. 'Strange thing though, the way he looks at you,' he said, smirking.

'Never! Although I did mention something - as a joke! Ryan thought it was hilarious. I'd never go out with that freak, even if you paid me!'

Danny grinned and glanced over to the far end of the hall, where Fitzpatrick was talking to his friends. They locked eyes for a moment, then Fitzpatrick reached into his pocket for his mobile.

Danny turned back to his sister, concerned. 'Probably a mistake to kick him. Other people do actually feel pain in their legs, even if you don't—'

'I wonder,' Anika said, staring airily into the distance, 'would Fitzy even know me if I didn't play football? I mean, is there another side to him? How did he end up being such a knob?'

Danny shrugged. 'You know what, Fitzpatrick's all right. He's got problems—'

'Yeah, right?'

'Seriously. He told me about it in a session of detention.'

'I don't believe you.'

'It's true. He made me swear never to tell anyone.'

'Well, go on, then,' Anika urged, nudging him. 'You can tell me.'

'I can't, it's a secret.'

'Don't be silly,' Anika implored. 'He told me yesterday his friends are going to kick the life out of me.'

'So. It's still no.'

'*Yes*,' Anika insisted. 'For curiosity's sake, and because it's sometimes better to know your enemy more closely than you know your friends.'

Danny wavered for a second and shook his head, even if Anika did have a point. 'Sorry.'

'*Pleeease*,' Anika begged.

'No.'

'*Pleeease*, Tassel.'

'God. OK,' he sighed. 'As long as you swear you abso-lutely won't tell anyone. And don't call me that name.'

Anika wobbled her head inconclusively.

'I mean it,' Danny said, 'don't breathe a word.' He eyed

her carefully. 'If he finds out he'll rip off my arms, suck my eyes out and give them to Olivia on a stick.'

'Yeah, yeah, I know. Not a soul. I promise.'

'OK,' he began, reluctantly, wondering how he'd given in quite so easily. 'The thing is, Fitzpatrick's parents died very suddenly when he was little. He never talks about it. And now he lives with his aunt, who he can't stand. There—'

'That's awful,' Anika said, her eyes wide. 'How?'

'What do you mean ... how?'

'Did they die?'

'Oh, I see,' he said. 'One night, driving along in an open-top car way up on the edge of the moors, they hit something, a deer, a fox – no one really knows.' Danny's voice turned to a whisper. 'The rest is properly grim.'

'Go on,' Anika said.

Danny looked over his shoulder, and noticed Fitzpatrick exiting at the far end of the hall. 'Apparently, the car skidded off the road, smashing into rocks as it plummeted into a ravine and blew up. Charred, disjointed remains were found scattered weeks later.'

Anika whistled. 'My God, I can see why he doesn't want anyone to know.'

'The worst bit is that it took several weeks before the car was found. And then, they discovered the bones of only one body.'

'No! That's terrible,' Anika said, staring at the floor. 'You like him a bit, don't you?'

'Yeah, I suppose, apart from when he's a jerk to you two.'

'Well then, come on, tell me more, I mean he's probably organising my death right now.'

Danny ran a hand through his hair. 'Beneath all that

macho stuff he's quite soft – it's a barrier he puts up to protect himself, well, that's what his shrink says—'

'*Shrink?*' Anika blurted. 'He has a shrink?'

A few heads turned their way. 'Yes, shrink, psychiatrist, whatever – keep your voice down.'

'They're not doing a particularly good job.'

Danny shot his twin a look. 'Tell me about it. He seems to snap in and out. I mean, in detention, when he said all this, he cried buckets and went on and on about wanting a normal life with a normal family. And then he thumped me really hard on the shoulder and ordered me not to tell anyone. Remember that massive bruise I had when I said I'd fallen out of a tree?'

'Oh yeah, I thought that was a bit odd.'

He shook his head. 'I couldn't move my arm for a week. He's sad, bored, and to be honest, lonely. Everyone hates him, and he knows it.'

'Even those sidekicks Jackson and Pulse?'

'Those freaks pretend they're best mates, but it's fear that glues them together. Ever seen how they jump to attention when he's around or their heads get cracked? One moment he's charming and funny, the next he's pure evil. It's like a switch flicks in his head – and he's strong for his age – the only boy who can match him is Williams—'

'Yeah, I noticed sparks flying between them earlier,' she said. 'But, Dan, why does Fitzy like you?'

'Because I'm probably not worth beating up.' Danny said, raising his eyebrows. 'And because I don't deliberately *piss him off.*'

Anika thumped him playfully on the arm. 'He's a loser, Dan. Why doesn't he try being nice for a change?'

'Apparently it's something to do with offloading emotional pain. That's why Wynn-Garry and the teachers leave him alone so he can do what he likes; they're terrified he'll go even further off the rails. I mean, think about it, if our parents got killed we'd probably go a bit nuts, although to be fair,' and he pinched Anika on the cheek, 'you're almost there.'

She smiled, sarcastically. 'Our parents are never around, so it's almost the same thing,' she said, a frown slipping onto the corners of her mouth.

Danny was glad that he wasn't the only one who missed them. 'Are you sure you're alright, you know, about the match?'

'Yeah,' she said. 'Thanks, Dan.'

'Another thing, Ani. Do you remember,' he began cautiously, sensing his moment, 'anything about your nightmare last night?'

'Which one?' she said too quickly.

'Put it this way, you woke me up.'

She looked confused. 'Did I? Was it loud?'

'Yeah! The entire Vale of York are waiting outside ready to beat you up. Ani, you screamed your head off – I thought you might remember, that's all. Wondered if you were OK?'

Anika shook her head. 'Now you mention it, I did have a nightmare about being in the middle of a storm.'

'And that's it?'

'And finding three eggs in a cave lined with totally random pictures.' She pulled a face and laughed. 'Crazy, huh? If I'm honest, it's a bit of a blur.'

Danny reeled. His face dropping. Eventually, he spoke. 'But nothing about me and, perhaps, the small matter of a murder?'

'A murder, Dan? Nah.'

'Sure?' Danny felt himself reddening.

'Yeah, think so. Why?' she thumped him gently. 'Was that scene this morning something to do with this? Mrs

Puddy's furious with you. And as for Olivia... So, tell me, who've you been bumping off?'

'It's not like that,' he replied, struggling to explain it. 'You see, I've had this recurring nightmare...' Danny petered out as if was too painful to broach.

'Actually, Dan—' she started, tentatively.

But Anika was interrupted by the figure of Mr Wynn-Garry blocking out the light. 'Anika, Danny, there you are. Now, where is that sister of yours?'

'Over here,' Olivia said, rushing towards them. 'Been showing how my project works for Mrs Douglas. I don't think she knows the slightest thing about paleomagnatism,' and she turned her eyes up as if reaching for the correct term.

'Her grasp of the matter is extremely *loose*, to say the least.'

GUDA

Guda flipped into his infiniti, arriving in the next moment on the planet of Halaria.

Wasn't it strange, he thought, how all the inhabited planets had been so similar, but then so utterly different. How Assyria and Cush had been vibrant places bathed in a richness of plants and sparkling seas, living mountains and animals that were happy both on land and in the seas' great depths. And how Earth embodied a range of static options. The trees whose roots remained fastened to the soil, the mountains who moved like sleepy tortoises, and sands which lay flat and lifeless on the ground.

Then there was Halaria. In every corner there were marvels of nature: towering rock formations from vivid blues, to ochre reds, to sparkly greys. Moving forests of colour co-ordinated trees, and the luminescent waters of a silver sea. Not to mention the rivers that defied gravity and chose to run, like snakes, above the land, or the snow and rain that covered the rock cities in multi-coloured droplets like confetti.

Guda remembered the golden ceiling and the glittering chandeliers that sparkled so brightly that people dared not look at them. He remembered the windows cut from jewels and the polished floors made from intricate patterns of coloured gemstones and shaded timbers. The wall of rock that made up one entire length of the palace, with clear, sparkling waters washing down its side like a waterfall.

Now, a veil of grey dust and grime smothered it like a thick blanket.

The Animais walked through the air feeling for Xinder's vibration. Soon, Guda found himself facing a huge piece of furniture with hundreds upon hundreds of drawers lined up row after row in neat columns.

A drawer opened, its contents spilling all over the ground.

It was Xinder, searching through his vast stores of precious stones and jewellery, looking for his branchwand.

'Who's there?' Xinder called out. 'Which rapscallion of a rascal is it? I'll have you. I'll have you right and proper when I find it.' Another drawer dived through the air, splintering on impact, diamonds splaying into the dust. 'Because, thief, when I get my branchwand back, I'll have just enough magic to turn you into a vile piece of slime.'

Guda materialised above Xinder's head, his opaque outline shimmering, his blue infiniti spraying from his midriff.

Xinder sensed it. 'Who are you and what do you want? I may be blind, but I see things. Do not underestimate me.'

'It is I, Guda, the Animais.'

Xinder thought about this for a little while. 'The Animais, again?' he said at length. 'Well, well, well, you're back. It is lucky I am blind so I cannot look upon your ugly body.' He floated a little further down. 'All this exertion exhausts me.'

'You talked with the Sacrum,' Guda said. 'What do you think?'

Xinder sniffed the air. 'I do not believe that those weak humans on earth are Sacrum? They are merely children.'

'It is as I said,' Guda replied.

'They have no magic, nor do they possess a sense of nature. IT IS WRONG! You jest, Animais,' he yelled. 'Tell me, foul sorcerer of dreams, who are the real Sacrum? Where are these strong, mighty men, blessed with power and incantations? Huh, tell me.'

Guda plucked his way across the air in silence and then spoke. 'Those protected by Mazeen become Sacrum. It has always been so. I have seen the writing. Even if the old wizard has forgotten it.'

'That's as may be,' Xinder snorted. 'It was always a foolish idea. You wish to tell me something, don't you?' he asked.

'On Earth, the clouds are building, Xinder, the sky is darkening—'

Xinder went quiet. 'Then you do not lie,' he said, his voice barely above a whisper.

'I come with a suggestion,' Guda began. 'The final part of the First Dream will soon be given—'

Xinder roared. 'While I am stuck here alone in this empty, dying land, the planet of Genartus may be reborn and inflict more useless creations on the worlds. It is diabolical.'

Two drawers flew out at the same time, sailed through the air and joined the heap of smashed wood on the ground.

Xinder floated to the ground and peered through the debris in silence.

'They will not succeed,' he said, softly. 'They require wisdom, strength and cunning —decades of learning and years of understanding charms. Physical training to the highest degree. But these infants are less than twenty years old. They do not even understand what is shown to them in their dreams. Is that right, Animais?'

'Yes.'

'They will never make it past the storm.'

'It is my conclusion, also,' Guda said.

'And what of Mazeen?'

'He wallows. He has grown old. He remembers nothing,' the Animais said. 'Earth has mellowed him. He may be more of a hindrance to the Sacrum, than a help.'

Xinder groaned. 'So, ugly Animais, why have you returned?'

'I can aid you,' Guda answered, his fingers vibrating the sound. 'It is time for a change.'

'Then, Animais, you have my ear.'

Guda took his time. 'The supply of dream-powders from Genartus that were stored in the great Atrium have ended. Now, we knit and spin from powders made from the spider webs on Earth and in Halaria.'

Xinder sounded genuinely surprised. 'Animais stored dream-powders from Genartus for all this time?'

'Yes. These are the dream-powders that nourish us and the creatures we give them to.'

'And so, Animais, by taking me to the boy Sacrum, you gambled they will fail?'

'Yes,' Guda replied. 'To me, their failure is as clear as air.'

Xinder sighed. 'What can I do? I was cut down from being a great man, a warrior, an artist, a lover and a prince to a restless spirit with the strength of a faun,' Xinder moaned. 'Yes, I have way more sway than those vile ghosts I see from time to time, but I have neither eyes for magic nor enough physical strength for a fight. You have a plan for that?'

Guda waited. 'I will tell you more of Animais—'

'Oh doo!' the ghost replied, his voice laced with sarcasm.

'If a solid being, that of flesh and blood, goes through our infiniti, it is said that we may suffer to the point of death.'

'What is your point?' Xinder shot back.

'You are not a solid being,' Guda responded, calmly. 'You are a spirit.'

'Yes, I know all this. Why repeat yourself? It is how you took me to the boy.'

Guda paused and then signed again rapidly, his slender fingers flashing in the air, humming.

'What if you were to absorb a body?'

Xinder paused for a beat. 'Ugly Animais, would this really be possible?'

'It has long been known to Animais that if a human were to freely and willingly offer its body to a spirit, there is not a law in the universe that says they cannot be connected.'

'Ha! You talk piffle-paffle of a bygone age.'

'I do not jest,' Guda replied. 'A merger would give you substance. You would move with purpose. You would have strength.'

'Intriguing,' Xinder mused. 'Get a human to absorb into me? I have never considered it. Why have I not known about it?'

'Because, Xinder, this feat is not so easy to perform—'
'Why so?'
'For many humans, ghosts do not exist. Furthermore, apart from you, spirits are weak. They have no desire for life. They move quickly to other places.'

Xinder let out a frustrated groan. 'But, Animais, in a physical sense, how might this happen?'

'A union cannot be forced,' the Animais said. 'It must be the true will of the person of flesh.'

'I see,' Xinder said. 'Yes, it isn't exactly the most ideal of negotiating platforms, is it?'

Guda dipped a long almost icicle-like finger into the blue, radiating hole in his stomach.

'However, as the storm approaches, you might form an alliance with one who realises that there is no further hope? One who might dream of a future elsewhere?'

'That would be possible?'

'Yes. For humans, life on Earth is cherished, Guda said, his vibrations softening. 'Better still would be an alliance with a child.'

'A human child?' Xinder spat.

'Indeed. But you would have to offer something great in return. Something almost more than life.'

Xinder circled the Animais. 'It is clever, you strange, dream-giving creature,' Xinder crowed. 'But if I was to merge with human flesh, wouldn't it curtail my movements to travel through one of you Animais? And then what?'

'I am unsure. It has never been tried. Yoking with a large human may harm,' Guda said. 'Though a child, perhaps, might only wear us down, over time.'

'The boy?'

'The boy, exactly.'

'A Sacrum?' Xinder chuckled. 'Oh, but just think of it. Stuck on that dead-end planet of Earth, harnessed to a revolting child,' he sighed. 'But, then again, a *Sacrum* with me ... in harmony. Do other Animais know?'

'I am alone, for now,' Guda said. 'Others will side with

me when they learn the path I have taken. Dreams must be given.'

'Indeed, they will flock to you,' Xinder said, clapping his hands together, although being a ghost it made absolutely no noise.

WYNN-GARRY

'A quick word, if I may,' Mr Wynn-Garry said, his voice kind and his manner fatherly but firm. He looked them over sympathetically. 'It pains me to say this, but this morning I received a communiqué from your parents who are somewhere in the Middle East. They will not be back for the football or indeed for the whole of half term.' He scanned their sad faces. 'It appears they have discovered something of great interest.'

Danny and Anika exchanged glances.

'What does it say – what are they doing?' Olivia asked, and she attempted to read the headmaster's notepad upside down.

The principal folded the pad into his midriff. 'Well, it's light on actual detail, which, given the circumstances is the very least you deserve. And to be honest, I'm not at all happy about it—'

'But we have—' Olivia started.

'Yes, I know you're fortunate with your caretakers at Appleside Farm,' the headmaster said, 'but this is the third time I've had to reprimand you in the last two terms. Your parents have an obligation to you and this school beyond the callings of their work, regardless of their fame and regardless of their accomplishments in archaeology. What if one of them should suffer a heart attack or a seizure or a fall?' he continued. 'What would you do?'

The children stared at the floor.

Olivia finally broke the silence. 'Sir, Mrs Smith's brilliant at helping out; I'll ask her tonight.'

Mr Wynn-Garry nodded. 'Very well, but before you go, Olivia, I'm going to entrust you as the eldest to take a letter back to your parents. Collect it from my office before you go.'

He cleared his throat and turned to the twins. 'I have given you some simple homework over the break. Please, at least, give it some effort, especially you, Anika. Your academic record is nigh on appalling, so I'd like you to do some reading on this topic and then think carefully about it – preferably before you dream up some hare-brained scheme that gets Danny battered into little pieces.

'In Chapter Four of your textbook there is a particularly valuable resource for your essay after half term entitled, *"Did God create the universe, or did the universe create God?"'*

Then, in one movement, as though suddenly aware of the time, Wynn-Garry straightened, and looked over the top of his half-moon spectacles. 'Now, for goodness' sake, over this half term, behave yourselves, children; I cannot and will not have the police and Social Services chasing us around with your parents nowhere in sight. Please do not run into trouble. Understood?'

'Yes, sir,' the children said in unison.

'Excellent. Very best of luck with the football tomorrow morning. There will be a big crowd cheering you on and several members of the press. The circumstances surrounding this game, and the fact that the final involves our rivals has caught the imagination of the entire region.' He darted a look at Olivia. 'Best behaviour, please. Now run along.'

Danny and Anika scampered off down the corridor, the noise of their footsteps echoing off the old sandstone walls. Mr Wynn-Garry mumbled something about the time and, as he turned, saw Olivia lingering.

'Excuse me, sir,' she said.

'Yes, Olivia,' the headmaster said, impatiently. 'What is it now?'

'Well, it's the weather, sir.'

Wynn-Garry sighed. 'Yes, what about it?'

Olivia hesitated. For the first time in her life, her brain had jammed. 'I've made a weather barometer,' she finally spat out.

'Yes, congratulations on your skilful endeavour,' he replied. 'Mrs Douglas notified me. And, atmospheric pressure isn't even on your syllabus—'

'From my readings,' she began, 'there's going to be a simply massive—'

'Storm?' Wynn-Garry interrupted with a wry smile. He bent down a little. 'Well, I'm pleased that your readings match up with the area forecast, but I don't believe there's anything to fear. A bit of rain and some thunder perhaps. As a precaution, do remind your class to take their umbrellas and waterproofs as I mentioned in assembly.'

The headmaster scratched his chin and smiled at her. 'While you're here, let me remind you that it would be a terrible idea to race on to the pitch again. Please leave events on the pitch to the referee and other officials – whatever the circumstances.'

Wynn-Garry smiled in a false, head-masterly way and straightened.

'I expect nothing less than immaculate conduct, Olivia. There will be drastic repercussions if you brandish that temper of yours again.' He paused for effect. 'Do I make myself clear?'

Olivia nodded.

'Good. Now, I really must fly,' he said.

That girl, Wynn-Garry thought, was one of Sutton's finest ever pupils. Making barometers in her spare time, for fun. He'd never have dreamt of doing such a thing, nor would ninety-nine per cent of pupils they'd ever had at the school. He liked that. And he rather liked the fact that she wasn't afraid to confront anyone who laid a finger on her brother and sister. And now that he thought about it, there were a surprisingly large number of incidents.

Well, it was perfectly sweet of her to try and warn him, but he had a leaving party and other pressing matters to attend to. Nothing would stop his celebrations, certainly not a little storm and a warning from a pupil with a home-made air-pressure contraption.

XINDER

Xinder knew the Animais had disappeared by the instant lack of the strange, intense energy they emitted.

He made a mental note to remember how the buzz tickled his aura.

For the first time in an age, Xinder had a sense of urgency and energy about him. But, he worried that he had confused this sensation with frustration, or, perhaps, trepidation?

Did the Animais not understand how incredibly difficult it would be to succour a child to become a part of him? To the common eye, he was nothing more than a sad old ghost. Would a Sacrum do such a thing? And, in any case, why would *any* human child willingly give themselves over to *him*?

Xinder hovered to the floor and lay back. He marvelled at the idea of being a little bit whole, a fraction human. Even partially flesh and bone and blood so that he might walk, dance, and maybe even see?

Was it truly possible?

His thoughts returned to the boy.

What had made him nick his cheek with the knife? Was it the thrill of leaving Halaria or the desire to see if he could use his sixth-sense with the human form? Or was it a tiny piece of revenge?

It was a stupid thing to do, though, and he knew it. How would the boy trust him again, willingly, when he'd already violated him?

Xinder threw himself at the door, flying straight through. He arrived in the old walled courtyard, scanned the area and hovered through it, dust puffing meekly to the side as he went. Xinder located his thin cane and tapped it over the ground. Moving in a straight line across the yard he touched on a lump, like a large, overturned saucer stuck down with glue.

Xinder sighed and knelt down.

'Hello, young one,' he said. 'One day soon, you, and all my people will once again see the beautiful world of Halaria all for yourselves. The moons, the sky, and the court of the castle. You will breathe the air and taste the honey of our bees. And, one day, when you are bigger, you'll drink the wines from our vines and press the flesh of others.' Xinder grinned as his mood changed. 'And you will sing and dance and fight and love. Just as I once did.'

'But, alas, as I have told you a million times, you will never see me,' he sighed deeply. 'And I, regrettably, will never see your dear, sweet face, unless I can fathom a way to join with a human.'

Xinder allowed himself a smile.

'And, on this score, my dear little fellow,' he said, 'I have news.'

Sas Smith looked up as Olivia opened the door, glad to see her best friend. When Olivia's straight brown hair hung like a curtain over her forehead it made her look older; more like a seventeen-year-old, perhaps, than her fifteen years.

'Hey, everything alright?' she said.

Olivia slumped into a chair. 'I told Wynn-Garry about my barometer.'

Sas gasped. 'You did *what*? Are you insane?' she said, turning pink.

'He said he'd seen the forecast. What was I thinking?'

Sas draped an arm around her and held back a smile. 'But at least you tried,' she said. 'Maybe the calibration's wrong.'

'No, not possible,' Olivia said, frowning deeper. 'Every time I reset it, the same thing happens.'

'Well, please don't spend too much time fiddling with it,' Sas said. 'You've got until the football match to sort it out.'

Olivia smiled. 'I'm not sure I'm going to watch. I'll just

lose control again and then I'll be looking at a red card from school.'

'Oh, come on!' Sas chided. 'It might be Ani's last game. You can't miss it, and anyhow, this time I'm going to look after you.'

She looked straight into Olivia's eyes. 'All of this,' she waved a hand at the barometer, 'is great – it's amazing, but it was only a dream don't you think—'

'I'm doing this because I believe you, Sas.'

'You do?'

Olivia drummed on the desk. 'Yes, of course,' she said, her breathing shallower. 'You see, I know it sounds crazy, but I think I've had the same dream.'

Sas nearly fell off her chair. 'You ... as well? Why didn't you say something? How similar?'

'Well, most of it was to do with extreme precipitation, but at the end, it goes a bit crazy. I just can't remember.'

'Didn't you write it down?' Sas said. 'If you don't scribble dreams the moment you wake up, there's no way—'

'Well, I never do,' Olivia replied. 'It's where we differ.'

Sas tapped the spreadsheet. 'But if your evidence stacks up ... shouldn't we say something?'

Olivia shook her head. 'Forecasters screwed up years ago before they knew what they were doing, before satellites and computer modelling,' she said. 'All we have is a homemade, slightly random experiment and a couple of freaky dreams. No one will believe us, look how Wynn-Garry reacted.'

Sas nodded. 'We'll be laughed out of school—'

'Yes, yes. I know,' Olivia said, rubbing her brow. 'I'll keep my mouth zipped, for now.'

'Me, same,' Sas said. She paused. 'Olivia, I really need to talk to you about something else—'

'Aha!' boomed the voice they least wanted to hear.

Olivia straightened. 'What can I do for you, Fitzpatrick, boys?' she said.

Fitzpatrick turned a chair around and sat down slowly.

'Look, I won't be long,' he said. 'Chief nerd, Mrs Douglas. She wants to see you right away. And seriously, it's a real request. I'm just being super-friendly.'

Olivia smiled, but her eyes were narrow and icy. 'Thank you, Fitzpatrick. You've delivered your message so now you can leave; we're busy.'

Fitzpatrick opened a book. 'I'm gonna stay here for a while,' he replied putting his feet up on the desk. 'I believe I'm allowed to and, furthermore, I'd like to see this experiment you're doing. What's it? A barometer—'

Sas' eyes flicked towards the desk.

Fitzpatrick's followed. Then, he smiled and ran a hand through his hair. 'You don't by any chance fancy a date, Sas—'

Sas stared back at his happy face open-mouthed. 'With a jerk like you?'

'There's no need to be like that,' Fitzpatrick said, standing up and grasping his heart. He turned to his mates and winked. 'One day, Sas, it'll be you and me? I can feel it in my bones.' He extended his arm and gave Sas's bottom a playful tap.

Quick as a flash, she rounded on him, slapping his face, the sound like a snapping twig. 'Don't you dare touch me, you animal.' Sas chided. 'You're just fourteen, Fitzpatrick, and your hormones are clearly going through ignition phases. So, let's get this straight once and for all.' She spoke slowly. 'I will never, ever go out with you, even if we're the last two people alive on this planet. Do you understand?'

'Are those real tears, or are you just pleased to see me,' Ryan said on finding Sas later, as he pulled a folded red and white polka-dot handkerchief out of his pocket.

Sas shot him a look but her face broke into a smile. 'Oh! I don't know. It's that oaf, again. He's got hold of Olivia's experiment and she's gone nuts.' She dabbed her eyes and offered it back.

'Ah. No, keep it,' he said. 'I've got a drawer full. Dad has a thing about them—'

'Thanks, Ryan.'

'Want to talk about it?'

She shook her head.

'You sure? I'm all ears, and teeth,' he said grinning. 'Look, don't worry about Fitz - I've got a plan where he's concerned. Right now, there are disturbing rumours leaking about these corridors concerning our headmaster.'

'Wynn-Garry?'

'Aye,' he said in mock way with an eyebrow raised. He paused.

'Well—'

He shook his head. 'Can't tell you,' he said.

'Why not?'

'It might cheer you up.'

The corners of her mouth turned up and she hit him playfully in the chest.

'Well, I just happened to be in the old school—'

'Just happened?'

'Yes. Taking an arbitrary stroll down the passageways leading to his study—'

'Ryan!'

'Do you want me to tell you?' he said, stealing a look over her shoulder.

She nodded.

'As you probably know, Wynn-Garry's having a massive party tomorrow night after the football. I happened to be standing outside when I heard this extraordinary noise.'

'What noise?'

'Well, singing, I think. Terrible sort of opera, like baritone cat-wails.'

Sas tittered. 'So?'

'That's not it,' Ryan said. 'You see, he then started talking but I'm sure there wasn't anyone in there.'

'How do you know?'

'He hadn't shut the door—'

'You didn't—'

Ryan pulled a face. 'Only quickly. I couldn't help it. Bet you'd have done the same?'

'No way!'

'Well, anyway, there he was, wearing a dress—'

'You're kidding!'

'Yeah. OK, so it was a kilt, I think. Green and blue criss-crosses, and, on his top, a white string vest.'

'A singlet? What was he doing?'

'Introducing himself.'

'What?'

'Practicing his how-do-you-doo's, his voice getting posher and posher. *"Oh how do you do, Mayor, how do you do Your Eminence, that sort of thing".*'

Sas laughed as Ryan raised his eyebrows.

'Then what?'

'I sneaked off. Told you it would cheer you up. Now, important stuff. I need some advice.'

Sas cocked her head. 'Go on.'

Ryan's face contorted. 'I need a date. Got a do on over half-term.'

'You're asking me for a date.'

Ryan coughed and blushed. 'Er. No. Not really. Just advice, or a bit of guidance as to whom I might approach.'

'Oh,' she said. 'Right.'

Ryan couldn't tell if her tone betrayed a hint of disappointment.

'Anyone spring to mind?'

'Annie?' he squeaked.

'Which one? Martin or Delaux.'

'Either.'

She rolled her eyes. 'Really?'

Ryan looked taken aback. 'Why not?'

'Annie Martin is pretty, but she's, you know, a bit soppy, forever sweeping back her hair and sighing. You'd be bored senseless. On the other hand, Anika might tear the place up, and, if there's dancing, you'd better have your dancing shoes on.'

Ryan's forehead rolled. 'I hate dancing.'

Footsteps made them turn.

Sas squeezed his arm. 'I've got to go. I'll think of something, don't you worry. I'll let you know before half term, OK?' She looked him in the eye.

Ryan smiled. 'Thanks, Sas. Discretion, please. Don't want it leaked around or everyone will think I'm desperate.'

'No problem. Hey, and thanks Ryan. Love the hanky.'

FITZPATRICK

'You'll have to swear on your life that you won't tell anyone,' Fitzpatrick demanded.

'Give me a break,' Danny replied.

'Danny, promise on your life that you won't tell anyone, that's all I'm asking. I mean, you can keep your mouth shut, can't you?'

'If you didn't want anyone to know,' Danny replied, 'why did you do it in the first place?'

'To protect the excellent academic reputation of Sutton School,' he said. 'And, anyway, your sister hates me and she cannot be trusted. Prove you're different.'

'Bog off, Fitzpatrick. My sister doesn't like you because you do idiotic things like throw barometers out of windows and sneak dead rats into sports bags.'

Fitzpatrick chuckled. Two years ago, he'd found a dead rodent by the river and hid it in Olivia's games bag. He waited. And every day he waited, getting more and more excited about the slowly decomposing rat. For the best part of a week, while everyone wondered what the terrible smell was, he waited. Then, on the afternoon of the school cross-country run, as Olivia put on her tracksuit bottoms, out plopped the remains, maggots spraying over her things like discarded rice.

Dynamite.

Danny sighed. 'Look, Fitzy, if it means that much to you, I'll do it, but only if *you* swear, on your life that you won't do any more harmful, stupid, bullying things to Olivia, Sas, or Anika.'

Fitzpatrick stuck out his jaw and moved it from side to side contemplating Danny's request. At last, he nodded and said, 'OK, I agree. But it ends when she gets me into detention again.'

Danny nodded.

'Come on then,' Fitzpatrick said, 'you say it first.'

'Do I have to? I'm not five.'

'Yeah, course you do – if you want me to do the same.'

Danny rolled his eyes. 'I swear, on my life, that I won't tell anyone that you dropped the stupid barometer out of the window. Satisfied.'

Fitzpatrick nodded. 'Easy, wasn't it?'

'Now you do it!'

Fitzpatrick looked him in the eye. 'I swear on my life not to harm your sisters, and not to play any more silly tricks on them. There, that good enough?'

'I suppose.'

Fitzpatrick's tone changed and he ushered Danny aside. 'Look, sorry, Dan. You don't have to say it ... I know, I know,' he said putting his hands in the air. 'I've been one massive tosser.'

'You're telling me!' Danny replied. 'Why, Fitzy? Why do you do it?'

Fitzpatrick shrugged. 'Dunno. Boredom. Can't seem to help myself when I see your sisters—'

'Look out!' Jackson said, as he ran back into the class-room. 'Steele's on his way.'

'Come on! Out of the window!' Fitzpatrick said.

They ran to the window and pulled up the blind.

Olivia, Sas and Mrs Pike stared up at them.

'Drat,' Fitzpatrick said, under his breath. He smiled pleasantly back at them.

'Fitzpatrick and Danny Delaux,' the old teacher hollered. 'Who would have guessed? What can you tell me about the mess down here?'

Fitzpatrick opened the window. 'Hello, Miss. Is there a problem?'

'You know perfectly well there is!'

'Sorry. I don't what you're talking about, Miss?'

'This debris, here,' Mrs Pike shrieked, pointing at the concrete.

Fitzpatrick peered like a sailor looking down from deck, a quizzical expression etched on his brow. 'I have no idea what you're talking about,' he replied. 'Window's been closed all along, hasn't it boys?' He shrugged. 'What is it?'

Olivia shrieked. 'Fitzpatrick, you know perfectly well what it is!'

'Glass?' he offered. 'A smashed Coke bottle perhaps?'

'No, Fitzpatrick, it was Olivia's barometer.'

'A bar-hom-tier,' Fitzpatrick repeated, thickly. 'What on earth is that?'

'Danny, did you see Fitzpatrick with it earlier?' the teacher hollered.

Danny stared at the floor.

'Tell me, what happened?'

'Dunno,' Danny said, running a hand through his hair.

'Danny, what do you mean, you "dunno"?'

'Dunno,' Danny said again, reddening.

Fitzpatrick looked straight into Mrs Pike's eyes. 'Honestly, there's been no one around. We've been chatting about fishing, life, and situation comedy—'

'Great!' Olivia stormed, addressing Danny. 'Fitzpatrick's made you swear not to tell or something childish like that, hasn't he? You, Fitzpatrick,' she said pointing at him, 'you were the last person to have it. It must have been you.'

'Then prove it,' Fitzpatrick said, thrusting out his jaw.

'I shouldn't have to,' she pleaded. 'Danny, all you have to do is tell us what happened—'

Danny shook his head.

'Expel him!' Olivia shouted pointing at Fitzpatrick.

'But I haven't done anything—'

Olivia stamped her foot. 'YES YOU HAVE.'

'PROVE IT!' he yelled back.

'You had it last! I saw it in your hands, admit it—'

'NO! Innocent until proven guilty—'

'*I DID IT!*' Danny yelled, his voice cutting above theirs. 'It was me.'

The school bell chimed, the echo circling around their heads.

'*You?*' Olivia quizzed.

'*Danny?*' Mr Steele said.

'Delaux?' said Mrs Pike.

'Yes,' Danny sighed. 'I was fed up with you two always getting at each other, so I thought I'd, you know...' He bowed his head.

Olivia looked from one to the other. 'Oh great! You two have done a deal or something, haven't you?'

3

XINDER, WEDNESDAY

With a swish of his hand, Xinder brushed off the top of the raised puddle. He had no idea if the boy stuck in the puddle beneath him could hear. But he liked to talk, nonetheless, for there was no one else; aside from his man-servant, Schmerger, and Schmerger's strange, elven-like kind.

'So, child, if I am not able to use force, how shall a union with a human be done?' he said. 'In another time, I would have snapped off a finger or two, or pressed hot oil into orifices, and, yes, they would beg to do my bidding. But, now, if I am to find a person to join me, they must wish to do it with their whole heart.'

Xinder tapped his cane on a cobble, thinking out loud. 'If these children are indeed the Sacrum as Guda claims, then how must they feel? Afraid? Fearful? Confused, possibly?'

Xinder jumped up.

'The prophecy! The First Dream! I must recall every detail,' he said. 'How did it go? If my memory still serves me, the dream states that they must solve three riddles in order to find three egg-stones. And these stones hold the clues to the one key of Genartus.' Xinder floated onto his back, thinking. 'They have one chance and all must survive. If they fail, Earth is destroyed and,' Xinder smiled, 'Halaria awakens.'

Xinder shot into the air startling a bird.

'Infants such as these Sacrum could never do it. Never!'

Xinder clasped his hands and returned to the ground.

I suspect that that boy, Xinder thought, *has an over-whelming desire to put the images he's seen in his dreams as far out of his mind as he possibly can.*

'It is quite simple,' he said out loud. 'To secure the boy, I must take away his greatest fear.'

Xinder grinned.

Love and fear, he thought, as the idea formed. *The two greatest weapons of manipulation known to mankind. And I do believe I know where his fears lie.*

'You must think I'm a fool, Dan. It's perfectly clear that Fitzpatrick put you up to this.' Her tone softened. 'Didn't he?'

Danny kept his eyes down.

She sighed. 'Have it your own way, Danny. I just don't understand how you can be friends with him. I just wish you'd been honest with me, Dan. That's what really hurts.'

'I'm sorry about your experiment,' he said, raising his eyes.

Olivia pressed her lips together. 'Don't be. It kept bottoming out. Actually, I've researched a better idea. I'm going to make a Fitzroy storm glass.'

'A Fitz glass?'

'No, a Fitz-ROY storm glass. It's a brilliant bit of kit, a kind of old-fashioned weather gauge, and, as a punishment for your behaviour, you can help me make it.'

Danny smiled. 'Why the craze about weather stuff?'

'Well, if you must know,' she said, 'there's a curious weather system developing. She hesitated a little. 'This may sound a bit strange, but Sas and I have had a premonition; a dream about torrential rain, flooding, that kind of thing.'

Danny reeled, and put a hand out to steady himself. 'You're always saying how unscientific things like dreams are, and that therefore they're irrelevant—'

'Nevertheless,' she said, curtly, 'dreams are viable mechanisms of the brain, Danny.'

Danny cleared his throat. 'Livi, do you dream a lot?'

'No,' she said. 'I never dream, well, not until recently. But I've got an intensely strong feeling about this one. So, I reckon there's no harm in trying to find out if there's any scientific substance to it.'

Danny scratched his head and wondered if he should mention *his* appalling dreams, and Anika's shouting in the middle of the night. Instead, he heard himself asking, 'How does this Fitzglass-thing work?'

'It shows what's going to happen to the weather through the liquid in the glass. A reflection of what's going on outside, I think. So, if the liquid is clear, the weather will be clear. If small crystals form, then snow is on its way—'

'And if there's a storm…?' Danny asked.

'When a thunderstorm is coming, the liquid should be cloudy with small star-like crystals in it, and so on.'

'Nice.'

'First, I'll need a few ingredients – and this, bro, is where you come in.'

Danny nodded.

'First, go and bat your eyelids at Mrs Culver. Ask for ten grams of camphor; she'll have some for food flavouring. Tell her you need some in Chemistry to show how a compound can burn without leaving an ash residue. If she starts asking questions, mention oxygen in a scientifically related question. For some reason, Mrs Culver can't bear the word "oxygen".

'Then, go and find Mr Pike in the Maintenance Department. Ask him for distilled water. Fill a large, plastic bottle if you can; he keeps some for his forklift batteries.'

Olivia scratched her forehead thoughtfully, making sure she hadn't forgotten anything. 'Have you got that? Camphor and distilled water. I'll find some ethanol and the other bits from Chemistry later on. Shouldn't be too difficult,' she added, almost as a reminder to herself.

'Where shall we meet?' he said.

Olivia smiled. 'The science labs are free straight after lunch. One thirty. I'll see you there.'

When Danny arrived, Olivia was talking animatedly to Sas. They reminded Danny of nurses in an operating theatre.

Sas threw a lab coat at Danny. 'Gotta look like you mean it, Danny,' she said.

Danny handed over the camphor and Sas filled a beaker with distilled water, which she began to heat.

In silence, as Danny and Sas looked on, Olivia added each component until the beaker was half full. The ethanol and camphor were poured in last. When these had dissolved, Olivia asked Danny to find a large test tube sealed with a stopper. She exchanged the liquid into the test tube and filled it almost to the top, and capped it off.

Danny put the test tube upright in a holding device on the desk.

'Danny,' Olivia said. 'Wash those beakers while we put everything away.'

Danny headed to the far corner of the laboratory, but, just as he was about to place the beaker in the sink, the door swung open.

Instinctively, Danny ducked under the table.

'Aha! *There* you are,' Fitzpatrick said, with big smile. 'Been looking all over for you girls.'

'GO AWAY!' they shouted.

'Whoa! Calm down. I've come to apologise.' He looked down at the desk. 'What's all this then? Doing some illegal experiments, are we? That's terribly exciting. Creating a bomb or some poisons or a wee bit of chemical warfare—'

'It's none of your business, Fitzpatrick. Leave us alone.'

'Biological warfare?'

'SOD OFF, Fitzy!'

'Mustard gas? Come on, I'm offering an olive branch. I am sorry about earlier. Got a little out of hand, didn't it? Actually, have either of you seen Danny?'

Olivia caught Danny staring at her from behind one of the desks, out of Fitzpatrick's eye line, and shaking his head vigorously.

'Er, no. Sorry. No idea,' she said, brushing an imaginary speck off her lab coat.

Fitzpatrick regarded her suspiciously before his eyes moved to the test tube on the desk.

'This is your experiment, is it? A test tube full of cloudy potions. Cor. Brilliant.'

'Thanks for your interest, Fitzpatrick,' Sas said, in the most condescending manner she could. 'But, to be honest, this is a very dull investigation we're doing, dealing with the creation of crystals using camphor, ethanol, distilled water, and a couple of other things you probably wouldn't understand.'

But Fitzpatrick was like a dog chasing after a scent, and his tone changed. 'So, if it's so boring, why are you doing it in lunch break?'

'As I said, Fitzpatrick, it's a simple experiment—'

'I don't believe you.' He stepped closer. 'It doesn't add up.'

'Please, go away, and leave us alone,' Olivia said, as sweetly as she could, remembering Danny's advice.

Her words fell on deaf ears. 'Why don't you tell me what you're doing?' Fitzpatrick quizzed.

'Why should we?' Olivia snapped.

Fitzpatrick smiled back. 'Cos, otherwise I'll smash it—'

'You wouldn't dare.' Olivia lunged for the test tube, but Fitzpatrick was too quick.

'Give it back, immediately!'

'No way. Come on, what's in it?' he said, inspecting it. 'A lethal poison, a nerve agent, a deadly virus—'

'Don't be stupid.'

'From where I'm standing, I'm not the one being stupid,' he said.

Olivia huffed. 'If you must know, it's a Fitzroy storm glass—'

'Well, well, well,' Fitzpatrick said, slowly. 'You're not still going on about this bleeding storm? When will you two grow up and do what everyone else does?' He shook his head. 'Watch the weather forecast on this thing called the telly. Oh, hang on, don't tell me; you're so far up in the hills that you haven't got one!'

'Of course we do,' Olivia raged.

Fitzpatrick raised an eyebrow. 'I'm not sure I believe you. Thing is, you Delauxs are so backwards I wouldn't be surprised if your mum has to shave Neolithic hair off her body. We'd never know, though, because she seems to have disowned you.' He cocked an eye at Olivia's puce face. 'And that old woman who looks after you, with whiskers coming out of her face like a cat!' He opened his eyes wide theatrically. 'Hey! I know exactly what you should make,' he paused, holding the test-tube in front of his eyes. 'A potion for hair removal! You've got customers in your very own home!'

Fitzpatrick brushed aside Olivia's howls. 'Now, clever clogs, let me fill you in. Last night the man on the TELLY,' he said in a deliberately loud voice. 'He said that there might be a storm over the next couple of days, but not a big one, and certainly NOT one with WHITE WATER RAFTING.'

Fitzpatrick marched to the corner of the room, near to where Danny was hiding under the table.

Olivia gasped lightly.

'I tell you what,' Fitzpatrick continued, 'I'm going to do you a favour, and put you out of this ridiculous weather fixation once and for all. I'm going to spin this tube thing like a spinning top. You do know what that is, don't you? By the time you get over here, it'll either be in bits on the floor, or, by some miracle, you may have grabbed it. But, if and when this happens, I'll be long gone out of the door. Then you can go and do what everyone else does, and watch the weather forecast on the box.' He grinned. 'You'll find it comes directly after the news.'

Fitzpatrick, with the test-tube in the palms of his hands, drew them quickly apart. The tube spun fast and straight, and, while everyone in the room momentarily fixated upon it, Fitzpatrick strode through the door, turning the lights off after him.

The sound of the latch clicking seemed to accentuate the wobbling of the glass. Instantly, the girls rushed over in near darkness, but, in their haste, they careered into the lab furniture. The noise of scraping chairs and upturned tables filled the room.

As the crashing receded, the test tube wobbled to its conclusion, followed, moments later, by the tinkling sound of breaking glass.

LUNA

The large Animais studied each of her delicate, long, slender fingers one by one, as if paying homage to them for their service. For the first time she noted the wear and tear; the way so many fingers had turned grey when once they were bright white. She noticed how her slender slithers of knuckles and joints were now worn down to thin, hardened bone.

As Luna seamlessly morphed each finger from a pincer, to a needle, then back to a long finger again, a deep sense of foreboding filled her.

What if these Sacrum do not understand?

She shivered at the possibility. Putting the thought aside, she sent vibrations from her rapidly moving fingers to the waiting Animais, the Elders of the Animais population: Sola, Juno, and Guda.

'The First Dream comes with a gift for each Sacrum,' Luna said, as she dipped three long fingers into her infiniti and withdrew some microscopic granules, studying the ends. 'These gifts are physical talents designed to assist each one to whom the prophecy has been given. They are known as the Gifts of Genartus.'

'Then the stories are true,' Sola vibrated.

'Yes. These crystals were passed to me by my mother, as once they were handed to her. If the Sacrum succeed in the tasks set before them they will open the planet of Genartus to life once more,' she said. 'Dream powders will be replenished. Wondrous times may begin afresh for all life.'

A strong vibration cut through the air.

'Why do we meddle?' Guda said, his fingers moving quickly. 'If you had not spun the First Dream, who is to say that life would not have continued just as before. Besides, the First Dream has been given to Sacrum who are but *children* of man. They are not equipped to tackle what lies ahead; the storm alone will tear them to pieces—'

'The riddles and tests were prepared by Mazeen the Great when he was a wizard at the height of his powers in Genartus. It is ancient magic—'

'But these children do not seek it. They do not even know of the consequences—'

'It is not the time to argue the rights or wrongs. The sequence of the First Dream has begun. Only the Sacrum can interpret because they represent the Soul, the Heart and the Ego of Earth—'

'Even though they have no training—'

'The time has come for change,' Luna said, her vibrations overriding his. 'That is the lore of the universe. It is natures will.'

Guda scoffed, his vibrations slowing. 'They are not equipped—'

'Enough!' Luna said. 'They are the ones who are protected by Mazeen—'

'But Mazeen does not know it. He does not even know his name—'

'He will remember,' Luna said, the vibrations from her fingers singing through the air. 'He must.'

The old Animais slowly dipped her hands into the blue electrical hole that filled her midriff.

'Juno,' she said, addressing a younger Animais. 'Have the last dream powders from Genartus been dispersed?'

'Yes, Mother. The Atrium is clear.

'Good. Then the final part of the First Dream will be given to the Sacrum this Earth night, as they sleep. Afterwards, they will be given the Gifts of Genartus. On the giving of the Gift of Strength they will have seven days to solve the riddles and unlock the key.'

'But they will die,' Guda said. 'It is such a waste. The suffering for all will be immense—'

'I will hear no more of your objections, Guda,' Luna snapped, as she lifted her wiry, opaque outline up into the air.

'The journey for the Sacrum to find the egg-stones and fulfil the prophecy is about to commence. Regardless of what you may think, these children of mankind are the Sacrum. The universal energy that combines the living in all corners of the universes has reasons for these things. Nothing can change it. When the gifts are given, life on Earth will be in the Sacrum's hands and theirs alone.'

DANNY

'Now then, now then!' Fitzpatrick said, flicking on the light. 'What's going on here?' he said, in a mock, policeman-like voice. He looked around to see an empty room and then, slowly, Sas got up. Her hair covered her face like a veil.

Then Olivia rose, too, rubbing her head.

Fitzpatrick's eyes were on fire. 'Brilliant. Blooming gold.' He pulled his phone out. 'Smile at the budgie.' The camera clicked and flashed. Fitzpatrick inspected the image. 'Lovely. You two look gorgeous. I'm gonna post this everywhere.'

Danny stood up, brushing splinters from his jacket.

'Danny!' Fitzpatrick exclaimed, his expression changing. 'Shit! Where did you come from?'

'I've been here all the time, you bloody idiot.'

Fitzpatrick's manner changed immediately. 'Are you alright?' He pointed at Danny's sleeve. 'Is that blood?'

Danny looked down at his hand. Blood was oozing from a gash at the base of his thumb and running over his hand.

'Satisfied?' Olivia said, as she tiptoed through the glass fragments towards him. 'Happy now?' she held Danny's arm and inspected it. 'Sas, get the first aid box, we need to stop the bleeding. And Fitzpatrick, be useful and find a brush and dustpan.'

Olivia led Danny to the tap.

'This might hurt,' she said, as she ran the water and placed Danny's hand underneath.

He winced.

'There's a fragment in there. Sas, I need a towel, and tweezers, and then we'll need to compress the wound.'

Danny gritted his teeth as she plucked out the tiny slivers before applying pressure on the wound.

After they had finished, Danny turned around. Fitzpatrick stood frozen to the spot. Danny looked him hard in the eye.

'You SWORE, on your life, that you wouldn't do this kind of thing,' Danny said. '*You swore – on – your – life*,' he yelled. 'I held my side of the deal, but at the first opportunity you couldn't resist it, could you? It's now entirely clear to me that you value your life as pretty much worthless. What would your parents think? Do you think they'd be proud?'

Fitzpatrick's face fell, and the colour drained from his cheeks. 'Sorry, Danny,' he said. 'I ... I didn't realise...'

With Danny's words ringing in his ears, Fitzpatrick fled for the door.

After a long silence, Sas turned to Danny. 'Right, Danny. Where is it?'

'Uh?' Danny cried, feigning shock.

'Where is ... what?' Olivia said.

Sas tutted. 'Oh, come along, come along, Sherlock Olivia. The storm glass, silly.'

'In fragments in the bin?'

Sas bit her lip. 'That isn't test-tube glass. That's a beaker, right, Danny?'

'Beaker?' Danny replied.

'*You've* got it, haven't you?'

Danny laughed. 'Indeed, I have!' He slowly moved his gaze towards his trousers and pointed at his crotch. He began to unzip his fly. 'It's right here.'

'No way!' Sas exclaimed. 'Oh … my … God!'

Danny reached in and teased it out. 'DA-NAH,' he said, his eyes sparkling.

He held the test tube up in the air. 'Sorry, couldn't think of anywhere else quick enough,' he said. 'Then, when I crouched down, I lost my balance, and knocked the beaker over.'

Sas clapped her hands at Danny's story but Olivia looked horrified. 'Well, well, Danny. A storm in your pants. First time for everything, eh?'

Danny slipped the tube into the rack.

'One thing, Danny. Do everyone a favour. Go and give it a proper clean.'

4

OLIVIA, WEDNESDAY

By the time the Delauxs returned to the stone courtyard of Appleside Farm, the charcoal colours of dusk lay sandwiched upon the buildings and the landscape. Danny and Anika immediately set about kicking a football. The scuffing, sandpapery noises of their feet, and the ball doffing back off the grey stone walls, roused Mrs Puddy. She waved enthusiastically from one of the two windows in her flat opposite the farmhouse.

Olivia's mind tracked back to the conversations with Wynn-Garry and Fitzpatrick, who had both been so rude about their house. *It wasn't that bad*, she thought, as she studied the exterior.

OK, so it was a bit of a mishmash of an ancient moors farmstead, but it wasn't too unusual, was it?

Constructed from irregular, Yorkshire-grey boulders, and old, thick timbers, its slate roof was covered in moss and lichen that hung over too far, as though badly in need of a trim. Looking at the blackened, slightly crooked chimneys, the higgledy-piggledy stone arrangements, and the odd sections of glass and brick intermittently nestled into the walls, Olivia was reminded of a bag of loose sweets squished together and charred until they were all the same colour.

As Olivia entered the kitchen, she realised that this was definitely the heart of the house, a place that oozed warmth, love, happiness, and appreciation of fine foods. Bunches of rosemary, lavender, thyme, and dried, cured hams and fruit dangled from a row of black hooks. The smell intoxicating.

Even the stone slabs, laid out in great squares, had a warm, glossy sheen from years of wear. As she looked up, grey, oak timbers fanned out in clean lines above their heads, protecting those within.

Down the middle of the kitchen ran a long, chunky, dark brown oak table fit for a banquet. Next to the table stood a pleasing, red-brick, inglenook fireplace where the old wood-fired cooker sat.

Fitzpatrick was wrong. Even if the kitchen was a bit of a curiosity, it wasn't entirely archaic. Two waggon wheels suspended by three heavy chains had spotlights beaming down from the rim and, on the far wall, was Mrs Puddy's pride and joy; a fifty-inch flat-screen telly.

ANIKA

'Well, come on then,' Anika said, slinging a bag on her bed. 'Show me this amazing thing that's been holidaying in Danny's pants.'

Olivia unwrapped the test tube from her scarf and leant the glass between two books on the table. Three pairs of eyes stared down at it.

'Bit foggy, isn't it?' Anika said. 'So, does that mean it'll be foggy?'

Danny raised his eyebrows. 'Don't be silly, Anika. This is serious science.'

Anika giggled and elbowed Danny as they continued to stare.

'Ooh,' Anika cooed. 'Look at those little stars. What does that mean?'

Olivia pulled out her crib sheet. 'I think tiny stars means that it will be stormy,' she said, and then read from her crib sheet. '*A cloudy glass with small stars indicates thunderstorms.*'

'Wow,' Danny said, sarcastically. 'Impressive.'

Anika spluttered. 'And ... is that it?'

'What do you mean, *is that it?*'

'Well, it's very pretty, but you know, as an award-winning scientist, I thought it might be a bit ... cooler,' Anika said, glancing to Danny for support. 'I mean, if you wanted to know thunderstorms were coming all you had to do was look at the forecast on TV.'

Olivia shot up. 'That's what that moron Fitzpatrick said.'

'Well, maybe he's right? Have you gone to all this trouble to find out something we already know?'

'I think there's going to be a terrible deluge,' Olivia fumed. 'Sas and I both dreamt about it. All I'm trying to do is prove it scientifically.'

'Don't get me wrong,' Anika said, picking it up and turning it round in her hands, 'but how will this crappy thing help?'

Olivia sat down slowly, took the storm glass off her sister, and twisted it through her fingers.

'To be honest, I had hoped for something a little more dramatic, like the crystals speeding up or something.'

'But how would that change anything?'

'I don't know,' Olivia shrugged. 'It might give us a warning, or...' she shrugged. 'Actually, Sis, I give in. I haven't a clue. But I had to try something.'

Anika handed it over to Danny.

'This must be the worst scientific experiment ever,' he said. 'If Fitzpatrick knew how poor it really was, then he'd rip you to bits.'

'Then don't tell him.'

'I'll never say anything again after what he did today—'

'Children!' Mrs Puddy's strange voice screamed up the stairs. 'Hurry! Tea's on the table.'

On the kitchen table sat four bowls, brimming with noodles in a thick, soupy broth. A Mrs Puddy "Ramen" experiment. The children slipped into their chairs and began sniffing like curious cats.

'Have you heard?' Olivia said, taking a small taste. 'Mum and Dad aren't coming back for half term.'

'What!' she cried. 'No. Well, I'm blown apart – oh deary!'

'Can't you say something to them when they get back?' Danny asked. 'They're never here.'

'Don't eat with your mouth full, little Danny,' Mrs Puddy said, before sighing. 'You know it isn't proper for me to tell your folks what they can or cannot do. If they choose to be away, then it is for good reason. I know you won't think it's true but I promise they miss you twice as much as you miss them.'

Mrs Puddy said this with as much conviction as she could, but she could read the disappointment in their eyes and wondered what on earth it was that so completely occupied their parents' time.

In any event, she wouldn't hear a bad word said about them. She only had to raise her left arm above her head or try and touch her toes to remember.

Sap had found her in the woods, miles up in the depths of the forest, on the verge of death, so they said. Her face and shoulder smashed, her clothes ripped to bits. Hardly breathing.

Sap had carried her all the way home, singing and keeping her going. She still sang that funny song, especially when she felt lonely or tired.

For several months, Sap and the children's parents nursed her, built up her strength, and tried to help her recover... and remember. But, her memory never returned. She had no name, no address, no family, no lovers, no pets;

nothing and no-one she could ever recall laughing with, or crying to.

Instead, she had had to learn everything again; although some things came to her quite naturally, like, strangely, making puddings.

The first time she recalled laughing was when the babies crawled to her and gurgled in her ear, especially little Danny. Olivia, on the other hand, would scowl and point at her scars, and continued to do so until she found she could see through the damage on Mrs Puddy's face and into her heart.

These were her first memories, and cherished ones too.

After a while she didn't want to go anywhere else. Why should she? She loved the children. She loved the quiet remoteness of Appleside Farm, with its ballooning views over the Vale of York towards the peaks in the far distance. She felt safe being close to old Sap, who, although he came and went, seemed not to have a harmful bone in his body. It felt right that she should look after the children while their parents were away, for a nurturing instinct ran deep within her.

As far as her name went, Olivia called her, affectionately, "the famous Mrs Pudding", and it caught on. She'd been Mrs Puddy ever since, living in the apartment on the top half of the converted barn across the courtyard.

'Evening, All,' Sap said, popping his head around the door. 'Smells marvel-wondrous.'

Anika got up and wrapped her arms around him.

Sap hugged her back, closing his eyes. 'Now then, littluns. I must say, I can't remember such strange weather. Feels like a storm is brewing right bang on top of us. An appley-big one at that. I can feel it in my old bones—'

Olivia slammed her fists on the table. 'That's what I've been trying to tell everyone. No one believes me; Wynn-Garry, Fitzpatrick, you two—'

'Whoa! Chill, Livi,' Danny chipped in. 'Your experimentation is a bit ... bonkers.'

Mrs Puddy piped up, 'That nice man the weather forecaster on my television said there might be a bit of a storm. Localised—'

'Arrggh!' Olivia cried. 'NO! NO! NO! Not you as well!'

Mrs Puddy turned puce and looked as though she might burst into tears.

'That's enough of that, Olivia,' Sap said, firmly. For a

moment there was quiet. He furrowed his brow, as though deep in thought. 'What's funny,' he began, 'is that I've been having real clear dreams about lots of rain, flooding and storms. Thing is, I'm so old it could mean anything.'

Olivia gasped. 'You ... you've had dreams too?'

The children stopped eating and stared up at him.

'Oh, yes. More than ever. Shocking stuff too. I should check those apples—'

'There's nothing wrong with them, I'm telling you,' Mrs Puddy fired back from the end of the table.

'Well then,' Sap said, 'I do believe there's going to be a storm and three-quarters.' He reached across, grabbed an apple, rubbed it on his patched-up jumper, and chomped. 'Now, you're old enough to know,' he continued, between mouthfuls, 'that once upon a time there was a story about a great storm and a flood that covered the world.'

Olivia groaned. 'You're not referencing the original flood story?' she said, her tone loaded with sarcasm.

Sap seemed surprised. 'Ooh. Yup. I think that's the one. You know about it, do you? With a man they called ... now, what was his name?'

'Noah?' Olivia said.

'Ha!' Sap clapped his big hands. 'There. That goes ding-dong. Been muddling that one for a while. So, you know about it. How marvel-tastic.'

The conversation was interrupted by a rapping sound at the front door.

The family stared at one another.

'Who on Earth?' Sap said.

Before anyone else could move, Anika tore off to see who it was. Shortly, she returned.

'It's Wynn-Garry,' she gushed.

For a minute they looked at each other, not sure what to do.

'Well, don't you think you should let him in?' Sap said.

The children headed towards the door.

'Mr Wynn-Garry, Sir.'

'Hello, Danny, Anika, Olivia. Please accept my apologies for the late hour, but I thought I may as well potter up. May I come in?'

They led him to the sitting room, where Sap was adding logs to the orange embers.

'Mr Sapwood, how nice to see you,' the headmaster said, as he eyed up the old man. Sap was just as tall and wrinkly as he remembered, and had the strangest little tufts of hair protruding from an otherwise bald and patchy scalp. In fact, the old man looked the same as he had when he met him twenty-five years ago.

He remembered thinking then what peculiar clothes the old man wore. His trousers and shirt were made of fragments of cloth that made him look like a moving patchwork quilt. It reminded him of Danny and his curiously modified school uniform.

Their clothes must have been stitched together by the lady who was loitering in the doorway. He strode over and shook her hand. 'Isn't that road terribly narrow and steep?' he said as a way of breaking the ice. 'It must be devilishly tricky to navigate when the weather turns. Do those parcel couriers ever manage to find you?'

Mrs Puddy froze, and turned as pink as a doll.

Sap rescued her by moving in and extending his hand. 'Now then, is everything in order? Perhaps I could offer you a glass of something: apple juice, cauliflower tea, my own marrow rum?'

'How very kind,' Mr Wynn-Garry said, 'apple juice will suffice. I shan't stay long.' The headmaster rubbed his hands; for a man his age, Sap's handshake crushed like iron. 'May we have a word in private?'

Olivia, Anika, and Danny streamed out of the room while Sap poured the drinks.

'Mr Sapwood, I'll get straight to the point. Can you give the children the kind of assistance they need if - and I do hate to say this - if anything goes wrong.'

'Depends what kind of ... wrong, Headmaster?'

'Well, say if Danny was to break his arm again. How would you get him to the hospital? And what if there's a house fire?'

Sap burst out laughing, his vibrant, joyful tones bouncing back off the walls. 'They are quite capable of looking after themselves, with or without me.'

His comments had the effect of making Wynn-Garry feel rather idiotic. 'With respect, Mr Sapwood,' he shot back. 'Even though Olivia has conducted herself outstandingly well in her academic studies, can we be sure she won't disgrace the school by violently interfering with the officials during our remaining football matches? And, while Anika shows exceptional sporting ability, she is on course to fail her exams."

Sap didn't know what to say, so he simply smiled back.

'And then there's Danny,' Wynn-Garry continued. 'Lovely fellow that he may be, he has no redeeming features, aside from his siblings, to earn a place at our school.'

Wynn-Garry wondered if the old man had listened to a single word.

'Mr Sapwood, I will be frank with you. I have no argument with your family in any way.' He removed his spectacles, rubbing them on a cloth before setting them back on his nose. 'But I must tell you that I am to retire at the end of the term, and I've heard through the grapevine that my successor - a modern, disciplinarian sort – is looking to shake up the school. 'I very much fear that the children's bursaries will almost certainly come to an end.'

Sap scratched an imaginary beard. 'I'll make sure the children's parents understand the situation entirely.'

'Good, thank you,' Mr Wynn-Garry replied. He cleared his throat. 'Are you fit and well enough to continue in the role as the children's caretaker? I worked out you must be nearing the heady heights of ninety years—'

'Oh, Headmaster,' Sap said, 'body and mind are ticking along quite nicely, thank you.'

'I ask for the children's sake—'

'Mr Wynn-Garry,' Sap chuckled. 'When you are as old as I am, you will find that love and well-being are the things that matter. While it is hard to hold on to the memories from one's youth, we are lucky to be in possession of decent health, and blessed that Mrs Puddy feeds and nurses us.' He flicked him a smile. 'But, you're right to be checking up. We don't have so many visitors up here in the hills. Have you made plans for your retirement?'

Wynn-Garry leaned back in the armchair.

'Yes,' he sighed, pleased to switch subject. 'As a matter of fact, I'm hoping to go to the Middle East to see some of the ancient tombs and archaeology for myself. It's a small passion of mine, if you will.' He exhaled loudly at the thought of the unknown life to come after he left his beloved school.

When the men stood up, scuffling noises scratched towards the kitchen. Sap and Wynn-Garry exchanged a smile.

'Children!' Wynn-Garry boomed. 'I have something to say to you, so you may as well come back here.'

The children emerged, sheepishly.

'I've decided the time has come to hang up my leather binder and my red marker-pen.'

'You're leaving?' Olivia said.

'Yes, my dear. It is time for some fresh blood at Sutton School. Please promise to keep this information to yourselves until I have made the announcement official, after half term.'

He looked each of the children in the eye. 'I would be hugely disappointed if any of you were to exit the school before me, so I suggest you work together to improve those areas that need addressing. For example, Danny and Anika, a mastery of the periodic table and basic algebra.' He gave them a knowing look over his half-moon glasses. 'I have a suspicion that these may feature heavily in your exams.

'The other thing is that I would like you to win the football trophy tomorrow. I don't mean to put any additional pressure on you both, but it would be wonderful to finish my tenure here knowing that we had reached the pinnacle of both sporting and academic endeavours. So, Danny, please hold your concentration for the entire game.'

'We'll do our best,' Anika said. 'I promise.'

He smiled and headed out of the oak door.

Olivia seized her chance. 'But what about the storm, sir?'

He turned. 'Olivia, this is Yorkshire, for goodness' sake.'

'But I've studied the charts and...'

The door closed in her face, Wynn-Garry's footsteps tip-tapped across the flagstones.

Sap pushed the thick bolt into the wall. 'What a fine man,' he said. 'I wouldn't worry too much about what he said. You're doing well at school, you're fit and well, and you've got friends – what more could you want, eh? Now, off to bed, right now.'

A rumble of thunder boomed high up in the night sky. Sap sniffed the air.

'Something tells me tomorrow is going to be a big, big day.'

5

LUNA, THURSDAY

The grandfather clock in the hallway chimed twice, its ring echoing around the old farmhouse. Two in the morning of the next day and the children's sleep was long and deep: the night-hour of dreaming.

Four Animais arrived in a flash.

Using their long, wiry legs, each Animais flew across the air until they stood above the children.

'You are here to witness the final part of the First Dream, for there must be no doubting it,' Luna said, through her vibrations. 'Their sleep pattern is flowing. It is time. Come.'

Luna walked deftly through the air towards Olivia. Bending impossibly forward, as if made from soft rubber, she pushed her head and one arm into her own churning, electrically-active void.

Moments later she held out microscopic-sized granules of powder at the end of a long pincer.

Fragments that hold so much power, she thought, realising

that power was the wrong word. *They were far more than that, these were the opportunity of life itself.*

Luna positioned herself so that her two long legs anchored above Olivia's sleeping head, steadying her for the dream Luna was about to deliver. She bent down, almost doubled-over, and soon her fingers moved freely by Olivia's lips, ready.

With her ovoid, jet-black eyes, Luna studied the girl.

Instinctively, she tuned in to the rhythm of Olivia's breathing.

IN … OUT.

IN … OUT.

'Sacrum,' she thought, '*interpret this dream as best you can.*'

Beneath her, Olivia inhaled. As she did so, Luna's two fingers spun at an incredible speed, releasing a fine dust which was drawn deep into Olivia's lungs.

Without taking her eyes off the girl, Luna plucked more dust from within her infiniti and, at the optimum moment, lowered her fingers towards the child's mouth and repeated the process.

After every breath, Luna stopped and gauged the girl's reaction, making tiny adjustments to the rate of powder in proportion to the volume of air drawn in.

So far, so good, Luna thought. *Already she tosses and turns. Soon she will begin her lucid and vivid journey. Nothing will wake her.*

Luna glided through the air, across the dark room, and settled above Anika. She repeated the procedure, scrutinising every movement, looking for signals, and making sure her dream was perfect.

Only the boy, now.

She noted the strong, intense reactions of the male sibling. But his haunting, wailing cries were reminiscent of someone else. Someone with whom she hardly dared to compare: Xinder.

Luna studied the reaction of the children, noting that the noises they made were not just the anguished cries of their previous dreams. These were sounds that exuded certainty and confidence; Anika laughing, Danny smiling, Olivia's face beaming with happiness.

Maybe the final part of the First Dream was a reassurance that it would be worth the trouble ahead.

She dipped a hand into her infiniti. *After all, there is always balance,* she thought. *Where there is fear, there is hope. And where there is life, there is death.*

Luna, tired and aching, addressed the Animais.

'Last of all, the Gifts of Genartus. And then their journey will commence.'

Luna's silvery-grey, ghost-like body now sat directly above Olivia's sleeping face, her infiniti emitting blue shards of light over the girl's peaceful, pale face.

Quietly, Luna began.

'For the eldest, yellow dust – for hands and feet. Hands that guide, heal and lead. Swift feet for running.'

She transformed the end of one of her fingers into a needle so long that it was like a sliver of pure ice that melted into nothing. She injected a tiny yellow speck into the soft flesh between thumb and finger on each of Olivia's hands. Moving down Olivia's body, she repeated the action on her ankles, the needle entering the tender skin by her Achilles tendons.

As she withdrew the needle for the final time, Luna noted a fizz of electric blue energy flowing through and over the girl's sleeping body.

The gifts are undamaged by time, she thought.

Without hesitating, Luna walked across the night air to Anika, moving directly over her face. As she extended her legs Luna signed again, the vibrations clear to the onlookers.

'Blue dust, for eyes to see when blackness falls, and ears to hear the smallest of sounds. With eyes so sharp and ears so keen, she will understand what others do not hear or see.'

A minuscule blue crystal fragment sat at the tip of the needle. With astonishing precision Luna injected the tiny particles through the delicate tissues of Anika's closed eyelids and into the retinas of her eyeballs. Carefully, she slid a needle down each of Anika's ear canals, and injected the crystals directly into her eardrums. As she withdrew the needle, Luna saw the same strange electrical effervescence momentarily splaying over Anika's outer body.

So skilful was her technique that, apart from the gentle rise and fall of their chests, Olivia and Anika did not flicker, nor spill one single drop of blood.

Now it was the boy's turn. Luna sensed the other Animais vibrating nervously nearby. She stretched out an arm and drew it slowly back in, twisting her slender hand from side to side.

'Animais,' she announced. 'His first gift is to the heart. When the needle leaves his body it will trigger a reaction that will herald the start of their quest to open Genartus, and to save the Earth from damnation.'

'From this moment forth,' she continued, her vibrations like a whisper, 'clouds will build. There is no turning back.'

Luna stood above Danny's chest, legs astride his face.

A roll of thunder drummed high above them as she steadied herself and vibrated.

'Yellow gifts for hands and feet,' she said. *'Blue to hear and see, but red is the one for heart and mind – for power – and understanding what may be.'*

With aching limbs, Luna galvanised herself.

'*Red Dust, a gift of power, when strength is needed.*' And on the word "power", Luna thrust her arm high into the air.

She paused and steadied herself, marking the exact spot on Danny's chest where she would thrust the needle.

Moments later, the needle swept down and pierced the boy's heart.

His body fizzed as his chest cavity rose. Luna held it as long as she dared, making sure every last speck of dust was instilled into the boy.

As she withdrew, a terrific thunderbolt spat out, rattling every window of the farmhouse.

Even Luna trembled. Nature was awakened.

A sign from one of the other Animais confirmed her suspicions that Danny's sleep waves were already changing. A strange feeling filled her. A sense of exposure, a sense she had known only once before.

My invisibility!

She concentrated hard on the boy.

Finish this.

She dipped a leg into her infiniti and withdrew her final gift. '*Red Dust,*' she vibrated quickly. '*One for strength – another for courage.*'

A minuscule red fragment flashed into the tender flesh beneath Danny's chin. But before she could fulfil the task, she heard a gasp and felt a movement.

She withdrew the needle as a pain seared into her, her face burning.

Luna looked up.

In front of her, with a face contorted by fear, Danny's eyes were open. Staring right back at her.

Sleep, on this quiet, sultry night, hadn't come easily to Sas. She'd tossed and turned, but something was niggling her, preventing her from nodding off fully.

Now, as she lay in bed, she flicked through the family photo albums.

She was particularly drawn to the pictures of herself as a baby, the ones in which she lay in her cot alongside Olivia. Friends from the very beginning. Friends now, and friends until they passed away.

There were only four pictures before she graduated to a toddler. One of the pictures was cut in half, the others were of Sas staring upwards on her tummy, always next to Olivia. A warmth spread through her.

She wondered why she'd been visited by the dreams. Why had she been lumbered with nightmares concerning the Delauxs?

Someone had once quipped that she and Olivia might be twins, but it couldn't be possible, not here. There would have been an outcry. People would have noticed.

Why would either the Delaux parents or her own

mother give away a child? Besides, if that outside possibility was true, then one of their parents would have told them by now, surely?

She examined one picture which seemed a little more grainy than the others. She noticed, in the corner, a large, old hand. She squinted as she tried to make out the background.

She pulled out her phone and applied the magnifying glass.

The picture rushed out of focus before regaining its sharpness. The camera phone blinked and, moments later, a 'bing' on her laptop told her the image had saved itself on her computer.

A couple of clicks later, and Sas was staring at an enlarged digital version of the grainy picture.

Opening her image-editing programme, she added the picture and started playing around with the options.

Zooming in on the background, she noticed a strange brown vertical wiggle in the corner, as if it might be a wooden beam of some kind. She sharpened the image and played with the contrast.

Quizzically, she slanted her head first one way, then the other.

An upright post, on a bed?

She thought about it and realised it might be a four-poster bed.

As far as she'd ever known, they'd never had one of these. Their house was modern and full of contemporary furniture. Sas knew it was the only thing her father had left her mother when she was small.

She looked again. That hand in the corner. So old and leathery, the nails thick and hard.

An uncle or her grandfather, perhaps. But her grandpa lived in Australia. She first met him when she was four years old. Her first real memory. And her uncle had brown, slender hands. Fit for an accountant.

Could it be …

She frowned.

Zooming back out, she looked at the overall image again.

She and Olivia were staring up at the lens, looking remarkably similar, although her mother insisted she was the baby on the right.

But now, zooming in on the picture, she queried this information.

She examined it close up. Wasn't that the same flop, the same little tuft of hair that fell forward on Olivia's brow, on the child on the right?

She realised whose hands they were: Sap's. The bed had to be the old four-poster with carvings that she had seen in his room.

She noticed her pulse racing.

Twins? It was impossible.

A plan quickly formed in her head. During half-term, she'd ask for her birth certificate. If that wasn't forthcoming, she'd head to the Town Hall and ask to see the registrar for Births and Deaths. That would, at least, confirm where she was from. She would then start asking questions, targeting those who might have seen them all those years ago: Hospital workers, perhaps, or the local postman.

With this knowledge, she'd be able to knock her doubts on the head.

She'd need a diversion, so that Olivia and her mother wouldn't ask questions. She'd also need a companion.

Instantly, she thought of Ryan. He'd been so kind to her earlier. He'd understand the situation and, moreover, he could be trusted. She was certain of it.

In return for finding him a partner for his 'do', she'd ask

him to join her on her investigations. He loved doing strange things like this, even if he was a bit of a dork.

And, if she couldn't find a girl to go with him to his party, she'd go herself — at least with Ryan it was bound to be a laugh.

She climbed out of bed and made her way to the window. Opening the curtains, she pushed the windows open and looked out over the rooftops of Sutton.

Glancing up, the cloud loomed larger than ever. Its blackness filled her soul with dread.

In bed, she opened her notebook. She read over exactly what she'd written down moments after she'd woken up, stains of her sweat still marking the pages.

All she had to do was tell Olivia. At least, that would unburden her from the feeling that a heavy chain hung around her neck.

She lay back and closed the book. Yes. She'd tell Olivia before the game.

After that, in secrecy, she'd get to the root of the twin thing once and for all.

She returned her diary to the desk and made her way over to the window, peering out over the eerie night sky with pinpricks of light from the streetlights in the distance.

As she looked, she heard a piercing cry from somewhere outside, the haunting notes of a scream caught on the wind. It chilled her to her core.

Quickly, she shut the window and raced back to bed.

She lay panting.

If that wasn't a cry of intense pain, then it was the cry of someone wrestling with agony.

Noting the direction, she wondered if it hadn't come all the way from Appleside Farm.

MRS PUDDY

Candlelight filtered in to the corridor, and a soft light spread under the door into the attic room. Mrs Puddy rushed in, out of breath, her hair hanging down to her waist and her sharp eyes accentuated by the glow of the candle.

'Goodness me! Oh, my dear boy,' she said, rushing over to him. 'I never heard such a terrible scream in all me life. I thought you'd died.'

Nursing him, she dabbed the sweat from his brow.

'I ... I had the strangest dream, Mrs P. I swear, I was about to be stabbed by ... by a—'

'Is that right?' Mrs Puddy cooed. 'Stabbed? Goodness graciousness me.'

'It had an electric hole in its middle—'

'Well, well, I'm sure it did. Now, I think you're old enough not to be getting all a-tizz with that kind of bunkum,' she continued, helping him back to bed.

'Come, now. Lie back and get yourself off to sleep.'

'Please, don't go.'

'I'm staying right here till you're back in the land of

nod,' Mrs Puddy said. 'Now, don't you worry about a thing.'

Mrs Puddy sat on the edge of his bed for some time. When he yawned, she stroked his hair and laid him down under the duvet, his head nestling into the comfort of a pillow.

A gentle, faraway tune came to her. A song that had been sung to her by old Sap, who had once sat by her bedside himself. She hummed it quietly, the music soft and soothing.

Before long, Danny's breathing slowed, and he slipped into a deep slumber.

Mrs Puddy kissed the young boy on the forehead.

What was it, she thought, *about this scruffy young lad? Sensitive, but coated with a layer of steel, just like old Sap.*

GUDA

Guda shifted uneasily. 'Time is moving, Xinder,' he said. 'On Earth, the storm spills its anger when the Earth's sun moves to the highest point in the sky. It is time to go to the boy. It is known that one of his Gifts of Genartus failed.' Guda hesitated. 'His "courage" may not be with him.'

'Excellent, excellent!'

'Soon, the boy sleeps. He has seen the Prophecy in his dreams. One part of it he does not understand at all. Death confuses him, for he is young. That part relates to your mother, the one female Founder of Genartus. To him, she is known as the Ancient Lady. He dreams of her murder but it frightens him.'

'Her death and her end,' Xinder replied. 'The power of life. I could use her murder to manipulate him.'

'Indeed. Come with me.'

Xinder guffawed. 'There is hardly a stone unturned in your scheme. But hear me out one more time. How will the boy trust a spirit?'

'It may not be enough to remain invisible,' Guda said. 'Can you bear garments?'

The ghost scratched a non-existent chin. 'There is a long, light overcoat with which I use to visit my primitive subjects. I have the strength to wear it for a short time.'

'Then gather it,' Guda said. 'Hurry. Bring anything else that you require.'

Xinder drifted away, his invisible presence marked only by the swaying movement of dust and papers wafting off the floor.

Shortly, he returned wearing a rimmed hat, a scarf, and a long overcoat.

Guda stretched out a spindly opaque hand. 'Hold me. Feel the energy of the infiniti pulling you in.'

'Yes. The force is strong.'

'Good. Now crouch down, and dive like a bird as you have done before. Do this quickly.'

A tingling, gassy fizz vibrated through his ghostly frame.

'When you are ready, go!'

Xinder thrust forward, a mild burning sensation shuttling through him. A millisecond later, he found himself lying on a worn carpet in a dark, creaking house.

He scoured the room, vibrations from objects and walls filling his mind with a picture, a sense of the world around him.

'You have little time,' Guda said. 'Do the rest alone. Return to the fireplace at the bottom of the house. When you are done, hide in the chimney. I will be back before the sun rises, before the old man stirs.'

Xinder floated towards the stairs.

'Remember,' Guda called after him, 'make an ally of the child.'

'If he fears the murder of the Ancient Lady,' Xinder replied, 'I will play on it.'

'Good. Arrange a place and time to meet him before the storm breaks. Go now, in haste, Xinder. Do your bidding.'

DANNY

Danny woke, his brief sleep disturbed.

He exhaled loudly, opened his eyes, and looked out into the blackness of the room.

Was there someone at the foot of his bed?

'Ani? What d'you want?'

A windy chuckle came back at him. It wasn't either of his sisters.

Danny shuffled into a sitting position, stretched his arms out, and searched the room. Before long, he was able to make out a figure. A human figure, wearing a long coat and a wide-brimmed, cowboy-like hat.

Danny slipped back under his duvet. 'Who is it?' he called out in a weak voice.

'Aha! Hello!' the voice said, huskily.

Shivers raced up Danny's back. 'What can I ... er ... help you with, Mister?' Danny eventually stammered.

'You are the boy, aren't you?'

This wasn't the kind of question a burglar would ask.

Danny couldn't think what to say, so he remained silent as his eyes adjusted to the light.

'Ah! Forgive me for another little intrusion,' a deep, crisp voice said, 'but I have something to share with you.'

The cloaked man approached. As he neared, he raised his head.

Danny's eyes bulged. Beneath the hat, he saw straight through to the curtain.

'Now, boy, I need to speak with you about a rather urgent matter. The thing is, this time I need a favour.'

'No!' Danny reeled. 'Not you, *again?*' he blurted.

'I tell you what,' the ghost said, moving closer, 'perhaps you need a reminder?' In a flash, Xinder whipped out a knife.

Danny froze as the knife floated through the air towards him. Moments later, he felt a nick just under the left side of his jaw. A drop of blood ran down his chin. Danny sidled down his bed.

The ghost moved closer, inspecting the damage. 'Goodness, now it matches the other side,' Xinder said, coldly. 'You do believe I exist, don't you?'

Danny's bones rattled. He nodded.

'Good,' the ghost said. 'Let's be quite clear about that straight away.' Moving a little further from the bed, he said, 'you might be aware that you are on the threshold of something rather extraordinary. There are mortal challenges you must face. I am sure you know of them...'

'The dreams?' he stuttered.

'Precisely,' said the ghost, chuckling. '*The dreams.*'

Danny shivered. 'I don't understand.'

The ghost sucked in a mouthful of air. 'You've heard about Genartus?'

Danny's brain fizzed. Why was this ghost so interested in a place that only figured as whispers in his mind?

Danny kept as still and as quiet as he could, hoping like

mad that the ghost would say his piece, not mutilate him any further, and go away.

The ghost stared at Danny for a few moments. 'Well, Genartus is where life began, where all things were created. But more recently it's been, how should I say, put on ... standby. The thing is,' the ghost continued, 'there's a slim chance it may operate again, which would mean terrible things must happen to my mother.' The ghost paused as though taking stock. 'Everything clear so far?'

Danny had no idea what the ghost was talking about, but nodded anyway.

'Good. Now this event is known as the Prophecy of Genartus, and it involves you, my boy,' the ghost said, leaning in. 'I would like to help you in your quest and, in return, you can give me a hand. How do you say it, a tit-for-tat arrangement?'

Danny tried to remember to breathe. His eyes strained in their sockets, forgetting to blink. He sensed that the ghost was smiling thinly at him.

'In due course, I need you to take good care of the Ancient Lady, see that no harm comes to her.' His voice trailed off as he searched Danny's face. 'You do know about the Ancient Lady?'

Danny stayed silent.

'Well, you see,' the ghost continued, 'she's my mother and a sad old woman who's been hanging on to a mere thread of life for an awfully long time. But she'll never see any of it again because, like me, she's blind. Eyes gauged out.' The ghost paused solemnly as if remembering her. 'One day, maybe, I'll tell you more about her, but, to cut a long story short, boy, she took the noble but worthless step of sacrificing herself to keep a spark alive.'

'A spark?' Danny said, barely able to squeeze the words out. 'Of what?'

'A spark of life, I suppose.'

Danny thought he'd better play along. 'If you save your mother, will it mean you stop being a ghost?'

The ghost was thankful Danny couldn't see his face. 'Of course not,' he sobbed trying to bury the amusement in his hurt voice. 'My body is gone, but my spirit is forever.'

'But will I stop having dreams about ... about death.'

'If you help me, then I solemnly promise that from this moment forth, this is exactly what will happen. No more violent, murderous dreams, young man.'

Danny exhaled. 'What ... what do I have to do?'

'In due course, you must protect her, that is all,' the ghost whispered. 'There are some people that would want her dead. These people may think they are right, but rest assured they are mistaken. Dreams often show what you fear; they indicate the opposite action to what you must do. In this case, you must protect her from harm – do you understand? I'm really asking so little.'

Danny smiled. Looking after this Ancient Lady seemed entirely reasonable.

He nodded, hesitatingly.

'Splendid,' said the ghost, whose invisible gaze seemed to rest on Danny for rather too long.

❧ 6 ❧

WYNN-GARRY, THURSDAY

Dancing! That's what he'd forgotten, the blasted Scottish reels! What had made him agree to that?

Goodness me, he thought. *All that twirling, stamping and clapping. The sets and the do-si-doing. He'd be expected to lead from the front!*

Wynn-Garry shook his head and rubbed his eyes. Drat. He hadn't done any reeling for years. It wouldn't do to make a tit of himself in front of his esteemed guests.

He climbed out of bed and studied his watch. Very early, even by his standards.

Drawing the curtains, he levered the windows open. Fresh air shot in and he breathed deeply, the oxygen waking him, and a soft wind brushing through the room. He frowned at the big cloud above, hoping that it might have blown away overnight.

He hummed a tune while moving downstairs to his office. He flicked through his old vinyl records until he came to the 'Scottish Reeling Classics'. Blowing the dust off, he pulled out the black disk and placed it over the gramophone deck.

He'd start with the "Dashing White Sergeant".

The sound crackled as the reeds of the bagpipes filled with air.

Wynn-Garry, clad only in boxer shorts and string vest, made himself a bit of space by moving a couple of chairs and exercise books off the floor. Placing a hand behind his back, he began hopping up and down.

Imagining a circle of his guests, he 'set' to an imaginary lady, clapped and turned. Yes, that was it. 'Set', clap to your partner, turn, figure of eight, and bow.

Onto the next.

The music of the Highland Band filled the room. Wynn-Garry skipped through the song, growing in confidence as the memories came flooding back.

Hop, clap, and turn. Bow and twist.

After the third tune, he collapsed into his armchair, and sipped a glass of water.

He wondered about his guest list. *Pity,* he thought, *that the Delaux parents couldn't have made it.* He shook his head. *One minute here, the next they'd gone.* No wonder the faces of the children had dropped when he'd passed on the news. Such was the archaeologists' life, he supposed.

In the public eye of archaeology, they were very much seen as stars in their field, even if they didn't show it. They would have fitted in happily with the guest list of prominent men and women of the area.

His train of thought moved on to the children. He had to admit the set-up up there on the moors was more than decent. The old man looked well, Mrs Puddy obviously cared for the children splendidly, and the house was in good order. Wynn-Garry examined his hand and wondered if he shouldn't have talked to Olivia further. Oh, well, the deed was done.

A passing thought struck him. He wondered whether

he should ask the Delaux children to come along to the party. Make a bit of a fuss of them. Perhaps they could help the catering staff with their chores. He nodded at the thought. Olivia was his most gifted pupil, a prize-winning scholar, and Anika their greatest athlete. He could make a show of them, and introduce them to his guests.

Danny could look after the coats. Then again, he'd probably lose them.

He walked over to the gramophone and turned over the record. It was a sterling idea. He'd ask the children after the football match, as a surprise. A consolation prize, or maybe even as a reward for Anika? The gesture would also show Olivia that he took her seriously.

Wynn-Garry smiled as he bowed to the music, clapped his hands, and, with one arm in the air, spun and hopped his portly frame around the room until the music ran its course.

After dinner, the disco. What better way to get everyone going, than by having a few of the youth around to start the dancing? Rumour had it that Anika was a very energetic dancer, particularly at a type called "rave".

He pondered this thought as he selected another disc from his collection, 'Disco Hits of the Seventies'. A cracker, if he recalled.

The music came on. Wynn-Garry nodded his bald head in time with the beat.

Feeling his body come alive, Wynn-Garry thrust a hand high into the air, and gyrated his hips.

'Anika Delaux,' he said, as he moved in time with the music, 'will be second fiddle to these kinds of moves!'

XINDER

The boy – this Sacrum – has absolutely no idea what is going to happen, Xinder thought, as he hovered into the middle of the room. *He has found no meaning in his dreams. Do these people ignore visions? These Sacrum will never survive the storm, let alone find the cave of riddles, the one place they must reach that shows the secrets to gaining the egg-stones that lead to Genartus. It is time to execute the plan.*

He floated back to Danny's bedside. 'There is another way,' he crowed.

Danny didn't move a muscle, the leadenness of sleep preventing him.

'I want you to consider joining me, physically, as my flesh and blood.'

Danny yawned. 'Really? Join you?'

'Not right now of course. I'd like you to think about it. But joining me will save your life.'

Danny stretched his arms out wide. 'Save my life,' he repeated. 'Sure.'

'Good-good. I'm thrilled ... delighted,' Xinder said, feeling the weight of his coat on his frame. 'About the knife,' he continued. 'I don't have time to explain things in great depth, so occasionally it pays to use other means.'

'But, Mister ... Sir,' Danny said, summoning up his courage, 'if I did this joining up thing, what's in it for me?'

'For you? Ah yes!' the ghost crowed. 'What's in it for you, aside from saving your existence on this planet?'

The spirit drew himself up as best he could.

'I hold the secrets of ages past, boy. I will give you strength and courage, so that you are feared and respected. You will have the power of a horse and the courage of a lion. I give you my word. All you have to do is meet me tomorrow morning. Somewhere safe. Then, I will show you alone what happens. When you know the facts, you will choose to join me freely.'

His voice turned darker.

'A terrible time is coming, boy. You have seen the Great Prophecy now, and, deep down, you know it is a hopeless quest. I offer you a different salvation.'

'The prophecy,' Danny stammered. 'It's the nightmare, isn't it?'

'Yes, indeed,' the ghost crowed. 'Meet with me in no more than nine hours, and no less than eight. Tell me a place where no one will see us.'

Danny tried to think. 'Er ... there's a back alleyway above the bank of the football field near the school,' he said, trying to swallow a yawn. 'You'll know you've found it when you see two houses leaning in on each other, sort of head-butting each other. It's usually pretty quiet.'

'Excellent,' the ghost gushed. 'Wear a long overcoat, like mine, and a scarf. Do you have a scarf?'

Danny didn't, but he lied and said he did.

'And do you like sweets, boy?'

'A bit,' Danny replied, feeling happier now that the ghost appeared to be wrapping things up, even with such a strange question. 'But Sap's the sucker for sweet things in our house. He's always dipping his fingers in the sugar bowl, and getting told off by Mrs Puddy.'

The ghost chuckled. 'Is that so?'

A groan from the bed nearby signalled that Anika was stirring.

'I must leave. We will meet in a few hours in the alleyway,' the ghost whispered, drifting to the door. 'Tonight's chat, young man, is our own little secret. Any tongue-wagging and the deal is off.'

Xinder stopped, as if an idea had popped into his head. 'Tell me your name, boy?'

'Danny Delaux.'

'I will save you, Danny Delaux.'

Danny caught a glimpse of the knife.

As the ghost reached the door, he turned. 'Be in no doubt that your life will change forever in a few hours from now. The strength of a horse and the courage of a lion! You will never regret it.'

Danny nodded. 'What ... what's your name?' he asked.

'Ah, yes. The fine detail.' His eye sockets bored into Danny, who felt as though his heart was briefly being sucked out. 'I am the ghost of Xinder, Frozen Lord of Halaria, Son of Mazeen and the Ancient Lady. Do you have a cup of water, boy?'

Danny pointed to the table just behind him.

Xinder hovered to it and dropped something in the cup. 'You will need this. Drink. It may give you strength.'

And with those words, Xinder slipped quietly out of the door.

Danny fell back on his pillows, rubbing his eyes. *What the hell was that about?*

He didn't know what was real and what wasn't anymore. He knew, though, that there was no way he was going to turn up at this meeting with the ghost, whatever powers had been offered to him in return.

Lions and horses! Twaddle.

He studied the clock. Three thirty-five.

He did a quick calculation. Eight hours from now and it would be … bang in the middle of the football match. Nine hours and the game would just be finishing. A classic Danny timetable cock-up.

He breathed a sigh of relief. Problem sorted; he wasn't missing the game, certainly not for a knife-wielding ghost.

Relieved, Danny closed his eyes and drifted back to sleep.

SOLA

Sola raced across the air to the boy.

Xinder, forever banned from leaving Halaria, had discovered a way to the Sacrum only hours after the last part of the First Dream had been given! This was beyond comprehension.

Sola anchored her legs either side of Danny's head, and spun a hazy-styled dream.

With any luck, as the sun rose and humans readied themselves for a new day, the meeting with Xinder might feel as if it had never happened.

XINDER

Talking to Danny, an idea so simple, and yet so brilliant, had popped into Xinder's head.

Xinder pulled a small jar out of his pocket and examined it, smiling.

Halarian toadstool powder. A lethal poison, with the power to kill those who came from Genartus. In one stroke, he'd reduce the old man to a spirit. Just like him.

Mazeen's value would be nullified, not that he had much worth anyway. *But why not take the chance, while he had it?*

Xinder reached the hallway. No Guda. *Good,* he thought, *better the Animais doesn't know.*

The ghost cursed. Wearing a coat for such a long time had sapped his strength. He let the garment cascade to the floor as he searched the room, sensing vibrations. In no time he had created a map in his mind's eye.

He headed down a corridor, and came to an open door. He slipped through and instantly sized up the energy in the room. Before long, the outlines of a table and chairs, and the vibrations of plants and foodstuffs came to him, hanging off the easy-to-identify metal hooks clasped onto the beams of the ceiling.

Turning to his left, he discovered the strong vibrations of a smouldering fire – a cooker. Good.

He thought about sweet foods, like honey or, how did the boy say it, *sugary-things*?

Yes! There, near the cooker, in a small container. Sweet granules, exactly as he hoped.

It's easy to see, he thought, *when one has aeons of time. It's easy to understand how energy spins, fires and vibrates around every single thing.*

Xinder cursed. His strength sapped by the coat, he found that pouring the Halarian toadstool powder into the bowl was more of an effort than he'd bargained for. As he did, tiny squeals emanated.

Perfect. The fungi are alive.

Xinder drifted out of the room, along the corridor, into the living room, and back to the fireplace.

He felt for the vibrations of the Animais.

Nothing.

Above him, he could hear yawns. The old man stirring. Feet padding on the ceiling above.

Come on, Guda, where are you?

A moment later, the stairs groaned with a heavy footstep.

Xinder didn't want to hang about. Even though he knew he couldn't be seen, he certainly didn't want to be found in the house of his father, the home of his greatest enemy.

As the footsteps neared, a small vibration squeaked out. 'Master, it is Guda. Lower yourself and dive. Do nothing else.'

'About time,' Xinder snapped.

Without waiting to be prompted, Xinder knelt down and sprang into the Animais, hoping like mad it was the right place. As he left, he heard a small cough as Sap entered the room.

7

DANNY, THURSDAY

Danny stretched his arms and thrust out his chin. As he did so, he felt the sting of a fresh cut. He froze. Cloudy images of the previous night rushed in. He dashed into the bathroom and stared back at his reflection.

A small incision, just as he expected, mirroring the cut from the night before.

Danny couldn't believe it.

And why were the words "horse" and "lion" swimming in his head?

'The weight of a horse and the looks of a lion? Nah,' he said aloud to his reflection, shaking his head. *The head of a horse and the body of a lion?*

Danny sprayed water on his face. *The bite of a lion and the kick of a horse? No, no.* Deep in thought, he headed towards the kitchen, letting the water spill onto the floor as he went.

Mrs Puddy looked up as Danny came sloping in. 'You taking an elephant for a walk?' she said.

'Elephant?' he repeated, before realising what she meant. He tried not to break into a smile.

'What is the matter with you lot?' Mrs Puddy complained. 'Slumping and skulking and screaming in the night.'

Danny coughed. 'Oh. Olivia and Anika had a bad night again. I think they're talking about some, er…, girlie things. You know…' Danny mumbled.

'Periods?' Mrs Puddy squealed. 'Anika's becoming a woman now, is she? About time, I suppose.'

Girlie things? Danny went bright red. Oh dear. This was absolutely the last thing on his mind.

He changed the subject, fast. 'My throat's sore, Mrs P, and my head hurts. It's like someone's tightened a clip around my neck.'

'Come here. I'll take a look.'

Danny sidled over to the sink, and Mrs Puddy took his head gently in her hands. 'What are these cuts on your chin? Have you been playing with your knives again?'

'Of course, I haven't,' Danny said, weakly. 'Caught my face on something.'

Mrs Puddy looked at Danny suspiciously. 'I won't tell anyone about your knife throwing, you know that. I know you like to disappear off to that old potting shed and practice, though heavens only knows why.'

She took his hand, before feeling his forehead and the back of his neck. 'It's your big sister who doesn't approve.'

Mrs Puddy finished her medical. 'Well, you is a bit sweaty, young man. Could be a fever coming on.'

She rubbed her chin, thinking about what might be the best cure. 'I reckon you need a couple of…'

'Apples?' Danny suggested.

Mrs Puddy raised her eyebrows. 'How did you know?'

Danny smiled. Mrs Puddy's medical knowledge was virtually non-existent and Sap's extraordinary variety of apples in the orchard just happened to be her number one cure for everything.

ANIKA

After an unexpectedly large breakfast, Danny felt it was time to question his sister. 'Ani,' he began quietly, 'last night you called out, "Ancient Lady" several times. Why?'

A shadow fell over her face. 'Another nightmare,' she began. 'I've had three, each one utterly disturbing, but this dream was the best ... and the worst ... and the weirdest.'

She turned to her sister for support. 'They've been so real. I could smell things, and understand everything. Birds, trees, and plants talked to me. *Talked, Danny*! It's so ... so complicated and bonkers and confusing. I don't know where to begin.'

Anika scrunched her face up and ran a hand through her hair, trapping a finger on a knot. 'One minute, there's this knackered old woman telling me about a wonderful, beautiful place. The next minute I'm in a terrifying storm, like an endless hurricane, and the storm is chasing me. Lightning, mudslides, and tonnes of water coming after me, beating me to death...' She tailed off, scratching the back of her neck.

'What is it, Ani?' Olivia asked.

'I dreamt I reached a sanctuary. It was only then that I was safe from the storm. Kind of like heaven, but with pictures on the walls.'

She shook her head. 'I still don't know what it's supposed to mean.'

Olivia set her books down on the table and pulled up a chair.

'Anika, in your nightmare, what happened to this Ancient Lady?'

'Well, I'm pretty confident this haggard old woman kept trying to tell us something,' Anika said. 'But each time she did, she died.'

'Are you sure?'

'Yeah,' Anika said, her eyes wide. 'A violent, horrible death, different every time. And it was like being there, standing next to her. I could feel myself screaming.'

She took the stunned silence from the others as a green light to continue. 'Look, I know it sounds nuts, but this Ancient Lady knew about us ... she knew *everything* about us, even though I think we were on an entirely different planet.'

Her eyes searched her elder sister's face, begging her to believe. Anika's bottom lip began to tremble, and tears moistened in her eyes. 'I've tried to blot it out, but I think I'm going crazy.'

XINDER

'You cut it fine, Animais,' Xinder snapped.

'I cannot pretend it was easy, Master. Another Animais is suspicious. I must go. There are dreams to knit and sow.'

'Find me in eight hours, as the storm breaks,' Xinder said. 'With luck, I will get the boy. There will be no hiding place for you then, Animais. Be prepared.'

'That is why I must go,' Guda said, before flashing through his infiniti.

Xinder gasped as a terrible realisation struck him. He had left the coat with the knife in the pocket!

His shock soon turned to chuckles, though, before belly-laughs bounced into the high ceilings of the palace.

The cuts on young Danny's chin might be explained by bumps in the night or the nick of a common thorn, but the coat will prove that I was there, he thought. *The boy cannot ignore such a thing. He will reach into the pocket and feel the knife. Then he will stumble and take the bait.*

Xinder thumped the air. Oh, if I could see the look on his face! And now he will come to me, like a fly drawn to sweet granules.

Enjoying the image of the bowl filled with Halarian toadstool powder, Xinder threw his head back and roared with delight.

Without warning, a teardrop spilled from Olivia's eye.

'Oh, Lord. Not you as well!' Danny said.

'Yes. Me, too!' Olivia cried, lines of water now streaming down her cheeks. 'Same, exactly.'

Danny's eyes nearly popped out of his head. 'But this is madness—'

'I know.'

Danny was confused. 'You're sure it was just like Ani's dream? You're not making it up?'

'Yes! I'm positive. It's the truth,' Olivia insisted. 'I swear. Three intense, clear dreams like Anika described, except I was in a hall of mirrors. I've never been so amazed or happy or terrified, and, just as Ani said, the dreams all ended the same. Death.'

She clenched her hand. 'I kept seeing lightning and rain. Torrential, terrible rain. You know how I've been going on about this deluge, it's terrifying me. It's as if this stupid storm wants to target us, alone, until we make it to this weird cave, just as you said.'

They both nodded.

'And, Livi, you saw this Ancient Lady?' Anika asked. 'What did you think?'

Olivia thought for a moment. 'She'd been stuck. Abandoned someplace, I think. She's pathetic, desperate, waiting. Waiting for...'

'For what?'

Olivia shrugged. 'I don't know. Us, perhaps?'

'Her eyes had been gouged out, so she didn't know where she was,' Anika said.

'Exactly! You're right.'

'No eyes, but she had a gentleness; an aura of kindness and love,' Anika continued. 'She was disgusting to look at, though. All shrivelled up, like one of Sap's prunes.'

'Probably even more withered,' Olivia added with a thin smile. 'I don't know how she's still alive. It was as if she held the key to something...'

Danny had become noticeably quiet over the past few minutes. As if by instinct, the girls noticed.

'What about you, Danny?' they said.

Danny swivelled and faced the girls, his face ashen.

'Yeah,' he said, shakily. 'I've dreamt of this storm and this Ancient Lady on three occasions – just like you.'

The girls gasped.

Danny stared at them, his eyes red and brimming with tears.

He dropped his head.

'The thing is, in each of my dreams, it's me who kills her.'

Eventually, Olivia spoke. 'Look. I know it's odd, but these are only dreams, you know. They're just our minds worrying about things. Dreams aren't real, however much they appear to be.'

'If you don't think there's any truth in them,' Danny said, 'why did you go to such lengths to make a barometer and a storm glass? You must have thought there was something to it.'

Olivia thought for a moment. 'Sas had had a similar dream, too. I suppose I wanted to try something – anything – to prove or disprove the dreams, scientifically.'

'So, four of us have had the same dream,' Danny said. 'Perhaps there's some kind of storm demon out there, hurling dreams at us, and we just happened to catch them?'

'But Sas had the dreams, and she lives miles away,' Anika added.

Danny guffawed. 'She does sleep over a lot.'

'Don't be silly, Danny,' Olivia sneered. 'Of course sleep demons don't exist.' She rubbed her temples.

Anika suddenly piped up. 'The Fitzroy storm glass! Where is it?'

Olivia stood up, plucked the glass out of the fire grate, and placed it on top of the mantelpiece.

The children stared at it, as though it held the answers to all their problems. 'It's still cloudy with little stars,' Danny said, mischievously.

Anika focused more intently. 'Actually,' she whispered, entranced, 'those little stars are belting around? What does it mean?'

Olivia sighed, 'I don't know what it means or what it's supposed to show. It's not my finest work.'

Anika wasn't convinced. 'Just out of interest,' she said, 'for simple-minded people like me, who never saw it before, what was the glass like when you began this mad project?'

'Cloudy,' Danny said, 'just like it is now.'

'Thanks, Danny, very helpful,' Anika said. 'Well, it's like a game of pinball in there,' she said. 'There's way more going on than simply cloudy little particles shooting all over the place.'

Olivia strode over and squinted. 'There's nothing here but a foggy substrate,' she announced. 'You're wasting your time, Ani. Come on you two, get your things. You've got this big match to play today, or had you forgotten?'

Anika frowned. 'You think we should just ignore it all; the dreams, the cave, the Ancient Lady, everything?'

'Yes, I do,' she replied.

'Really?'

'Absolutely. One hundred percent. I believe it's purely a coincidence, that's all. These dreams are parasites of fear.'

The twins grabbed their sports bags, Anika stealing one more glance at the storm glass.

'We need to get a move on,' Olivia said, slipping the storm glass into her bag as she went. 'My guess is that, somehow, this big cloud sitting above us is making our brain patterns react oddly in advance of a storm breaking. With my scientific hat on, I'd say we ignore the whole thing. Yorkshire storms are never that bad.'

The twins shrugged. Olivia was the boffin. Much as they hated it, she was generally correct.

'I realise I'm pretty rubbish in Chemistry, or whatever science category the glass belongs in,' Anika said, earnestly. 'But I'd keep a really close eye on that Fitzroy storm thing-a-me if I were you.'

SAP

The children had barely stepped out of the door when Sap's deep voice stopped them short.

'*Wait!*' he yelled from the doorway. 'Did any of you leave this coat? Found it in the corridor.' A large overcoat dangled over his arm. 'Nice one too, with an unusual pattern on the lining. Sure I've seen it somewhere before.'

Danny missed a step and stumbled, righting himself before his nose split the floor.

Sap noticed. 'Yours, is it, Danny? Looks a touch big for you, mind.'

Danny doubled back, his body trembling. Without looking at Sap, he inspected the coat and shoved a hand inside one of the pockets. The hairs on his back shot up.

'Back in a second,' he yelled, as he flew up the stairs.

Danny sprinted into the attic room where he spied the cup of water, tinged slightly blue, exactly as he'd left it. In one movement, he drained the glass.

'Everything alright, Danny?' Sap asked.

'Fine,' Danny answered.

'Right-oh,' Sap said. 'Your coat?'

'Oh, yeah, a friend's. Must have grabbed it by mistake, in a rush.'

'Big fella, is he?'

'Yeah. I suppose,' Danny said, as casually as he could.

Sap handed him the coat. But as he did so a knife slipped out of the pocket and tinkled onto the paving slabs.

'A knife, Danny? You know you shouldn't carry one of those at school.'

Danny's heart skipped a beat. 'It's only plastic. A stage knife, you know ... drama stuff.' He smiled, bending down to pick up the knife, and beating Sap to it. 'The bloke who owns the coat is the lead part in the play.'

'He certainly has an interesting taste in knives,' Sap commented, raising an eyebrow. 'Well, on you go, young Danny, and remember to save those footballs.'

Danny set off to catch up with the girls. As he ran, his heart was thumping like a huge bass drum, and his head buzzed with a mixture of dread and excitement.

Sap knew it was a beauty; a knife worthy of a powerful man. From the clinking noise it made when it dropped on the floor, he would have bet a coin or two that it was made from silver and steel. From the way the light reflected through the stones on the handle, he'd have taken another wager that its jewels were unique; most likely rubies and pink diamonds.

It wasn't a plastic knife. Not in a million years.

He couldn't remember how he could tell a cheap knife from a proper knife, but he had been the one to show Danny how to master a knife all those years ago: how to test the balance and weight that would determine the revolutions and power of the throw.

Sap mulled this over, wondering what light his brain might shed on the subject. No, nothing there, just a deep penetrating pain in his mind, like toothache.

And why did that funny old coat stir his curiosity? The lining had taken his breath away. Was it the pattern?

He'd seen thousands of patterns of snakes and trees, or snakes slithering around poles, all the way through his long life.

Why did this one make him feel nervous and thrilled at the same time?

He replayed the moment he glimpsed the lining for the first time. That odd feeling again, as if the snake had actually moved, as if it had slithered up into the tree right there on the fabric itself.

Sap paced around the room.

He'd noted the buttons too. A matching crest of a snake winding through branches.

Nothing I can do about it now, he told himself, *whatever it might mean.*

Suddenly, a thought smashed into his head, electrifying his entire body.

He sat down in his large, worn armchair, cupping his face in his big, leathery, old hands.

What if the fabric from that jacket wasn't from Earth?

He'd never seen fabric that had the ability to change shape here on Earth before, but, if he remembered correctly, the marks of the snake and the tree were from ... Genartus?

A surge of energy rushed through his body, making him feel strong for a second or two.

Time to research those old carvings, he thought, *to shed light on that overcoat's true home.*

8

DANNY, THURSDAY

Assured by Olivia's dream diagnosis, the girls had a spring in their step as they headed down the track. From the top of the hill, the banks on either side of the road gradually increased in height, as if a giant digger had gouged the lane out of the hillside. The lane acted as a drain taking the water off the hill, and even in the driest summer a constant trickle dribbled from the moors to the river below.

Branches of oak, ash, maple, wild cherry, crab-apple, blackthorn and hawthorn made a thick canopy high above the road and today, it was coloured in a mat of rust, red and gold autumnal colours.

On a clear day it looked as if glitter had been sprinkled on the track as the sunlight flickered through the trees. Today it was almost pitch black, and the tree roots supporting the bank twisted through the rock and soil, reaching out like the arms and legs of decaying corpses. Sas still called it 'the big graveyard ditch', but the children were used to it; it was their daily walk to school. The idea of it being scary had long gone.

Nonchalantly, Danny told the girls that the coat was Fitzpatrick's dad's, and they must have got muddled up in the cloakroom. But although he slumped along quietly, his heart was thudding in his chest, and his brain worked overtime as he tried desperately to remember what had happened during the night.

The girls didn't bother to question him further.

For someone as disorganised as Danny, mistaking a coat was as common as being late for a lesson.

Half way down, they stopped by a large oak with a huge bough that leaned over the road. Anika climbed nimbly up the steep, tall bank, using the roots as handgrips. At the top, she uncoiled a rope wrapped around the branch and tossed down the slack end.

Danny went first. He took off, climbing the rope until his feet settled on a large knot at the bottom. Swinging backwards and forwards, the warm wind rushed through his hair.

As the line slowed, he jumped down, running to a stop.

'Pathetic, Dan,' Anika said. 'What's up with you?'

'Nerves,' he replied. 'Not really in the mood.'

Olivia went next. She sat on the knot and swung backwards and forwards at a leisurely speed, as she always did. Finally, Anika mounted the rope and asked Danny to pull her up the hill as far as he could.

'Watch this,' she said, her eyes glimmering.

Danny let go, and Anika soared forwards, hair flying, until she was horizontal with the bank, touching the canopy. She swung back, screaming in delight, and bashed into the bank on the other side.

'Anika! Enough. We've got to go to school,' Olivia said, trying to catch the rope. 'Kill yourself on the way back, but we're running late as it is.'

'Oh sure,' Anika said, coming to a stop and tucking the

rope around a protruding root system. 'I bet we'll be too tired, or it'll be too dark, or some other rubbish excuse as always.'

'Ani,' Olivia replied, 'after today, you have all of half term to swing yourself into hospital.'

At last the steep track levelled out and the height of the bank lowered, like the end of a playground slide. At the old wooden bridge, the children peered over the handrail at the water running beneath and looked for fish gliding in the pools next to the chunky oak uprights.

Olivia noted how, in the strange light, the school tower to their left looked enormous compared to the tiny boathouse by the river. She wondered if the old rowing boat they'd once played around in was still fit for purpose.

The children arrived at the lush, velvety green football pitch. White posts all the way round balanced safety ropes to keep the spectators at bay. Set back from each corner, the moveable floodlight towers dominated the pitch like metallic giants standing guard.

Anika ran across the bold, alternating stripes with its tattoo-like, fresh white markings. She practised kicks, flicks, and tricks and commentated loudly on the goals she was going to score later.

Before long, they were across the playing field, and heading up the steps to their form rooms.

Luna drew her arms together, taking comfort from the warm glow of her electrical current.

She soothed the burns from where the boy's eyes had scalded her, and wondered whether Guda was right.

Had nature, the universe, got it wrong?

Could the Sacrum, mere children, survive nature's fury, and nature's power, and go on to find the egg-stones of creation?

This undertaking had never been designed for children of mankind. But nature's wishes cannot be resisted. Not at any cost.

What about the old man, too? Time had taken its toll. He was old, but was he now, in a curious twist of fate, a *liability?*

One by one, she dipped her slender fingers into her infiniti.

She would make sure a dream was given to Sap every night that would somehow, *somehow*, stir him into action.

Luna stretched out a digit, dipped it in her infiniti, and

watched the blue light swirl in and around her finger like thread spinning around a stick.

With these thoughts, she dipped her head and inverted through her infiniti, vanishing into thin air.

DANNY

Danny noticed Fitzpatrick sitting quietly at his desk, reading a book.

Let sleeping dogs lie, he thought, *especially unpredictable dogs*.

Without any fuss, Danny made his way to the other side of the room, draped the coat over the back of his chair, sat down, and put his head in his hands. He desperately tried to remember what the ghost had said. A meeting, something about a lion and a horse? After writing down a couple of variations, Danny realised that it might be something to do with strength and courage.

He remembered that he would be saved, *but from what exactly?*

Hadn't he agreed on something as well, such as joining the ghost in some form of partnership? It didn't make any sense but, and it was a huge BUT, the ghost's coat and dagger were right here in this room. So it couldn't be a false memory, regardless of Olivia's certainty that their recent experiences were figments of their imaginations.

Danny teased the nicks on each side of his chin. Another reminder.

He pulled out a piece of paper, and nibbled the end of a pencil.

"*Possible meeting place*", he wrote.

He racked his brain. Was it down by the boatyard, or up by one of the big willow trees? He wrote both down, but shook his head. No. Neither option rang true. He wondered if it was the alley above the football pitch, and he wrote that down as well.

He underlined it twice and leaned back in his chair. Yes, that one rang a bell.

His thoughts were interrupted by a friendly, slightly painful, wallop on his shoulders. It was Ryan Williams who had bounced into the room. 'Morning Danny. You're not by any chance writing a "to-do" list, are you?' he said sarcastically.

Danny smiled. If Fitzpatrick was an otter with big lips, Ryan was a laughing donkey. 'No, don't be ridiculous,' he said.

Ryan read the list. 'Lost something?'

'Nah. Just trying to remember a dream.'

'Oh, well that's OK,' Williams said, cheerily. 'So long as it wasn't a big and complicated one?'

'Well, as a matter of fact, it was.' Danny smiled. 'Now, go away and leave me to think.'

'News alert!' Williams announced to the room, his grin almost completely covering his face. 'Danny Delaux is thinking! Give him plenty of room, oxygen at the ready.' Ryan leant down again. 'Next, you'll be telling me Anika's caught the same bug,' he whispered. 'Good luck!'

He smiled and sprang off like a big, energetic puppy to his desk at the back of the room.

FITZPATRICK

Fitzpatrick listened in to Danny's conversation with Ryan. He'd bet money that Danny had forgotten something again. By the looks of it, this time the object was more important than usual.

Fitzpatrick stood up quietly. 'Morning, Danny, everything cool?'

Danny groaned. First Ryan, now Fitzpatrick.

'Not really, Fitzy,' he replied.

'Lost something?'

'No,' he started. 'Well, kind of.' Danny groaned. 'Actually, I had another dreadful nightmare. Trying to remember it.'

'Oh, yeah?' Fitzpatrick replied.

'Yeah,' Danny said. 'A couple of really strange experiences, but, poof, gone for ever.'

Fitzpatrick laughed. 'Want to talk about it?'

Danny stared at Fitzpatrick. 'I told you, I'm not talking to you after what you did yesterday.'

'Really?' Fitzpatrick sighed. 'Look, I had a think and last

night I decided that I'm going to change. No more jokes, no more pranks. I promise—'

'You said that before, and let me down. In fact, you lied to me. Christ! Fitzpatrick, I had to own up for your stupidity, and you made me feel like an idiot. Luckily Olivia didn't believe me.'

Fitzpatrick sucked in his cheeks. 'I've told Jackson and Pulse that I don't want to be part of the gang. When I'm with them, I act like a ... well, like a total dickhead. I don't know what comes over me. The bottom line is that I'm actually sick of it, too.'

Fitzpatrick noted Danny's look of disgust. 'Dan, if you don't believe me, go and ask them,' he continued. 'They're over there in the corner playing on their phones like happy little freaks. Seriously, I don't want to hurt anyone anymore. I really don't.' He dropped his voice and briefly stole a look over his shoulder. 'I want to be your friend.'

'Blimey, Fitzy, this isn't the time. Right now, I've literally got a nightmare on my hands. I'm not going to trust you until I know you mean what you say.'

'What do you want me to do? I've promised I won't be nasty to either of your sisters. I'm going to put all that anger behind me. I won't even speak to your sisters if you don't want me to.'

'I bet you've already arranged with your Newton mates that Anika's going to get a kicking though, haven't you?'

Fitzpatrick winced. 'There's not much I can do about that now, is there?'

'The only reason you're being 'Mr Nice' is because if they kick her out of the game we'll lose and she won't play in the team after half term. That would leave room for someone else. And that person will probably be you.'

Fitzpatrick's expression had changed. 'You know what,

Danny,' he spat. 'I meant what I just said. Throw it back in my face, why don't you.'

'Well, that's rich, coming from you,' Danny said, standing up. He looked him in the eye. 'I swore on my life that I wouldn't tell anyone about the glass and I kept my word. You, Fitzy ... well, you're a lying, deceitful disgrace to your dead parents, your aunt, your school and, more importantly, to yourself.'

Danny noticed an unusual silence.

From the corner of his eye, he noted how the whole class had stopped and stared at them, their mouths ajar.

The Animais was astonished to learn a couple of things. First, that it was Xinder who knew about the children's dreams and their gifts. Second, that Danny had no idea about his own gifts; but Xinder knew enough about them to exploit him.

Sola thought it through, reaching the same conclusion. One of *them* must have gone to Xinder. But Animais were neutral in all things. They did not meddle, and they never had.

Only four Animais Elders had seen the gift ceremony: Luna, Guda, Juno and herself.

Was Luna bitter about appearing in front of the boy? No, it didn't add up.

What about Guda? He was the one who had objected to the Gifts of Genartus being given to children, but he was also the most passionate Animais about giving dreams.

Or Juno, the quiet one?

Yes, Sola thought, maybe it was her. Why? What was her motive?

Another thought whistled into Sola's mind. Xinder was

a spirit, so what if he had travelled through one of their infinitis, or perhaps the infiniti of another Animais, to escape Halaria?

It was the only possible explanation she could think of.

She searched her vibrations.

Nothing close by.

This Animais would have to be caught in the act. But Animais moved so fast through the universes, it was as if they were a multi-dimensional fluid.

Catching one would not be easy.

FITZPATRICK

The silence was broken by the bell.

'By my watch,' Mr Steele said, hitching up his sleeve and twisting his arm as though showing off a priceless treasure, 'the time is approaching half past nine. After I have dismissed you, you have an extended free period. Please use this for last minute drama rehearsals; like learning your lines, Mr Ford; or practising your clarinet, Miss Buxton; or for recital practice before the programme this afternoon, Mr Anderson.'

Mr Steele stuck his nose in the air and twitched his moustache. It was a signal that he was going to say something profound. 'Now, about the weather. There is a rather large cloud b*rrr*ewing right above us.' He rolled the 'r' rather dramatically.

'To put your minds at rest, our headmaster has been in touch with the Met Bureau to find out if this might be a cause for concern. I am happy to report that, as far as they know, there are none. This morning and this afternoon, there is a high chance that we may get a little wet; indeed there may even be a possibility of a heavy downpour. But all school activities are scheduled to go on as usual.

'Anika Delaux, please remove that lipstick from your desk. Now, remember, class, just in case lightning strikes, what would be the best course of action to take? Anyone? Ah, yes, Alexander?'

'Put up your umbrella, sir.'

'No, you do not, Alexander. And stop laughing. Allen, will you desist from flicking paper balls at Anika please?' He glared at the boys, 'Umbrellas, as you know perfectly well, are for repelling water. I'm talking about lightning strikes.'

Steele raised his eyebrows in anticipation. 'Fitzpatrick, what would you do?'

'I'd get the hell out of there before I was shrivelled to a crisp.'

The class laughed.

'Well, it's better than holding up an umbrella, but where would you go?'

Little Jimmy Nugent put up his hand.

'Yes, Nugent.'

'I've been told that, if you get in a car, the rubber tyres would earth the strike, wouldn't they, Sir?'

Mr Steele clasped his hands together. 'Very good, Nugent, and you're absolutely correct. Either get indoors, or hop in a car—'

'My granddad,' Nugent continued, 'got killed by a bolt of lightning in 1983, while walking his bull terrier called Plank—'

'Did he, Nugent?' Mr Steele sensed one of Nugent's stories coming on. 'How fascinating. Perhaps you might fill me in another time.'

Steele turned back to the pupils. 'Now, Class, do your

best today and make us all proud. Afterwards, have a safe and relaxing break. You are dismissed.'

The pupils instantly divided into several small groups. Danny remained in his chair, twiddling his pencil.

Fitzpatrick quietly made his way over. 'Come on, Danny, it can't be that bad. You look terrible. I can help if you want ... if we're still friends?'

Danny shrugged. 'Sure. Sorry about the outburst. Been a bad morning, that's all.'

'Sounds terrible—'

'You have no idea,' Danny replied. 'Really. If I told you, you would never, ever believe me.'

'Try me.'

Danny sighed. 'Nah. You'll only laugh.'

'Go on. I promise I won't tell a soul.'

'Look, Fitzy, we've been there.'

'If you don't talk to someone, it just gets bottled up. My shrink told me that.'

Danny fingered his pen. What did he have to lose? 'You won't believe me,' he heard himself say.

'I promise you I won't judge. I'll just listen. That's what friends are for, right?'

Danny exhaled. 'OK,' he began. 'If you really want to know, last night I was visited by something that, as far as I could tell, was a ghost.'

'A ghost?' Fitzpatrick coughed. 'Really?'

'Yes. Really.' Danny fired back. 'I told you that you wouldn't believe me.'

Fitzpatrick eyed him suspiciously and raised his hands. 'OK. A ghost ... carry on.'

Danny rubbed his forehead. 'Well, this ghost promised me stuff if I met up with him.'

'Yeah? What did you say?'

'I think I kind of agreed. I was half asleep. What would you do?'

'I'd probably agree too,' Fitzpatrick said. 'Was it a nice ghost or a nasty ghost?'

'Bit of both, I think. It was wielding a knife, but at the same time I'm pretty sure it wanted to help.'

'Well that's alright,' Fitzpatrick said, sounding like an authority on the subject. 'So, the ghost had a knife and it didn't kill you. That's a start.'

Danny hadn't thought of this.

'Any idea where you're hooking up?'

'That's the problem. I can't remember. I thought it was a dream, so I agreed to everything and said the first thing that came into my head.'

'What makes you think it wasn't a dream?'

Danny pointed at the coat. 'This.'

Fitzpatrick looked at it. 'An overcoat! Bleeding heck, Danny.' Fitzpatrick wondered if Danny hadn't entirely lost his marbles.

'I know,' Danny said, quickly realising it must sound idiotic, 'but I swear it's the same coat the ghost was wearing. I remember those buttons with the snake up a tree.'

Fitzpatrick thrust out his jaw and furrowed his brow. 'How do you know it isn't Old Whatsisface's?'

'Sap,' Danny said. 'His name is "Sap".'

'Yeah right, chill your boots,' Fitzpatrick said, holding the coat up. 'I mean it's pretty big – about his size – are you sure he wasn't ... giving it to you? You know, offloading it before he took it to the charity shop.'

Danny shook his head. 'No, definitely not. Sap only has patched up clothes, certainly not an overcoat like this one. Anyway, there's more.'

'More?' Fitzpatrick raised his eyebrows. 'Blimey. I mean, great.'

Danny turned his head up. 'Look at these. Cuts from the blade of the knife I was telling you about—'

'From the ghost?'

Danny nodded.

Fitzpatrick inspected Danny's face. 'Nah, I don't believe you. You could have got those from a bramble or a branch when you ran to school yesterday.'

Danny shook his head. 'No, honest to God, look how neat they are. The ghost definitely arrived in the middle of the night.'

'You're one hundred percent sure?'

'Yes.'

Fitzpatrick guffawed. 'Look, Danny, everyone knows ghosts don't carry things like knives or hit people.'

'This one did.'

Fitzpatrick struggled to contain his laughter. 'Don't get me wrong, Danny, but it doesn't stack up. Why would a ghost want to harm you?'

Danny thought for a second. 'To prove it was real.' Danny felt in the coat pocket and slowly withdrew the knife, shielding it from prying eyes.

'Here. Look.'

Fitzpatrick's eyes fell to the gap under the desk where Danny held the knife. He swore under his breath.

'Blimey, Danny, that's a beauty,' he said. He could hardly prise his eyes away. 'So, what did this ghost say?'

'That's where it gets blurry,' Danny began. 'He said he was on a mission to save his mother. He said that she was going to die, and that I had to help protect her at any cost.'

'Epic. He sounds alright to me,' Fitzpatrick said. 'I'd do anything to protect *my* mother.'

Danny realised he'd hit a raw nerve. 'Sorry, Fitzy. I didn't mean—'

'Chill, Danny, I know you didn't mean anything by it.'

Fitzpatrick was fully intrigued. 'So, was there anything in it for you?'

'Well, as I said, I think he talked about a partnership of some sort. That's the part I can't remember. I would find out at this meeting, I suppose, not that I can go.' Danny laughed and turned a little red. 'I think I agreed to meet it bang in the middle of the football match.'

Fitzpatrick chuckled. 'Blimey. Even with the dead, your planning skills are crap.'

Danny screwed up his face. 'Somewhere along the line, he went on about power and strength, or something,' he said, scratching the desk. 'Maybe it's in my head from a general lack of sleep?'

Fitzpatrick was intrigued, but also concerned about his friend. If Danny's story was completely made up, this was nigh on madness. You had to hand it to them, though; these Delaux kids were damn interesting.

Danny studied Fitzpatrick's face, and quickly reached a conclusion. 'You think it's bollocks, don't you?' He put his head in his hands. 'I've been sucked in, haven't I?'

Fitzpatrick shrugged. 'Probably your old Sappy friend playing a joke or something—'

'Or I've been hallucinating from one of his bitter apples?' Danny added.

'Yeah,' Fitzpatrick said, as though this would have been perfectly normal. He'd heard about the old man's curious apple collection. 'Probably one of those apples. I can't believe you didn't see it all along.' He slapped Danny on the back. 'You ought to be getting along, don't want to miss your warm-up.'

Danny cocked his head and looked at his watch. 'RATS! Is that the time?' He rushed his things together. 'Hey, Fitzy, thanks for the chat. Please don't think I've turned into a nutter.' He slung the bag strap over his shoulder. 'Promise me, don't tell anyone about this.'

'You lot are all nutters,' Fitzpatrick said. 'But you, Danny, are the only one worth your salt.'

Danny noted that the look in Fitzy's eyes had turned harder. Maybe his thoughts had moved on to his sisters.

Danny ran to the door. 'See you later.'

'Sure.'

Fitzpatrick shook his head.

If it wasn't strange scientific experiments, or an infatuation with ghosts, or girls being brilliant at games designed for men, then it was some other random thing in the Delaux family. Extraordinary disorganisation, say, or manic recklessness, or unbelievably old helpers and missing parents.

Mr Steele reappeared. 'Time to lock up,' he said. 'Please gather your things as the school won't re-open until after half term. Take everything you need.'

Chairs scraped against the floor as the remaining students stood up. Fitzpatrick slipped into his overcoat and gathered the contents of his desk, dropping them haphazardly into his bag. He tucked in his chair and headed towards the door.

'Fitzpatrick,' Mr Steele called out, 'haven't you forgotten something?'

Fitzpatrick looked puzzled.

'Your coat?'

'That? It's Danny's,' he said, too quickly. 'But, er, don't worry, I'm seeing him later. I'll take it for him.'

At that moment, he saw the slip of paper covered with Danny's scrawny handwriting.

Fitzpatrick scanned it for a second, and noticed the underlined location. It must be where he was meeting this so-called ghost.

He folded it and crammed it into his pocket.

'Jolly good,' Mr Steele said running his hand over his chin. 'Have a nice break, Fitzpatrick. It's good to see you've decided to watch the game, after all. That's the spirit we like to see in you.'

DANNY

Danny tore down the corridor, almost colliding with a bevy of girls.

Anika stood in the middle of the pack, holding centre stage.

He reddened. 'Ani, shouldn't we be getting ready?'

'We've got plenty of time,' she said, studying her watch. 'It's only just gone ten. At least half an hour before we need to change.'

Danny blushed even more and shook his wrist. Stupid watch. 'Yes. Sure. Right.' It wasn't going well. Individually the girls were fine, but as a group they scared him to death.

'I'm going to see if I can find Olivia. Want to join me?' Danny said.

'No. Not really.'

Danny's face went purple. 'Please,' he squeaked.

Anika caught his eye. 'OK, Ladies,' she said, 'I'm off to do battle with those big, bad, beastly boys, and kick the damn house down.' They shrieked their approval. 'Wish me luck.'

Each of the girls made a big play of kissing her on her cheek, before breaking into a chant.

'*GO, GO Ani Delaux! GO, GO Ani Delaux! GO, GO Ani Delaux! Go Ani! Go Ani! GO Ani...*'

Anika put one hand in the air as she waltzed away, wiggling her hips and fluffing up her wavy blonde hair.

As the twins turned the corner the chanting changed to the old *Queen* anthem: '*A-D-L, A-D-L, A-D-L – SHE WILL, SHE WILL, ROCK YOU!*'

'You're awfully glum-faced, what have you done now?'

Danny groaned. 'Oh, Ani, I think I've done something insanely foolish. I told Fitzpatrick about my nightmare. I don't know why I did it. He'll probably tell everyone, like he usually does.' Danny caressed his temples with his fingers. 'It's social suicide.'

'Yup.' Anika pinched him playfully on the cheek. 'When will you ever learn? He's a moron. You're best off keeping well away from him.'

They found Olivia in the physics lab with Sas. They were running over an experiment, their heads buried in calculations while an assortment of rubbery tubes and glass devices lay strewn over the counter.

Anika was full of bounce. 'Ready to go, girls?' she said.

Her jollity didn't really have the same effect on the science students.

'Anika,' Olivia said, in her most serious tone. 'I want you to wear these, in your boots.'

Anika looked at her in amazement. 'On my boobs?'

'Don't be stupid. In your football boots.'

She fingered the rubbery, gooey material that Olivia handed to her. 'What is it?'

Olivia peeled off her lab glasses. 'In short, it's a de-energising unit that we've created.'

'A what-erising-unit?' Anika said. 'Why?'

'Just in case, that's why.'

'I don't understand.'

'Just do it, will you,' Olivia demanded. 'One for each boot.' She handed her a second one. 'You too, Danny.'

Danny studied it. 'What's it for?'

Olivia squealed. 'In case either of you gets struck by lightning. It might help you not fry, that's all.'

Danny stuck the strips to the insoles in his boots. 'Aren't you're taking this a bit far—'

A huge roll of thunder shook the building rattling the windows. They looked at each other.

Olivia raised her eyebrows. 'No, we're not. These could save your life.'

'Where's your Fitz storm glass thing?' Anika cut in, her tone serious. 'I need to see what it's doing.'

'Next to Olivia's desk,' Sas said, wafting a hand.

Anika picked the storm glass up before quickly putting it down again. 'I don't mean to be rude, science-y nerd folk, but have you analysed this lately?'

Olivia marched over as though it was a complete waste of time. 'What?' she snapped.

'This storm test tube thing,' Anika began in an unusually serious voice. 'Have any of you noticed a) how hot it is, and b) that it's literally crammed full of crystals moving incredibly fast.'

Olivia stared at it for a moment or two. 'I have no idea what you're talking about, Anika. Yes, it might be a little warm, but so what? As I told you earlier, I'm not sure how it works.' She dismissed it with a wave. 'We've moved on.'

Anika shrugged. 'Well, you're supposed to know what you're doing. I'd keep an eye on it, if I were you.' She stretched out the gooey strip. 'Can I put this in my hair?'

'Please, Anika,' Olivia said. 'It must be on the bottom of your shoe. Attach it to the underside of your boot using the sticky Velcro patch or in the insole.' Olivia sounded irritated by the intrusion. 'Now, run and get changed or you'll be late.'

Anika skipped off, singing to herself and punching the air.

As her footsteps receded down the corridor, Danny picked up the storm glass. Immediately, he put it down again.

'Whoa! It's boiling, seriously. Try it.'

'I've just done that,' Olivia said.

Sas put her finger to the glass. 'OW! Scorching!' she sucked her fingers. 'Olivia, look! It's steaming.'

'A mild expulsion of water vapour, that's all,' Olivia said nervously.

'You think so?' They all started to back away.

'No, not necessarily,' Olivia admitted.

The test tube was beginning to glow, steam seeping out of the top.

'Has anyone added anything to it?' Olivia asked.

Danny and Sas shook their heads.

The activity in the test tube increased. They could hear crystals popping against the glass.

'Get out!' Olivia yelled. 'It's going to blow!'

They ran for the door, shutting it firmly behind themselves before diving to the floor. Seconds later, the storm glass blew into smithereens.

Sas shivered. 'What does it mean?' she asked.

'I think it means that we were right all along.' Olivia's voice quaked. 'Here, above us, lies the storm from hell.'

OLIVIA

Olivia barged past Sas. 'Where are you off to now?'

'To see Wynn-Garry and have it out with him. This time properly.'

'Oh, no you don't!'

But Olivia was already on her way.

'Wait! I'm coming with you.'

Olivia marched off, her eyes hard and her chin up. Sas had to run alongside to keep up. They wove through the maze of school buildings, up worn stone stairs and down dark corridors, until they reached a colonnade. Halfway down, below a striking, pointed arch was a dark brown, studded wooden door.

Olivia thumped it. 'He must be in,' she said, turning the handle. It creaked.

'You can't just let yourself in,' Sas hissed, remembering what Ryan had told her.

'Watch me. I'll wait for him inside, then he can't get away.'

'You're being ridiculous—'

'Now, then,' said the familiar voice of Mr Wynn-Garry

as his head appeared around the door. He prised it open and peered over the top of his glasses. 'Olivia, Sas.' A thin and rather fake smile appeared as he studied their faces. 'Is everything alright? What can I do for you?'

Inside, Olivia saw books piled up on tables, crammed into shelves, and stuffed into every nook and cranny of the room. Reading lamps shone light over large leather armchairs, while the floor was littered with exercise books for marking. Portraits of past headmasters dotted the walls.

The room had the immediate effect of dampening Olivia's temper.

Wynn-Garry caught her staring past him and invited them in. 'Can I get you both a cup of tea, perhaps?'

Olivia hesitated. 'No, thanks.' She turned to Sas as if for encouragement. 'I've constructed a Fitzroy storm glass, you see, and it has just blown up—'

'A Fitzroy storm glass?' Wynn-Garry interrupted. 'Goodness me! Seventeenth century weather forecasting apparatus?' Wynn-Garry laughed dryly. 'I haven't heard of one of those since I was a student. In fact, I'm sure we had one here, once upon a time. It was in a cabinet, as a curiosity. I'll have to dig it out.'

Olivia frowned. Wynn-Garry knew about Fitzroy storm glasses. She felt a pang of uncertainty.

'You're concerned about this horrid cloud again, aren't you, Olivia?' Wynn-Garry said gently, noting that he'd unsettled her.

She reddened a little. 'Yes, Sir. I am. You see, I ran some programmes on global weather data with specifics exactly like those we have above us. Then I did another experiment with a different band of metrics, which simply confirmed my suspicions—'

'How fascinating,' said Mr Wynn-Garry, with a plastic grin. 'Rest assured, it worries me too.'

'Really?'

'Of course! I have just this minute put the phone down from a further conversation with a senior forecaster at the Met Bureau. According to them, there will be little to concern us. It's a localised cloud. At worst, we may hear several growls of thunder and see a few flashes of lightning, or perhaps experience some heavy rain. Nothing too unusual for the time of year. They assured me that the storm was unlikely to break until this afternoon. Satisfied?'

'But—'

'There you have it, Olivia. I'm afraid there's nothing more to say about the matter. The match is on, and the other performances will continue as planned.' Wynn-Garry's tone changed. 'I am particularly busy at the moment finalising this evening's celebrations, so, please, don't pester me with this again. You should know by now that I really do have everyone's best interests at heart. Safety is my number one priority.'

Olivia stared at the headmaster. He wasn't telling the truth one bit, and she could smell it. 'Can I ask who you spoke to at the Met Bureau, Sir?'

Wynn-Garry glared at her. 'If you must know, it was a man by the name of Mr Fish.'

With that he smiled and ushered them out, shutting it firmly behind him.

Fitzpatrick reached into his pocket, pulling out Danny's scrap of paper.

He leaned against the stone wall outside the school hall and held it up. If that Sap had played a prank on Danny and given him the coat to wear, then what were the others capable of? Perhaps this was an elaborate set-up, dreamed up by Olivia in order to get him to fight with Ryan Williams.

Fitzpatrick could smell Olivia's cheap perfume all over this.

He glanced up. The sky was ridiculously dark and ridiculously huge. What if Olivia's experimental madness had some foundation?

Fitzpatrick's eyes returned to the paper. He read the middle, double-underlined, option.

'Alleyway behind kissing houses.'

Fitzpatrick thought about it. If he was going to meet a knife-wielding ghost in a quiet spot, it was a pretty good choice. It had the advantage that you could get out at both ends, and it was close enough to the playing fields for a quick getaway.

Clever Danny. Not just a scruffy boy.

The alleyway was also the perfect place for a fight. He clenched his fist. He remembered the look on Williams' face, the glimmer of madness in his eyes. Fitzpatrick twisted the fabric on Danny's coat. It was nice and strong, and light, too. A layer of protection if Williams came at him.

Fitzpatrick sucked in his breath. It was a set-up for sure. It had to be. After yesterday's performance, Danny had been duped by his sisters.

Oh, well.

Fitzpatrick tapped his pocket, feeling the metal object within.

If he was right, and Williams was coming after him, Ryan Williams was in for a mighty big surprise.

WYNN-GARRY

Wynn-Garry leant on the oak door, and listened as their footsteps receded down the corridor. He let out a sigh. Had she believed him? It was hard to read her expression.

Returning to the soft leather armchair, he picked up his schedule. Olivia's persistence was admirable, if misplaced. No, no. Nothing was going to stop today going ahead, neither a big storm nor a few drops of rain.

Goodness me, he thought, *this is Yorkshire, the finest county in all of England, God's Own Country! Thunder and lightning go hand in hand with the rough landscapes of the moors and the dales.*

Kids these days were getting soft.

He chuckled to himself. Met Bureau? What nonsense. He simply knew that the only way he'd be able to stop her in her tracks was to throw something scientific back at her.

But why Mr Fish? It was an implausibly good name for a weatherman.

In any case, he had a busy morning ahead. Press were turning up, and there were place names to sort out for the banquet in the school chamber. It was an evening he'd anticipated for years. How much sweeter still if they won the cup?

He hoped that sister of Olivia's, Anika, would play her heart out again. What a player! He'd never seen the like. She was George Best, Pele, Messi, and Ronaldo, all blended into one slender slip of a girl. Brave as a mercenary, tough as leather, quick as a pike and slippery as ice.

He sighed before returning to the matter of wondering who he should sit next to tonight. Geraldine Forbes, perhaps. The star of Summerdale, the TV soap. Yes, perfect. Famed for her gritty Yorkshire one-liners, in reality she was a delightful, attractive lady, with beautiful green eyes and lips as full as cushions.

He pictured the scene in his mind; the hall decorated to the nines in the school's scarlet and green colours, candles accentuating the Gothic arched windows, and trophies and cups sparkling in the atmospheric light. Magnificent!

It would be a banquet that the governors, his friends, and their exclusive guests, would never forget.

Afterwards, he'd make his retirement speech and receive warm, generous, and heartfelt thanks from those whose lives he had touched. Yes, he mused. It was to be a glorious swan song.

Nobody, certainly not Olivia Delaux, was going to stop it.

His mood turned from happy to jovial. Mr Fish. Ah yes! The forecaster who in 1987 told the whole nation there was no need to worry, shortly before a devastating hurricane ripped across England.

Wynn-Garry laughed out loud and dabbed his brow. What if Olivia rang up the Met Bureau and asked to speak to Mr Fish?

Whatever will they think?

FITZPATRICK

From the road above the football field, Fitzpatrick scanned the crowd lining the perimeter of the pitch. They stood four deep behind the barrier rope at times, with smaller kids kneeling at the front. Fitzpatrick ached to be part of it, to have them cheer *him* on. He'd never play alongside Anika Delaux, though. Never.

It made him feel like puking just thinking about Anika, even if she was Danny's sister. That was an unfortunate twist of life.

He kicked a loose stone on the ground, which skipped across the raised pebbles and smacked a small boy in the knee with a dull crack.

The boy collapsed on the path as Fitzpatrick clenched his fist. *Nice one*, he thought, wishing it had been Anika Delaux's knee.

Fitzpatrick climbed further up the slope, towards the houses above the playing fields. He kept going until he was on his own, high above the pitch. As he walked, he thought about how he could occupy himself over the break with his dreary aunt. Last time, he'd nearly died of boredom, being dragged around endless museums, antiques shops, and flea markets. Sure, his aunt was pleasant and she tried hard, but her never-ending jollity and the way she talked to everyone about the same things over and over again drove him mad.

She was too nice, too wet and too dull.

His mind turned to his lost parents. They would have done awesome, cool, outdoor stuff, and they'd all get stuck in together, like sailing, or mountaineering, or holidaying abroad.

He imagined a trip by the side of the river next to a large campfire. Looking at the stars, his mother by his side playing guitar and singing, and his father smiling at him proudly, sharpening a blade.

It was a fantasy, of course. It was the idyllic family life he'd never have. Every time he thought of it, it brought an overwhelming sadness into his soul. He couldn't remember if his mother used to sing to him and he had no idea what his parents even looked like; but to him, the fantasy felt right.

A long rumble boomed in the sky above. Fitzpatrick spied another round pebble, and took a mighty swipe with his heavy, black boot. The stone connected sweetly, skipped a couple of times and then, on the last bounce, lifted quickly and seemed to whistle past the head of someone lurking by a lamppost near to the alleyway.

What was an old bloke doing standing over there in the first place? He didn't even flinch! Bloody weirdo. The stone must have missed him or else he'd have been knocked out cold.

Fitzpatrick put his head down and sauntered on as if nothing had happened. A few paces on, Fitzpatrick noticed a man just inside the entrance to the alleyway. He was sure no one had been there a moment earlier.

His heartbeat quickened.

Fitzpatrick pretended to read Danny's bit of paper while he studied the man.

It was a hunched over old man, he thought, shrouded in a long, dark cloak, with a thick scarf wrapped round his chin and nose. He had a kind of wide-brimmed hat pulled down over his head in such a way that Fitzpatrick couldn't identify a face. The figure leaned on a stick like a blind man.

Maybe, Fitzpatrick thought, *this* was Danny's ghost.

9

SAS, THURSDAY

'Sas, we need direct action,' Olivia said. 'Wynn-Garry clearly doesn't want to know about the storm, so we're going to have to either disrupt the match, or figure out an exit strategy—'

Sas couldn't face direct action. 'A leaving strategy gets my vote—'

'Good. If I can get Dan and Anika over the bridge, then I think we'll be fine. When we get to the lane, the canopy of the tunnel should protect us. It's you that I'm worried about.'

'*Me?*'

'Yes. You.' Olivia confirmed. 'How are you going to get out of here? You'll need to get home fast, or get to high ground. Have you ever driven a car?'

'No. Stop being ridiculous—'

'I'm not. You could steal one.'

Sas glared at Olivia, who shrugged back. 'I'll think of something, but you're getting weird.'

'That's not good enough,' Olivia snapped back. 'You need a plan. Come home with us.'

'I can't. Mum wants me back.'

'In that case, start engaging that brain of yours.'

As the two girls trudged slowly back from the science laboratories in silence, they could feel the buzz of the crowd making its way down towards the football pitch.

'I feel so edgy about this match' Olivia said, as a couple of boys ran past nearly knocking her over. 'What if Anika gets a kicking and can't run? Then they lose, and the storm breaks, and she can't get home?'

'Olivia, that's not going to happen—'

'And what about Danny? He's all over the place, have you seen him? He looks ill, the poor boy. I'm worried he won't save a thing. He's even more scatter-brained than usual.'

'Well, it is the final—'

'I know that,' Olivia said. 'It's just that I've got a hollow feeling deep inside me.' Olivia closed her eyes and shook her head. 'You know, I'm not sure I even like football—'

'What tosh! You love it,' Sas replied, 'you're jealous of Anika, just like everyone else.'

'That still doesn't mean I like it—'

'You're her sister and you're as sporty as a mole yourself, so it's natural for you to want her to do well.' Sas looked up at the sky. Her heart seemed to skip a beat. She whistled.

'Blimey. Wynn-Garry's floodlights are on,' Olivia said, her tone betraying her nerves.

'Every time I look up, my body starts shaking like a jelly,' Sas said, inspecting her watch. 'We've got five minutes.'

Sas slowed down and grasped Olivia's arm, as if setting herself up to say something important. 'Listen, Olivia,' she began, 'I've been meaning to tell you something important—'

'Important?' Olivia noticed that her friend had gone a little pale. 'You put the wrong mix in the storm glass—?'

'No. It's not about that ... it's about—'

'You added something to it—'

'Olivia, I haven't touched it. I'm quite sure it did what it did perfectly naturally.' Sas added. *It's about you*. It's personal.'

'Me?' Olivia's mind whirled. 'What? You've got a boyfriend and you haven't told me—'

'For goodness' sake, you know full well I haven't—'

'OK, someone out there fancies *me*—'

'NO. Of course not. Listen, Olivia – it's got absolutely nothing to do with boys—'

'Sure?'

'YES.'

'Good,' Olivia said, 'they're toss—'

'It's *about* you,' Sas said.

'Me?' Olivia said. 'OMG. You ... and ... me?'

Sas shrieked. 'For crying out loud, Olivia. NO! *Will you please let me speak?*' She took a deep breath. 'It concerns YOU, in fact it concerns all of you Delauxs. You, Danny and Anika. All those things I told you about? Well, there's more.'

'More?'

'Yes! I wrote a whole lot of stuff down the moment I woke up. I'm pretty sure it's about you, and that in some way you're linked—'

'Linked? With what?'

'SHUT UP! Listen! just for a minute.' Sas said, trying to compose herself. 'What I'm trying to say is that—'

The long shrill of a whistle and the roar of the crowd swept over them. Sas followed Olivia's eyes towards the floodlit football pitch.

'We're late!' Olivia cried. 'Your damn watch is slow.'

Sas tapped the face of the dial and compared it to the clock on her mobile. 'Oh no!' But when she looked up, her friend had already gone.

Olivia tore off down the track. *What was I thinking? I bet someone's scored.*

'Come on, keep up!' Olivia yelled over her shoulder, as she took off down the shingle path. 'You'll have to tell me later! I mean, it's not like it's life or death, is it?' she yelled.

'There are things you absolutely ... must ... know,' Sas said, her voice trailing off as she watched Olivia zoom away with extraordinary speed. In fact, she couldn't remember seeing Olivia run as fast in her whole life.

Sas felt empty, the moment lost. Everything that had happened in the last hour had started to confirm that what she had seen, heard, and felt was going to come true. If there was even the tiniest chance of this happening, she needed to tell Olivia everything.

Because, increasingly, it really was about life or death.

A roar rang out from below. Fitzpatrick spun back to the game. He picked out the chant of *"Ani Delaux, GO, GO, GO"* and smacked his fist into his hand. Dammit. She must have scored.

Fitzpatrick reached into his pocket and his hand touched a waxy piece of paper. It was a sweet wrapper. With a frown on his face, he tried to work out how it had got there. Of course, it was from a pack of Haribo he'd stolen from one of Anika's girlie friends at break. He'd stuffed the sweet in his mouth and nonchalantly tossed one of the wrappers into the headmaster's rose garden, where it stuck comically on a thorn and flapped in the breeze.

So, how come this one was folded, and in his pocket?

He pulled the wrapper out, opened it up and stared at it. Strangely, the sweet paper not only looked larger than he remembered, but scribbled all over it were random lines like spaghetti plonked on a plate.

Just as he was about to trash it, a few of the lines started to look familiar. *Faces?* he thought. Fitzpatrick scanned it, turning it sideways and then round again. Three figures came out at him, like a "magic eye" puzzle revealing itself on the wrapper.

There were three clear faces staring back at him.

Then it struck him. It was the Delauxs! Absolutely, definitely, them, all smug and cheerful and ghastly. As he studied it, their faces seemed to melt away into the paper, like slush dripping through a gutter.

The next time he blinked, he was staring at nothing. Not a damn thing.

He turned the sweet paper over.

Blank.

Fitzpatrick felt a surge of excitement run through him. Was this some kind of joke?

He slapped his cheeks and rubbed his eyes. He looked at the wrapper again. Its colour was changing gradually from white through grey to almost black, like the vast cloud above them. The words "HELP ME" started to form in tiny molten streaks of lightning on the paper, as if the words were being burned into it.

Fitzpatrick crumpled the paper up and tossed it in the gutter.

His heart raced. For a moment, sickness overwhelmed him.

Instinctively, he started walking faster and faster, as if walking might make what he had just seen go away.

Fitzpatrick bounded up a series of wide stone steps back to street level, and tentatively made his way towards the street's beamed dwellings. He peered down the dark alleyway but it was empty, save for the black wheelie bins guarding it like mini soldiers.

As he took his first step under the buildings, he noted how the houses on either side weren't leaning over the street as if they were kissing, more leaning towards each other like fighters braced for combat.

He heard a groan from the crowd below, and moved to the roadside to figure out what was happening.

Bodies lay all over the pitch. Had Newton won a penalty?

Was that Danny staring up at him?

He waved back, before turning and walking into the alleyway.

Halfway down, he slowed. He sensed something behind him. Who? A teacher? Nah, unlikely. They'd be watching the game, or making last minute plans for the performances later on. In any case, by now they'd have said something.

Ryan Williams. He almost spat his name out. Williams was coming after all. It was exactly his style to creep up on people.

Fitzpatrick curled his fist into a ball. 'Williams,' he said, 'I'm warning you. Stop, and walk away, NOW.'

There was no reply.

He could feel the presence edging closer.

Fitzpatrick bent down, pretending to tie his boots. His pulse raced. He readied himself. He sensed the person behind him was now only a couple of paces away.

'I've been waiting for this,' Fitzpatrick said, and in one movement swung around and threw his biggest punch. His momentum carried him forward, his fist unstoppable.

But it wasn't Williams. It was the old man.

Instead of connecting, his arm careered straight through the man, propelling Fitzpatrick onto the grey stone. His head cracked on the paving as he went down.

'You don't have to do that, Danny,' said a gravelly voice from behind the scarf. 'We're on the same team now.'

Olivia dashed down the touchline. 'Sas, thank God I've found you,' she said. 'What's up with you? We're on drinks duty!'

'Hell,' she said. 'You're right. My watch...'

They rushed over to the old Volkswagen Combi ice cream van, known as the 'catering-cart', which acted as refreshment centre and mobile sweet shop.

Olivia and Sas pulled out a few tables, and lined out paper cups ready for jugs of orange squash. A steady stream began queuing for drinks, chocolate bars, and crisps.

Sas took the money while Olivia handed out cups, but Sas could barely keep up.

Olivia was working at an astonishing speed, darting here and there, handing out confectionery and drinks. She talked to everyone about the current score, or Anika's brilliant goals, or the curious weather.

'How did you manage to serve all that in ten minutes?' Sas said, as she squeezed a few more cups into the overflowing bin bag. 'We've made a killing.'

Olivia breathed a sigh of relief. With no rain appearing so far, perhaps Wynn-Garry was right. Maybe the cloud would break later that afternoon. From inside the van, she looked out over the scene. The crowd was still three or four deep the entire way around the pitch, and she could just make out the steep rise of the bank on the far side that led up to the village.

The floodlights shone down, giving the players a strange, quadruple shadow. If it hadn't been nearly midday, there would have been no reason to suspect that they weren't playing a night match.

'Olivia,' she called out. 'Get a place left of the halfway line. I'll join you in a minute. I'm going to cash up.'

The feeling of dread that Sas had experienced before was building again. The vast black cloud seemed to be growing even thicker, and sinking even lower in the sky.

She knew she should get out of there and run to higher ground, but she was too swallowed up by the drama, and swept away by the skill of Anika Delaux.

A heavy challenge sent Anika flying. The crowd swayed, and spilled onto the pitch.

The noise levels increased.

'That was late. Too damn late,' Olivia shouted, peeling off her scarf.

'Careful, Olivia. Watch it,' Sas said, firmly. 'You mustn't. You'll get expelled. I promised—'

'It was deliberate and dirty—'

'NO, Olivia!' Sas snapped. 'Bite your tongue.'

'But they're targeting Anika exactly as Fitzpatrick said they would. They're going to kick her out of the game!'

Sas closed her eyes. Great, just what she needed! Still ten minutes to go, and Olivia sizzling like a firework.

'What was that noise?' Olivia said.

'That gargantuan thing up there?'

'Th ... thunder?' Olivia said, momentarily removing her eyes from the action.

Sas nodded.

Several members of the crowd started to leave, while others gestured upwards.

This is it, Sas thought. *This is where it starts, exactly as I saw in my nightmare. It even feels the same too. I've got to tell Olivia. I've got to tell her NOW.*

A ghastly feeling of panic swept over her.

They should stop the game. Get everyone away.

Sas's thoughts were interrupted as Anika stole the ball and sprinted down the field.

Anika skipped inside one tackle, then dummied inside looking for support.

The crowd roared, but, from nowhere, a couple of Newton boys smashed into her from opposite angles. All three lay on the ground as the ball was kicked away by another Newton player.

Play continued, but it was a poor decision.

'Yellow card,' yelled a senior boy. 'C'mon ref!'

The atmosphere flipped. Suddenly, late tackles flew in and players were being kicked indiscriminately out of eyeshot of the referee.

One of the Newton strikers stole into the penalty area, as a massive crash of thunder reverberated around them. At that exact moment, little Jimmy Nugent, running back, tapped the forward's foot and the player fell face-first onto the turf.

The whistle shrilled and the ball was placed on the spot.

'I don't believe it!' Sas said, quietly, 'the end of Anika's dream.' She turned. 'Olivia, what on earth are you doing?'

Olivia was scribbling furiously in her notebook. 'Just watch for me a minute. You know, commentate, like on telly.'

She didn't need to. The groan told her everything.

'What happened?'

'The ball trickled past Danny. All he had to do was put his foot out. Two-all.

'He is absolutely useless sometimes,' she said.

'Well, he's only in the team because no-one else would do it.'

'And to keep Ani company, though, to be fair, he has improved, ' Olivia said as she thrust the paper into Sas's overcoat pocket. 'Ye of little faith, Sas Smith,' she said. 'You'll see, she'll score again.'

Another roll of thunder boomed and cracked. More spectators started running away.

Sas's stomach lurched. It was now or never.

'Olivia, we've got to get out of here, now. I mean it. But listen to me first. There's something important I've got to share—'

'Please, Sas. Just shut up!' Olivia snapped. 'Get the ball to Ani Delaux,' she screamed. 'Give it to Anika!' Olivia turned to Sas. 'Listen, hon, tell me whatever is so damn important at the end, OK. There's less than five minutes to go and it's two-all in the most important match of my brother and sister's life. Can you please just give it a break for five minutes? Five minutes. That's all I'm asking.'

With that, Olivia sidled out onto the pitch, ran down the touchline, and dived in among the spectators further down.

FITZPATRICK

Fitzpatrick reeled, wondering if he should play dead.

'Believe me, it is excellent news that you've arrived on time.' The old man moved almost directly above him, his face covered by the scarf and hat. 'I sense that you have brought my coat back. Well done. Did the old man recognise it?'

Fitzpatrick simply didn't know what to say. His voice stammered as a chill swept through him.

'Are you ready to join me, Danny Delaux?'

Fitzpatrick's skin crawled.

He needed more time. 'Join you?' Fitzpatrick stammered, scuffling backwards, trying to keep his face hidden. 'Can you remind me again? I was shattered last night.'

The ghost hesitated. 'Well, let me put it this way. I've got what you want.'

Fitzpatrick shivered. *What I want?* 'What do you mean?'

The old man moved to one side and appeared to look up towards the sky. 'Why, me, of course.'

'You?'

'Yes, me,' said the ghost. 'You see, I'm the only one here

who can help you escape from this place. You have only about fifteen minutes in your time to decide.'

Fitzpatrick's brain went a little fuzzy. Bile swilled in his mouth. *Fifteen minutes? In your time? Decide what?* Fitzpatrick stole a look down the alley.

He needed to get away, fast.

The old man sensed his unease. 'You see, in a short time the skies will open and it will rain for forty days and nights in a way you cannot even begin to imagine—'

Fitzpatrick looked confused. 'Forty days and nights?'

'Yes. That's what I said, forty days and nights—'

'Forty days and nights—?'

'Yes!'

'What, like in Noah's Ark with the animals—?'

'STOP repeating what I say and listen!' the old man spat. The words seemed to smack Fitzpatrick around the face. He cowered.

'I can assure you that in a short while,' the old man said, bearing down on him, 'all of this – everything here, everything you see – will be destroyed.'

'Danny,' the ghost continued, his voice mellow once more, 'there will be nothing left. You see, boy, there is a shift happening, a shift in time, a shift in the way of the universe. It is happening right here, right now. The wheels are turning and they cannot be reversed.'

DANNY

Danny stomped around the penalty area, his face burning with shame at the unsaved goal.

For some reason, just before the Newton player stepped up to hit the penalty, it had come to him. The person he'd seen way up on the steps heading into the alley was Fitzpatrick. It could only have been Fitzpatrick. For a start, his hair was a complete giveaway, and he was wearing the ghost's long coat, which made him look like a monk.

All he could think of was running up there to find out what the hell Fitzpatrick was up to.

If Xinder *was* there, and Fitzpatrick had gone to find him, would Xinder know the difference between them? Would he care?

Then, in the next instance, the ball had trickled past him into the goal.

Danny kicked the base of the post. The more he thought about Fitzpatrick and the ghost, the more certain he became that he was right.

All I ever do is look on hopelessly, he thought. *When will I stop being so pathetic?*

A slow-burning fury moved through his body, an anger borne of frustration and annoyance. It began to build up in him like a glowing light, as if he were being charged up like a battery.

Danny was about to kick short from the goal kick, but, from out of the corner of his eye, he saw Anika in yards of space on the halfway line, catching her breath after the last attack. It was worth a try. He pushed the ball ahead, ran up, and thumped it hard. The ball rose high into the air.

Anika saw it, her eyes never leaving the ball. She took it down in her stride and, with a burst of speed, tore past one player then another. She then stopped so suddenly that another player over-ran, and she side-stepped one more player who fell over. The crowd roared.

'*... She will, she will – ROCK YOU!*'

Anika side-stepped again and, with an injection of pace, flew towards the penalty area with real menace. Four Newton players lay sprawled on the floor, leaving only one more to beat.

'Go on Anika, you can do it,' Danny screamed.

Danny watched as the remaining defender was sold a beautiful dummy, which Anika seemed to do with such ease that it was laughable. As she pushed the ball past him and effortlessly made her way around, he slid out a leg and tripped her up quite deliberately. Anika stumbled and fell but she wasn't giving up. She crawled towards the ball and then, even as she lay on the ground with the ball wedged between her knees, she managed to keep moving.

But a warning cry went up as three Newton players and the goalkeeper converged on Anika. It felt as if Anika had fallen into a trap as the Newton boys cocked their legs and kicked out, striking more of Anika than the ball, kicking her again and again in a kind of frenzy.

Still, she refused to give the ball up.

The crowd swayed and screamed before falling silent.

They could quite clearly see Anika's face contorting in pain as the assault rained down on her.

10

SAS, THURSDAY

For the first time in her life, Sas could feel a sensation of utter panic building up in her veins like one of her bubbling chemistry experiments. A series of flashes filled the sky, mirroring the extraordinary scenes on the pitch. Lightning fizzed then crackled. For a brief moment, it formed a picture of a boy in the sky.

Sas gasped. *A boy?*

A thunderclap smashed overhead so loudly that the crowd cried out. Shrieks and screams filled the football field.

Sas fell to her knees, barely able to think, her body shaking. *No! It can't be! It's not possible. It's … it's … Fitzpatrick's face!* The lightning was Fitzpatrick's face superimposed in the cloud. How was it possible?

She looked around. Where was Olivia? She couldn't have gone already. Sas followed the eyes of the crowd.

Olivia was striding towards the pitch.

'NO! OLIVIA, STOP!'

There was no reaction from Olivia.

Without thinking, Sas took off after her. 'Olivia, LISTEN!' she yelled as she ran. *'It's you!'*

She ran on further.

'The dream is about your family, the Delauxs.' She sensed Olivia slowing down.

'You must ALL survive until sunset and find a cave. Do you understand?' She took a deep breath.

'SUNSET. YOU MUST STAY ALIVE.'

Her voice was petering out as she realised she was screaming herself hoarse. She sucked her breath in again.

'Find clues in your house, Appleside Farm. *You must find the clues.'*

Sas coughed and then repeated the last part, adding, 'GET HOME! NOW!'

She noted some of the crowd staring at her as if she was a madwoman. But she didn't care, not one little bit.

DANNY

Danny couldn't believe it.

First Sas screaming at Olivia, and now this! Where was the referee?

He thumped the goalpost, shook his head, and looked up. The giant, angry bruise of a cloud stretched above him like a monstrous airship. It sagged so low in the sky that he felt he could jump up and burst it as easily as pricking a balloon.

The heady smell of damp filled his nostrils as another crack of thunder escaped. Danny felt his blood boiling inside him. Now, five Newton players surrounded Anika. She managed to stand, but one of them pushed her over.

That was the final straw. Anger flooded through him. *No one*, Danny seethed, *does that to my sister.*

He tore down the pitch, the crowd baying and shouting. The referee was desperately trying to separate the players, but everyone was fighting.

'NO! Don't retaliate, Danny—' he could hear someone yelling. It was too late, though. Hell had broken loose.

One of the Newton boys was holding Anika's hair and

leering at her, screaming in her face. Danny grabbed him by the collar and threw him away, the boy sailing through the air and landing in a heap on the ground. Danny punched another boy hard on the nose. He thought he heard crunching sounds, then found himself receiving blows although he couldn't feel them.

Blood coursed through his body. He felt strong and powerful. Invincible.

A couple of Newton boys jumped him but he picked one up with one hand and tossed him over his shoulder. The other boy he wrestled to the ground until the boy under him squirrelled away. Then he found another hitting Jimmy Nugent. He smashed the boy hard in the stomach and tossed him to the side like a piece of litter.

The whistle shrilled again and again.

Finally, a sharp, stern voice rose up out of the melee. It was Olivia. Danny could see her marching towards them. *Oh no!*

Danny looked around. Three Newton boys and the referee stared at him with their eyes wide open. *Was it in fear?*

This was a sensation he'd never really experienced before.

Danny wiped his brow and allowed himself a smile. It felt strangely good.

WYNN-GARRY

'Sir,' a small boy said, running up to him. 'Sir. What shall we do?'

Wynn-Garry smiled, badly. 'I've been assured that there won't be any rainfall until this afternoon,' he said. 'I'm sure we'll be fine.'

'But, Sir. Look. I don't think it's safe.'

Wynn-Garry stared up at the throbbing deep bruise that filled the sky to the horizon. His heartbeat quickened.

'If you're worried, Stanwick, make your way indoors. Are your parents around?'

'No, Sir. They're coming to the music concert this afternoon.'

'Then I suggest you go to the library and find a good book. How does that sound?'

Stanwick ran back to his friends, and together they scampered over to the old buildings with the tower.

Wynn-Garry's knees were shaking. In fact, now that he noticed, his entire body shook, as if he'd been swimming in a cold sea. Nerves about the match, probably.

At the back of his mind he wondered about Olivia. I mean, *really*? Bah! It wasn't going to happen.

This was a small lightning storm with a bit of thunder. It would probably pass them by, or they'd have a bit of heavy rain, but nothing like the deluge she was suggesting. That sort of thing never happened here in good old North Yorkshire.

A crack of lightning fizzed above. He noticed how the crowd were dispersing. How students flicked their eyes towards him.

'Come on Sutton!' he yelled. 'Jolly good play, Allen. Give it to Ani.' He clapped his hands as the play moved from one end of the pitch to the other, Anika narrowly missing to the right of the goal.

BOOM!

Wynn-Garry felt the ground shake.

'Sir—'

'The team need your support,' the headmaster said, loudly.

Suddenly he noticed how the players were almost attacking each other.

Oh Lord.

Moving quickly, he headed down the touchline.

'Coach,' he shouted.

The coach swivelled on his heels and ran towards him. 'For goodness' sake, watch out for Olivia Delaux. If anything happens to Ani—'

They watched as the Newton boys set upon her.

'Goodness. I'm quite tempted to get stuck in myself,' the headmaster said.

'Best you don't, Headmaster,' Coach said.

They both stared at the scene, their mouths open.

'Should we call it off?' Coach asked.

'No, no. It's nearly over—'

'Who's that, yelling?' Coach said.

'Well I never. That's Sas, isn't it? Whatever is she going on about?' Wynn-Garry said.

'No idea. Something about it being their fault?'

'Whose fault?' the headmaster queried.

'The Delaux's. If you ask me, I think they've all gone mad. Oh no, is that Danny? It's not poss—'

'Lord above. He's beating them up! What has the world come to,' the headmaster said. 'Steel, Coach. Look! There! Olivia's on the march. Be good fellows and grab her before this melee gets completely out of hand!'

XINDER

'Now, look here,' Fitzpatrick said, 'you need help.' He felt a slither of confidence returning.

'Look at me, Danny,' the ghost said. 'You see that thing there—'

'Yeah, right,' Fitzpatrick said. 'A large, dark cloud. Big deal. Excuse me, freak, but I'm outta here—'

'No – you – are – not,' the old man said, spitting each word out so severely that Fitzpatrick fell to the ground.

'Out of all the people on this puny planet, I've selected you. So be grateful, boy, because I'm giving you the chance to save your life. There is no other way for you.'

Fitzpatrick squealed, and looked down the passage. What was holding him back? Why didn't he go for it? Why didn't he say that he wasn't Danny? He felt oddly dizzy, as if a force was holding him against his will.

'I see you need convincing,' the old man said, his voice as smooth as honey once more. 'I'm going to show you something to ... reassure you. All I'm asking for is a little co-operation.'

The old man took a step back.

Fitzpatrick stood up, his knees barely able to hold him.

'You see, I'm going to tell you the story of what has happened so far, and then I'm going to tell you what will happen next. Do you understand?'

Fitzpatrick nodded.

'Good. Let me tell you about that piece of paper in your pocket, and how I generated your image in the lightning,' the ghost said, this time softer. 'Then, Danny Delaux, I'm going to tell you who you are and how we are going to help one another.'

'STOP IT – ALL OF YOU!' Olivia strode towards the players with a sense of purpose.

The teams almost instantly ceased brawling. Olivia's direct approach had that effect on people.

'Pathetic, all of you,' she shouted, pointing at various individuals. 'It's like a wrestling match for the Under 5s. Newton, you three especially, should be ashamed of yourselves.'

Olivia scooped up the ball. 'As for the refereeing. Twelve deliberate fouls totally unaccounted for and you haven't even got the balls to book them, let alone send them off for repeated violent conduct.'

The football smacked into the referee's hands. 'You should be struck off—?'

Before she had a chance to finish, she was grabbed by Coach and Mr Steele. They hauled her off her feet and away to the side line.

The referee responded by pointing belatedly at Olivia.

'You'll be dealt with later by the authorities,' he roared, blinking, trying hard to pull himself together.

Why couldn't he remember the procedure for dealing with a brawl?

It felt as if his brain had emptied.

'And along with that madwoman,' he continued, 'Sutton numbers one and eight, and Newton players five, seven and four,' he said pointing at the Newton players, 'GET OFF THIS PITCH.'

He waved his red card at the players and scribbled in his book.

Another huge slap of thunder exploded almost directly overhead. The ground shook. A terrible feeling tiptoed up his spine, sending his hairs erect.

'Direct free kick to red,' he said, pointing to a spot just outside the penalty area. 'And the quicker we're out of here, the better.'

The ref studied his watch. 'Last couple of minutes,' he announced.

The girl was right, though. His had been a truly woeful performance.

DANNY

Danny ran.

He had to find out what Fitzpatrick was up to, and fast. If he was right, there wasn't much more time left.

His stomach churned, and darkness seeped into his bones.

Thunder crashed and boomed as spectators began to flee to their cars and the school buildings.

Danny sprinted and scampered up the steep bank, pulling himself up on the longer tufts with his hands and using his studs to give him grip. At the top of the bank he caught his breath.

Another dramatic roll of thunder rattled the ground as Danny watched Olivia being marched off the football pitch. People were streaming away, pointing skywards.

Wow. What a mental couple of minutes. He couldn't believe his strength.

He shook his head and smiled. *Was it from the strange glass of water left by the ghost?*

He spied the alleyway and ran over, the studs of his boots clacking on the stone beneath him. He thought for a minute about taking them off but really, was there any point? *This ghost,* he thought, *couldn't really exist, could it?*

He peered down the alleyway and saw two shapes.

A sudden burst of lightning brought the pair to light and he could make out Fitzpatrick's hair, as well as another figure beside him wearing a long coat and a kind of wide brim hat. Danny's heart pounded. They were moving towards him.

OK. OMG. Wrongo. So, the ghost *did* exist and Fitzpatrick had got there first.

Danny shrank down, wiping rivulets of sweat off his forehead.

Xinder was blind, wasn't he? He'd gone on about the fact that he didn't have any eyes, like the Ancient Lady, so perhaps the ghost couldn't see Fitzpatrick.

So, what if the ghost thought Fitzpatrick was him?

Danny stood up from behind the wheelie bin so that only his head might be seen. Fitzpatrick was about ten paces away and Danny could definitely make out that the figure next to him was a ghost by the simple fact that he didn't have any feet and his face was mostly covered by a scarf.

A crackle of lightning fizzed above them and, from the light it momentarily threw out, Danny saw Fitzpatrick's face.

And his expression was one he'd never seen before on his friend. One of pure terror.

SAS

There was more, Sas thought, but she'd finally said what needed to be said. Thank goodness she'd had the presence of mind to scribble down her dreams the moment she'd woken up.

'*GO! Run! Run, all of you,*' she screamed at the spectators. '*It's going to break. The storm's going to break.*'

Thunder rolled.

She sprinted up the slope towards the buildings.

As she passed the top end of the ground she spied Ryan leaning on the lamppost, near to the leaning houses. She headed directly towards him. 'Ryan. What are you doing?'

'Following Fitzpatrick. He's been acting weird all afternoon. Are we winning?'

'Listen, Ryan,' she said as she caught her breath. 'Rain,' she panted, 'like you've never seen ... get out of here ... fast. You've got to believe me.' Her hand touched some paper in her pocket and she pulled out Olivia's note.

Ryan rolled his eyes.

She read it out loud.

'Sas, there's a boat in the old shed. Key under a pot by door, oars on the side. Think there's a canopy in cupboard ... just in case. Love you. Be safe, Olivia.'

Sas kissed it in relief. Clever, brilliant Olivia.

Ryan grabbed the note. 'What is it with you two?'

'Look at the sky, Ryan. When that "thing" bursts it will rain harder than you can possibly imagine. In minutes, the water will flash flood. I've had a premonition. I'll tell you about it'

'A premonition? Blimey. Cool. You sure?'

'Absolutely. No one has a chance. Can you drive? Do you have access to a car?'

'Of course not!'

'Nor me,' she fired back. 'Some of the kids have gone but I'm being picked up later, after the music concert.'

'Same,' Ryan said, trying to keep pace with her.

'Then we're stuck, Ryan,' she said. 'Properly screwed. There's no way out.'

'Screwed? What are you talking about? Why should we be stuck?'

'Look up, Ryan,' she said. 'I promise you I am not crazy. I am being absolutely deadly serious. This cloud isn't holding an ordinary storm. When it lets go the result will be catastrophic. Come on, keep up.'

Ryan frowned. 'You're really serious, aren't you?' he said, the smile slipping off his face.

'Never more so.' She stopped to catch her breath. 'Please, Ryan,' she began, 'I need your help. Will you help me? Please?'

Ryan scratched his nose. He liked Sas, and he'd certainly never seen her quite so animated. 'OK. I'm going to have to trust you on this one. Where do we start?'

'Oh, great! Thanks, Ryan,' Sas said, moving in and bear-hugging him. If she was going to do this, better to do it with big, strong Ryan Williams than by herself.

'First off, provisions. Food: high-energy snack bars; chocolates; lemons; dried fruit; tinned food like tuna and baked beans; sweetcorn;, a couple of lighters and fire-lighters; bottled water,' Sas rattled off, 'and blankets—'

'Blankets?'

'Anything you can get hold of.' She urged him to keep up. 'You're a Scout leader, aren't you? So, you know, stuff we can survive on.'

'To the shop, then,' Ryan said, smiling his keen smile and feeling rather important.

'I've got about twenty pounds from the footie snacks and drinks. I'll pay it back later.' Sas did some calculations in her head. 'Actually, that's probably not enough. Have you got anything?'

Ryan shoved his hands in his pockets and pulled out some change. 'Just short of four quid.'

Sas grimaced. 'In that case, Ryan, I hope you don't mind but you're going to have to steal. Come on, there's not a second to lose. When we get in there, grab some bags and start filling them. Don't hesitate or stop, understand? When it's done, I'll drop the money on the counter and we run. Alright?'

'Blimey, Sas. What if we get stopped?'

'We won't. Oh, and if necessary, use force.'

Ryan nodded, and handed over his money. His eyes were bulging with surprise. 'Where are we going afterwards?'

'The boat shed.'

'Boat shed? What boat shed?'

'By the river.' She waved her hand in its rough direction. 'We should have time to sort out some kind of cover and find survival things, then we're going to have to hope for the best. I don't know what we'll find when we get there, but, right now, it's our only chance.'

Ryan smiled. He loved a girl who meant business. If there was to be a catastrophe, this girl had the whole thing planned.

DANNY

Danny gasped.

Fitzpatrick's eyes widened as their eyes met.

Now, he could discern the ghost's words, like 'power' and 'magic' and 'strength'.

Danny was stunned. *This spook, Xinder, did think Fitzpatrick was him!*

Danny realised that the ghost was holding Fitzpatrick around his left arm. Was Fitzpatrick moving them, or was it the other way around?

He listened harder as they came to a stop just on the other side of the wheelie bin.

He heard Fitzpatrick's quivering voice. 'Tell me again about the Prophecy. I need to be absolutely certain before I make my final decision.'

'Did you not listen, Danny?' the ghost complained.

Danny reeled. *He was right! What was Fitzpatrick playing at?*

Why was he asking Xinder to tell him about this Prophecy one more time? It seemed a pretty odd thing to do.

Was it for his benefit?

'I need to be sure,' Fitzpatrick said, his voice wavering.

'Very well.' Xinder tipped his head to the sky as though sniffing it. 'But we are running out of time.'

Danny stole another look at Fitzpatrick from around the corner of the wheelie bin. When he caught sight of Fitzpatrick's face, tears were streaming down his cheeks.

Why? Why was Fitzpatrick crying?

He crouched down and listened to Xinder's deep, powerful voice. 'There is a great shift that occurs every now and then in the way of the universe, Danny,' the ghost began.

'Every now and then the world changes. There is a change in the world's relationship to its surroundings, the infinite and beyond. The process of these movements have been given to you in the form of dreams. These dreams are the Prophecy of Genartus and they are given to three people who are known as Sacrum,' the ghost paused. 'You and your sisters are the Sacrum. You are the anointed ones, charged with undertaking the tasks that have been shown to you.'

Danny's gut turned. *WOAH! Anointed ones! Blimey. The strange creature above Anika had been feeding her dreams.*

The ghost coughed and carried on. 'It is complex. This is not the time to tell you the ways of the universe. All you need know is that the Sacrum face fearsome challenges. The first of which begins with a terrible storm aimed entirely at you. If any of you do not survive the storm, it will rage for forty days and forty nights. It will wash away the world, bit by bit.' Xinder paused. 'When the waters recede, there will be a different world and a new beginning.

'I tell you now. You children stand little chance. There is no ark to save you, nor any place you can go where you will not find yourselves shot at by lightning or washed out by torrents of rain. The earth will slip down hillsides, the rivers will swell, and trees will crash down. There is nowhere you can hide. I do not tell you this with any joy, but the storm was designed when men were strong, lived long, and knew how to fight with nature through other means such as magic. You are about to enter a time you are not equipped to cope with. Do you understand?'

Fitzpatrick nodded and his eyes bulged. 'Why?' he croaked.

'Young man, the Prophecy is a measure; a test, if you like, to see if the people on this planet are equipped to move into a new age. It was designed to test the strength, courage, intelligence and skill of mankind.'

Xinder stopped for a moment and chuckled.

'You and your sisters, the Sacrum, are now the measure of human life on Earth. Together you must survive until sundown and locate the cave of riddles.'

'Then what?' Fitzpatrick stammered.

'Then, the destructive force of the storm will cease and the Sacrum must look for the clues that will open Genartus and save Earth, as you know it today.'

Xinder sniffed the air. 'There is no more time,' he barked. 'It will break in a few moments. You must willingly make your choice.'

ANIKA

Anika dragged herself up and flicked a fleck of mud off her shorts.

What a crazy match! Her being kicked to bits, Sas screaming at Olivia, and Olivia going mad again and screaming at everyone else. Danny missed a total sitter and then beat up the opposition like a prize-fighter before getting sent off, while thunder crashed overhead, lightning fizzed, and everything was deafening.

Now, with the last kick of the game, Anika had a chance to win the match. *Boy, pressure kicks don't come much bigger than this*, she thought. *Better make it a good one.*

'Come on, Sutton. Come on, Anika Delaux, you can do it,' roared the small section of crowd still remaining. They continued their chant.

"*Oh, Ani, Ani. Ani, Ani, Ani, Ani, A-A-Ani-iii*".

Anika rubbed her tired, bruised legs, and drew her hands through her muddy blonde hair. She fixed her boots and selected a slightly raised patch of turf on which she carefully placed the ball.

She stood back and studied her route to goal. Twenty,

twenty-three yards perhaps? Perfect. Just as she'd practised time and again with Danny.

She rubbed her eyes and concentrated hard. It was now or never. Everything she'd ever played for came down to this one shot.

She sucked in a large mouthful of air, her eyes focusing on the ball so intently that she felt she could see its entire trajectory and the precise spot on the leather where she aim her boot.

The whole atmosphere of the crowd, and the rumbling sky seemed to disappear for a moment, leaving behind a strange hush.

The referee blew.

Anika exhaled. It was time to step up.

RYAN

Ryan hurried after Sas, his arms nearly dropping off with the weight of the shopping bags. In the shop, he'd rushed round and shovelled everything he could find into three carrier bags, much to the proprietor Mr Ranji's increasing curiosity. Sas was on the other side doing the same, before she ran up to the counter and literally threw money at the shopkeeper. Notes fluttered through the air like leaves and coins sprayed the counter. Sas spun on her heel and fled out of the door with Ryan right behind her, burning with shame.

'Come back here!' Ranji shouted. 'Stop them! Thieves!'

Ryan bit his lips and shrugged his shoulders, as a sort of apology, then ran off as fast as his legs could carry him. He headed down the hill, hoping like mad that a thunderbolt wouldn't get him. When he took a little breather, he spotted Fitzpatrick in the alley looking nothing less than utterly terrified.

What the hell was he up to?

DANNY

Danny trembled. Everything Xinder said rang true.

Danny heard Fitzpatrick's voice, strangely muffled. 'So, there's little hope for me and my sisters.'

'There is always hope, young man,' the ghost replied. 'But in comparison to the thickness of a rainbow, the chances that the three of you will survive this storm are but an atom wide. You are a child. You have neither the strength, nor the skills, to combat what lies ahead. You have no magic, and you do not understand nature. What chance do you have?'

He paused for effect. 'None. That is why you must join me now, Danny. While the world is washed away, I alone offer you the chance to escape through me. You have the opportunity to start again. All I need is the use of your body.'

'Will this help save your mother?' Fitzpatrick said.

The ghost seemed a little surprised. 'Yes. You have seen her and you know that she holds a great secret within her that others seek to destroy. By joining me, Danny, she will be saved. I guarantee it.'

Xinder was laying on the charm. His persuasion was intoxicating. 'Here, on earth, the suffering will be great. Together, Danny, we can build a new future. I am nearly useless without you, and you are helpless without me.'

Fitzpatrick looked over at Danny whose terrified face had risen from the other side of the wheelie bin. 'But, I still don't understand,' Fitzpatrick whimpered.

Xinder growled. 'These things are beyond your understanding. Open your mind. Give me your body.'

Fitzpatrick tried to make a run for it. He attempted to loosen the grip on his arm by suddenly charging at the wheelie bin. 'GO!' he screamed at Danny. 'RUN!' But the ghost held him tight and forced him to the floor. Fitzpatrick whimpered at the stabbing pain in his hand.

The ghost moved into Danny's path and began to unfurl the scarf wrapped around his face. 'I see,' he said. 'There is another.' His head moved. 'Only one of you is Danny. You have deceived me,' the ghost said.

'It is your choice, Danny. If you choose to come with me, you will be saved,' the ghost continued. 'My mother will be saved. Run, and you die.'

He released Fitzpatrick, who stumbled to the floor. 'Which is it going to be?'

Fitzpatrick's cheeks were streaked with tears. He caught Danny's eye, and stared at him. Imploring him, begging him to understand.

Fitzpatrick began to speak to his friend. 'Fitzpatrick, you are my only friend,' he said, 'and, not long ago, I swore on my life that I would never hurt you or your family. I failed.'

Danny frowned. *What? What was Fitzpatrick talking about? Had Fitzy figured that the ghost was blind?*

Fitzpatrick began again, 'Run, Fitzpatrick, save yourself. GO!'

'Uh?' Danny said, confused.

'Yes, Fitzy, you moron, get out of here! Flee to safety.'

Danny stared at Fitzpatrick.

And then Fitzpatrick said it again. 'Look, Fitzpatrick, you bloody great big oaf. Go now while there's still a chance. Leave this to me, but promise me one thing.'

'What?'

'Look after that fishing rod.'

'Fishing rod?'

'Blimey Fitzpatrick, how stupid are you?' he said. 'Go! Now. Run you idiot – GO!'

Danny stared deep into Fitzpatrick's tear-stained eyes and could see a spark of light.

Danny curled his fist into a ball and punched his friend lightly on the shoulder. He winked and mouthed the words, 'Thank you'.

'So long, Danny Delaux,' Danny said. 'See you in the next place.'

Taking a deep breath, Danny turned and ran for his life.

11

RYAN, THURSDAY

S as' fingers shook so much that she couldn't lift the plant pot under which the key sat. Eventually Ryan put his bags down and calmly tried it for her. The old and rusty key stuck in the lock, turning only fractionally. Ryan forced it first one way and then the other, loosening it gradually until it clicked and let them through.

If that was the condition of the lock, he thought, *then what sort of state will this boat be in?*

The door whined open, as another crash of thunder and lightning crackled in the sky overhead. Ryan shivered and brushed away a few old cobwebs.

'When was the last time this was used?' he asked.

'No idea,' Sas replied, searching for a light. She flicked the switch and a solitary light bulb sparked into life.

In the middle of the boat house, covered by a large tarpaulin, an old rowing boat rested on two large pieces of wood. It had three bench seats, and Ryan reckoned it was probably twelve feet in length by four feet wide. He laughed. 'This is it? This piece of junk is going to save us? It should be in a museum!'

He dragged off the tarp, shook away the dust, and whistled as he inspected the vessel. Layers of peeling varnish and thick dust covered the wood.

'We need to build a canopy,' Sas said.

'Why?' Ryan quizzed.

'So we don't spend the entire time bailing water out, that's why.'

Ryan pulled the oars off the wall and nestled them in the rowlocks before searching the boathouse for wood. He found several lengths of two by four inch cut timber, as well as planks intended, he supposed, for repairs.

'How long did you say we would be stuck in this?'

Sas shrugged. 'How should I know? A day, a week'

'A week?'

'Maybe a month?'

'Jeez. A month.' Ryan sprang into overdrive. He ran around the room finding things that might be useful and tossing them into the boat: rope; wood; a couple of buckets; a crabbing line, and a fishing net. He found a handy-looking wooden box and a sealed plastic container, which he told Sas to clean before putting in the matches and anything else that needed to be kept dry.

How would they anchor down the canopy? What would they sleep on? What would they drink?

He yelled over to Sas, who was still busy cramming the tarpaulin under a seat.

'A month? Really, a month! You think so?'

A huge crack of thunder smashed overhead.

They cowered.

She stretched her arms out. 'How long is a piece of string?'

Ryan spied four, fifty-litre plastic containers. He ran over and smelled them. No foul odours. Good. He took two to the tap, then rinsed and filled them before heaving them up onto the boat. It creaked ominously under their weight.

'Make room for these,' he instructed Sas, 'one at each end.'

Ryan tied the two empty ones to either side to act as bumpers or emergency buoys.

With this task complete, Ryan spotted more loose planks on the far wall. He marched over and, without hesitating, levered the first plank off. As the nails bowed to the pressure and the length came away, he pulled two more weatherboards away and slipped them into the boat. 'Hammer and nails,' he yelled out. 'Have you seen any?'

Sas pointed in the direction of an old workbench.

It was a long shot, but if there were any tools it might make all the difference. He flew through the drawers and cupboards, finding paint and rags, paintbrushes and sandpaper. He dragged out a thick canopy and laid it aside. How would he attach it? To the right, another pile of workman's bits was covered by two large, crumpled dust sheets.

He handed the dust sheets to Sas, indicating that she needed to shake them out and fold them away.

Underneath all this he discovered a selection of woodworking tools hidden in an old, blue canvas bag.

Ryan thumped the air. Clearly, someone had set out to repair the building and left everything behind.

Right, Ryan thought. *I reckon I've got approximately twenty minutes to build a world class, life-saving canopy.*

XINDER

'It has started,' the ghost cried, his hat angled upwards towards the sky. 'Something more powerful than you can possibly imagine has begun.' He raised an arm towards the lightning and thunder.

'If you want to see your friend for the last time, follow his path. I doubt he will last long. You too may run now, but you would be a fool, Danny Delaux.'

Fitzpatrick moved towards the end of the alleyway.

People were scattering even though the players were still on the pitch.

Fitzpatrick watched Danny hare towards the steep bank and out of view. Then he reappeared, running flat out, waving his hands in the air, sprinting onto the football field.

Fitzpatrick shifted his gaze.

Anika struck the ball...

CRACK!

With a deafening roar, a massive thunderbolt flashed out of the sky right on top of Danny.

Fitzpatrick's heart missed a beat as he watched Danny

collapse to the floor like a rag-doll, his body spasming one moment, then still the next.

Smoke drifted out from his friend's body.

Sounds of screaming filled the air.

Fitzpatrick recoiled. Everything the ghost had said had happened; the sweet paper, the lightning in his own image, and now the thunderbolt aimed at Danny who lay dead on the ground.

Laid back Danny, with his scruffy hair, who was always late for everything. His fishing pal, the only person to whom he'd ever told the whole story about his parents.

He'd sent him to his death.

Xinder hovered behind him. 'I am nothing more than a sad ghost,' he said, almost forlornly. 'I was stripped of my flesh and bones, but not my spirit. It means that I cannot move or touch anything with any great purpose, so I require flesh and blood to partially restore me. This is where you come in. I cannot do it alone.'

The ghost removed his scarf and sniffed the air around Fitzpatrick, who felt a chill on his neck.

'Rest assured, boy,' the ghost said softly, 'I have no intention of taking your life, only *borrowing* it for a little while. When my work is done and my mother is safe from harm, I will put you back near this spot. That is my solemn promise. But nature's curse is now upon us. A decision needs to be made.'

Fitzpatrick remained frozen to the spot.

'You must freely decide,' the ghost continued. 'The window is closing so you must decide now. I very much doubt you will get such an offer from the storm.'

SAP

As the morning wore on, Sap had been consumed by a feeling of utter dread, as if a toxic stew brewed in his stomach and a splinter had played darts in his heart.

Whatever he did, his anxiety would not go away. He marched around the house looking for something – anything - to alleviate this terrible feeling.

He studied the wooden carvings, tracing his fingers over the rich detailing on the panelling in his room. He inspected the old pictures for a clue, anything that might shed some light on the nightmares he'd had and help temper the worry that filled him from the top of his head to the tips of his toes.

Did the carvings and paintings mean something? If so, *what*?

Was a vital clue staring him in the face?

The more he played with this notion, the greater and deeper his feeling of despair grew, like a festering skin boil.

He wondered if he shouldn't go down to the school and watch the football match, but it didn't seem right.

Instead, he headed up to the ruin to check on the sheep and cattle.

The herd appeared quiet but jumpy. The same as him, he thought, and he wondered if the animals sensed something unusual. He made sure that the shelter was sound, before counting them: eleven sheep, three cows, six bullocks, and Himsworth the bull.

Sap sat down on a grey boulder at the head of the ruin and looked out across the vale. In front of him a sheer drop of solid rock disappeared into thick forest seventy metres or so below, before levelling up near the valley floor. He could just make out the river curving around the rock face and, from there, it slipped around the corner.

Sap shuffled his boot in the dirt. He was too old for this, too old for riddles and memories.

Why the dreams every night, what were they trying to tell him? Why did he have that aching feeling in his bones which he hadn't had for ages?

He stood up as a deep roll of thunder boomed and crackled through the valley. He kicked a stone, which flew off the ledge and sailed through the air before crashing into the canopy of the trees below.

Looking out at the school buildings in the distance, lost in his thoughts, Sap saw a lightning bolt shoot out of the sky right into the heart of the village. This was followed by another, and then another. Each one came with a blast of light so bright and a crack so loud that Sap shielded his eyes and his ears.

A searing pain walloped into his chest. He bent over and cried out. The sky fizzed as another huge bolt crashed out of the sky directly onto the playing field.

This time the pain was unbearable and Sap crouched low, clutching his chest, struggling for breath.

Was this pain linked to the storm? He needed to lie down.

Sap straightened up as best he could and stumbled back down the pathway, stopping occasionally to view the tempest playing out over the school.

Wasn't it funny, he pondered, *how the storm seemed to focus only on the school?*

As he concentrated on this thought, his feeling that the children were in terrible danger accelerated. He hurried back, lay on his bed, and massaged his heart, as another thought crossed his mind.

If the storm broke, how would the children get back? The river would swell, and the track to Appleside Farm would act like a storm drain. What if they were trying to get home and were swept away?

He dabbed his handkerchief on his forehead. He had to *do* something.

But as he was preparing to get up, an instant tiredness washed over him, and a powerful urge to close his eyes enveloped him like a drug.

His head fell back onto his large pillows and a moment later the old man was snoring like an old tractor.

Fitzpatrick stumbled, dizzy and sick with fear. He faced Xinder head-on for the first time.

All Fitzpatrick could see was a transparent gap between the hat and the overcoat. His teeth were chattering. 'If I don't—?'

'You'll almost certainly die, or be drowned in the rains. Or in the landslides, or the tsunamis which will sweep the land…'

'Will you kill me?'

'Me? Kill you?' the ghost chuckled. 'No. As I said, I'm just going to *borrow* you for a while. Why would I kill you when my purpose is to save so many? You must *trust* me.'

Fitzpatrick looked up at the sky. It was fizzing with electricity like an angry nest. A terrible boom rattled every bone in his body as a thunderbolt walloped into a nearby chimney pot.

He ducked and his head vibrated like a jack-hammer mashing up a road.

Fitzpatrick stared down the path, preparing to run. As his eyes focused on the dark shadows between the buildings, he found himself looking at a familiar face: Ryan Williams laden with shopping bags. They locked eyes for several seconds before Williams simply ran off, as though someone had called him away in a hurry.

'Animais!' the ghost barked, impatiently. 'Open up. It is time to go! This boy is not the Sacrum.'

'Wait,' Fitzpatrick croaked. 'Please! What do I have to do?'

'Put on the coat and hat. Quickly. But you must want to survive and you must desire to go with me.'

Fitzpatrick's mind was made up.

In a flash, he threw both of his overcoats to the ground and moved in close. As he did so, he felt a strange coolness wash over him.

'Ignore that I am here,' the ghost said, as Fitzpatrick fumbled with the cloth. 'Put the coat on, as you would any other.'

Fitzpatrick grabbed the collar and pushed his arm into the sleeve, amazed by the sudden freeze that enveloped it. Then his other arm slid in. Fitzpatrick had a wonderful feeling of deep strength building up in him, as though a syringe was powering him with a thick energy juice.

The feeling started in his fingers, moved up to his wrists, through his elbows and on to his shoulders. All too soon, it was spreading down through his loins and into his legs and feet. Syrupy liquid, like freezing treacle, coursed through every vein and into every muscle and sinew of his body.

Fitzpatrick drew the coat across his chest as the curious feeling crept towards his heart and lungs.

He cried out and stretched his arms wide, as the ice-like goo rushed into his vital organs and washed through his body. He let out a cry of pure ecstasy, his shouts bouncing back off the old houses.

Fitzpatrick only had one more thing to do. He lifted up the hat and pulled it down over his head. Suddenly, he could feel the cold charge oozing up his neck and through his mouth.

He shut his eyes, enjoying the extraordinary tingling sensations of the liquid ice entering his brain and slowly dispersing through the back of his skull, tickling parts he never knew existed.

The surge of power moved around the skull and headed towards his eyes.

As it flowed into his eyes, everything changed. With a rapidity that took him completely by surprise, Fitzpatrick felt a searing, burning pain scream into his head, expanding like a balloon filling with air.

'What's happening?' he screamed. 'MY GOD, *my eyes!*'

He desperately tried to rip off the hat and wrestle out of the coat.

'My head! MY EYES! What have you done to me? Help me! *HELP! I'm burning!*'

As Fitzpatrick carried on screaming, the ghost chuckled.

'Welcome to me,' Xinder said, his voice laced with triumph. 'Welcome to the burnt-out body of Xinder, Frozen Lord of Halaria.'

12

DANNY, THURSDAY

Danny prised his eyes open and attempted to focus. His head! It pounded as if a road roller was travelling backwards and forwards in his brain.

He caught the sharp, acrid smell of burning hair.

When his eyes finally hooked up with his brain, he could make out a burning net and a smouldering goalpost.

'Danny!' Anika cried as she rushed over. 'Please...'

Several inaudible words mumbled out of his mouth.

'DANNY!' Olivia screamed as she too tore across the pitch.

She placed her hand on Danny's forehead then felt for his temperature, checked his pulse and inspected his tongue.

'Thank God!' she said, cradling him. 'I thought you were toast. Say something – can you move?'

Very slowly he lifted an arm, his fingernails black and his charred clothes singed.

He smiled weakly.

'At least he's showing signs of mental stability,' Olivia

said. 'Anika, get the tracksuits! I'll make sure his internal organs are functioning.'

Shortly, Olivia declared that Danny was well enough to try a couple of little sips of water.

Danny shut his eyes then opened them. Then he slurred some words.

'My strips must have saved you!'

'Urgh?'

'The strips I made you put on your boots.'

Anika returned with their tracksuits, slipping into hers before helping Danny into his.

'We won!' Olivia said. 'You did it!'

'Don't be ridiculous,' Anika scoffed as she pulled Danny's top over his stiff hair.

'I'm not,' Olivia replied. 'The ball's in the net. It was blown into the goal. You actually scored!'

Anika didn't know whether to hit her sister or cry. 'No,' she said furiously. 'I missed and Danny got fried. Look at him, it's a miracle he survived.'

'But you're fine now, aren't you, Danny?' Olivia cried. 'Anyway, you're wrong. Your free kick was heading towards the corner flag but the lightning bolt deflected the ball into the goal. I swear. The charge of particles must have generated a force to deflect it without blowing the ball up. It is therefore, the most extraordinary goal of the millennium—'

'Shut up! Please,' Anika said, sharply. 'Stop it.'

Coach was running over towards them. He went straight to Danny, spending some time checking him over.

'WOW-ee,' he whistled. 'That is one lucky escape, young man. I thought you were brown bread. It looks like the Gods spared you. You may feel a little groggy for a while, but, amazingly, I think you're gonna be alright. Try standing if you can.'

Danny smiled and, with the support of a person on each side, he stood up.

'How do you feel?'

He couldn't quite hear or see them. He tried smiling.

'That's the match ball in the net, isn't it, Coach?' Olivia asked. 'I've taken a picture of it on my phone, for safe-keeping.'

Coach clapped his hands. 'You know what, you're right! Looks like we ruddy well won. We're only the bleedin' champions!' He slapped Anika on the back, almost knocking her over. 'Quite amazing...' He stopped mid-sentence and looked up, his tone serious once again. 'Listen, if you think you can make it, Dan, you'd better get off now, up that funny track to your cottage. Otherwise, I'll give you a lift back, via the school.'

'Thanks, but don't worry, Coach,' Olivia said. 'We'll get him back in one piece, I promise. It's not so far. Anyway, you're not that bad, are you, Danny?'

Coach eyed them. 'You sure? You'd better get going then. Best scarper before another of them thunderbolts zaps us.' He patted them on their backs. 'As fast as you can! I reckon it's going to bloody piss down.'

Coach skipped off towards the car park singing loudly. Then he yelled back at them. 'Great goals, Anika, and bloody brilliant hairdo, Dan. You're all legends!'

ANIKA

'Is anyone else finding this boomingly loud?' Anika asked. 'I've had to put tissues in my ears. Look!' She pulled out her makeshift ear defenders. Suddenly, Anika's face drained.

Olivia spotted it. 'Ani, what is it?'

'I think there's another incoming thunderbolt.'

'*What?*' Olivia said.

'RUN! NOW!'

Draping Danny's arms around their shoulders, they set off.

'What did you hear?'

'It's like a build-up of collisions.' Anika froze. 'DIVE!'

A moment later, a massive crack tore across the sky and unleashed a lightning bolt that smashed into the exact spot where, moments earlier, they had been huddled together.

'Bloody hell,' Olivia whispered, her knees buckling. 'That was close. It's like it's after us.'

They huddled together, trembling.

'It is,' Danny eventually mumbled. He closed his eyes

and tried to work more saliva into his mouth. 'Survive ... dusk, cave.'

'That's exactly what Sas said,' Olivia said. 'Survive until sunset.'

'Where do you get that from?' Anika said. She twitched. Olivia noticed. 'What is it, Anika?'

'Another one, same kind of noise!'

They reached the tree and slipped under the branches. 'We should be safer here.'

Anika held her hands over her ears as a couple of tears rolled down her cheeks. 'Oh shit! Here it comes!'

A lightning bolt smashed into the branches.

The children screamed as a huge branch sheared off and crashed a couple of feet away.

Olivia and Anika held each other, paralysed with fear, shaking.

Danny gurgled a few words. It snapped them out of it.

'Home. We've got to get home now. Hurry!' Olivia eventually said, hauling Danny to his feet. 'COME ON!'

WYNN-GARRY

Wynn-Garry felt a sharp pain in his chest. He looked at the schoolchildren and the adults streaming in from the pitch.

In an instant, he knew what to do.

He ran to the Newton coach. 'Go, directly,' he ordered. 'Please don't argue, get in your bus and drive as fast as you can away from this place. I believe this fearsome cloud is about to break.'

He didn't wait around. He ran on, sweat breaking out.

'Children,' he boomed to the nearby crowd 'All those staying till later, do not go back to your classrooms. Go directly to the library in the tower. Hurry, there's not a moment to lose. Grab anyone you see on the way.'

Wynn-Garry rushed towards the buildings and ran panting into the classrooms.

'Get to the tower, now,' he roared, rushing in. 'Leave your things, just go!'

A terrible realisation filled him. Children were scattered around the school. The noise overhead, like heavy artillery fire, made his eyes water.

He bumbled into the gymnasium, where a last rehearsal was underway.

'Stop what you're doing,' he ordered, climbing on to the stage while trying to catch his breath. 'Get to the library. Immediately.' He hoped his firm tone would not go unnoticed.

Children poured out of the entrance. 'Good. Hurry,' he called out after them. 'You too, Mrs. Rose.'

He rushed back into the yard and shot into the canteen.

He gasped for breath. 'Chef!' he called out, as an idea popped into his head. 'Take as many provisions as you can to the library, this instant. Bread, milk, anything.'

'Are you alright, boss?' said the chef.

'Pile the contents of the fridge, the store cupboards, the larder into containers this very instant and head directly to the tower. NOW.'

The chef stared at him in disbelief and stole a glance towards his assistants.

'Everything?'

'Yes, chef. Trust me. There's not a moment to lose. And remember milk and orange juice. Do it now - all of you,' he roared.

They hesitated.

'Now! GO! There's no time!'

Wynn-Garry sped out of the kitchen then, as fast as he could, outside across the yard and into the art department. He struggled to breathe. 'Skinner, Moloney, run to the tower this instant,' he gasped, falling into a chair.

He wiped his specs. Who else?

The building splintered, the sound rattling the windows.

Good Lord. The changing rooms!

Then he heard the whooshes of wind, no doubt whipped up by oncoming rain.

No time!

Out he shuttled, his body screaming at him to stop.

Three boys sat on the benches, staring out of the window.

'Don't just sit there,' he cried. 'Come with me.'

'Where to?'

'Safety,' he gasped, collapsing onto the wood.

'Sir, are you alright?'

Wynn-Garry clenched his eyes. 'Yes, yes. Now run along! Go to the library. I'll follow.'

'But, Sir?'

'NOW!'

The headmaster took several deep breaths. He'd rounded up as many as he could.

Where were the Delauxs, he wondered. Then it struck him. They would be heading home across the playing fields. A twenty-minute walk at the very least.

He summoned his energy and threw himself through the door, rushing out into the corridor and then down the stairs.

As he ran outside, he saw far off in the distance three figures huddling together, heading slowly towards the bridge.

Oh my God, he thought, a feeling of utter despair gripping him. *They haven't got a chance.*

But as he sucked in a lungful of air to call out to them, his fears were realised, and the first drops of rain smashed into him.

Within moments, water edged through the cracks of the boat house and stole down the sides, drumming like a carnival on the barn's tin roof.

Ryan stared in disbelief at the rain. *Holy moly*, he thought, *she's right*.

Quickly, Ryan stretched the canopy, which in truth was a thick, heavy-duty plastic sheet covering the length of the boat from bow to stern. It would fit perfectly. Then, he formed a tent frame over the boat, hammering in nails as fast as he could go.

He stepped back. *Uneven*, Ryan thought, *but it would do, so long as the nails held*.

Ryan listened to the downpour. It needed to be a super strong boat. He'd take more wood and prop up the midsection if he had time later, once they were underway.

Next, he nailed two rough planks on both the port and starboard sides, leaving a gap in the middle for the oars. As fast as he could, he nailed batons over the canopy on the outside of the boat. He repeated this on the other side. In no time, the boat was covered in a tight tent. Better still, if it worked, water would run off the canopy and out of the boat, not into it.

Sas looked on in awe. She tried where she could to help, amazed at his dexterity and speed. Ryan didn't come across as the brightest spark in school, but my goodness he was practical.

She ran around the boat pulling bits of the canopy tight while Ryan hammered, sawed and stretched the plastic sheeting. So immersed in their project were they, that they hardly noticed water seeping in, up and over the floor.

ANIKA

'OH, NO!' Anika cried.

'What is it with you?'

'It's like a power shower ... RUN.'

A warm gust of wind blew in, nearly blowing them off their feet. The first few large rain drops, more like mini water balloons, began to plummet.

'Move, NOW!' Olivia cried. 'It's the storm we predicted—'

'*Predicted?*' Anika yelled.

'Yeah, Sas and I...' Olivia's voice trailed off. 'We've got about five minutes before this playing field becomes a river.'

'Terrific!' Anika yelled.

Olivia and Anika put their hands under Danny's armpits, and folded his arms across their shoulders so he was properly supported.

'Move your legs, Dan. HURRY!' Anika screamed, forcing the pace. The rain intensified as the wind blew in several directions at once. In no time, a wall of water sluiced out of the heavens, pounding them from all sides, beating their heads, shoulders, and backs.

Olivia removed her coat and draped it over their heads.

'Where's the bridge?' Anika shouted, above the din of the rain. 'I can't see ANYTHING!'

Olivia slowed and stared at the ground. Without knowing why, she pointed her free arm ahead of her, closed her eyes and allowed her arm to guide her.

Soon, the soft wet turf underfoot made way for hard gravel. They followed it, but every step was tricky and they couldn't be sure exactly where they were going. Olivia rubbed the ground with her foot every so often in order to feel the stone underneath. By the time they reached the bridge, the children were cold, soaked through, and exhausted. More worryingly, water was spilling out of the river at an alarming rate. It was up to their ankles and rising fast.

'Bind – tighter – scrum!' Olivia yelled. 'Move together, in time. I'll count.' She realised they couldn't hear her so she signed with her fingers: ONE, TWO, THREE and then she flicked out her thumb.

'Where's the bridge?' Anika yelled, before suddenly losing her footing. Danny hauled her to her feet.

Olivia shook her head, imploring her to keep going. 'DON'T FALL OVER.'

They nodded.

Olivia counted each step, the force of the water gaining by the second, pushing hard at their legs. Every breath was a struggle, and their heads bowed from the pressure bearing down upon them.

Olivia had no choice but to trust her hands and, as if by a miracle, they arrived at the handrail. She breathed a deep sigh of relief. The children shuffled on, still huddled together, their feet searching for the wooden boards.

Anika suddenly went stiff, holding the others back. She turned to the others, her eyes bulging.

'GO!'

They scampered up to the brow of the bridge, Anika leading the way and holding Danny's hand on one side. Suddenly she dived, hauling Danny forward with all her might.

Bits of wood splintered around them, the noise deafening.

Anika pulled herself out of the water, her feet grateful for the feeling of land, and found Danny next to her. He was fine, but where the hell was Olivia?

She grappled about. 'Olivia,' she screamed.

Anika called out but it was hopeless; she wouldn't be heard over the din. As she listened, the only thing she could hear was the roar of the rain and the rush of the water flushing everything downstream.

RYAN

'Almost time to batten down the hatches,' Ryan yelled, smiling.

Sas ran up and hugged him. 'I couldn't have done this without you,' she said, and she genuinely meant it. Sas climbed into the boat and sat under the canopy as a deep sense of foreboding filled her. She desperately hoped they were doing the right thing. She hoped like anything that Olivia and the twins had got away safely.

Ryan slipped a few remaining planks into the boat and a couple more of the two by four inch sections. He grabbed the remaining nails, the hammer, a saw, a small axe, a hand-drill and a chisel, and threw them all in the box. Just before the water covered the whole floor, he scanned the shed looking for anything else. Sas's umbrella, for starters, and a couple of old empty paint pots with lids. More rope, string, a whole reel of strimmer cord, and another large dust sheet, this one already neatly folded. He rummaged through the cupboards like a man possessed, and found an untouched bag of barbecue briquettes. He threw them in; maybe they'd need fire.

Sas packed them away. Then with a few last-minute alterations, as the water reached the upper limits of his boots, Ryan clambered in to the boat. He hoped like mad that, with the weight of the fresh water and timber and the two of them, they wouldn't all simply disappear through the bottom.

The boat creaked as it rose. No holes nor rotten timbers so far.

Sas shook, holding her hands against her ears as thunder and lightning blazed outside. It felt as if they were waiting in the depths of the Colosseum before being fed to the lions in front of an angry, baying crowd. The boat continued to rise, finding its buoyancy. Then it started to drift.

'Here we go,' Ryan yelled. 'Hold on tight.'

A moment later, the boat clunked into something.

Ryan squeezed past Sas to the bow. He looked out and muttered something under his breath.

'What is it?' Sas cried. 'Is there a problem?'

'Technical difficulty,' he said, scratching his chin. 'Pass me that hand axe.'

Sas scrabbled around in the box and handed it over.

Ryan disappeared, and set about trying to smash the weatherboards. A short while later, his banging stopped. 'It appears,' Ryan said, popping his head back under the canopy, 'that the water has risen higher than the gap the boat was meant to go through.'

'What does that mean?'

'It means we're stuck!' he said, smiling his huge grin again.

'For crying out loud,' Sas howled. 'Can't you get the boards off?'

'What do you think I've been doing? Knitting?'

She rolled her eyes. 'So how are we going to get out? I

was hoping we might be able to save Danny and the others.'

Ryan raised his eyebrows. 'There's a window directly above, so panic ye not. I've got an idea,' he said. 'Pass me the saw, and move to the other end, please.'

Ryan took the saw and stood on the seat right at the prow of the boat. He began sawing as fast as he could through the timbers surrounding the window. The boat sloshing from side to side.

After several minutes of sawing and hacking, Ryan put his drenched head back under the canopy. 'Don't think that's going to work, either.' He smiled again. 'Rain's quite warm.'

Sas looked appalled. 'What are we going to do?'

Ryan stretched out his legs, closed his eyes and took a deep breath. 'We wait.'

'Wait!' Sas roared. 'You must be joking. We'll drown if we stay in here. Can't you see that?'

Ryan ignored her and smiled toothily again. It seemed to act as an anger-deflecting shield. 'You know what we haven't done?' he said, his large eyes sparkling.

'What?' Sas snapped.

'Named our vessel.'

Sas eyed him warily. 'Seriously, Ryan, before we start thinking up names, do you actually think we'll get out of here?'

He raised his eyebrows.

'How?' Sas said, raising her eyebrows back at him. Getting a straight answer out of Ryan was proving to be a bit of a nightmare.

Ryan jabbed a finger upwards.

'God?' she yelled, sarcastically.

Ryan's whole body galloped up and down with laughter.

He moved close to her so they could hear each other without yelling. 'No, you banana-cake, through the roof. So long as the water continues to rise,' he peered out of the end of the boat, ' - and it is rising, just as you said it would, - then up we go.'

Sas grimaced. 'Really? You sure it'll work?'

'Oh yeah. Far easier this way. There's corrugated iron sheeting up there, they'll lift off and then, whoosh, into the river.'

Sas couldn't help but admire his confidence, although she wasn't convinced. Wasn't corrugated sheeting heavy, especially with water beating onto it? 'So, what do we do now?'

'Well, let's see. We could start by naming our boat. It's definitely good luck before a maiden voyage. You got any ideas?'

'Not really. You?'

'Yeah,' and he smiled his big smile again.

'Well, what is it?'

Ryan opened his eyes wide. 'I think we should call it the 'The Joan of'.'

'That's it?' Sas said. She looked mystified. 'The Joan of ... what? What does that mean? It doesn't make any sense. That's not a name for a boat.'

Ryan feigned a look of shock. 'Now, come along, brain-box. This little teaser shouldn't be difficult for super-smart Sas Smith.'

13

SOLA, THURSDAY

Sap hadn't reacted to any of the dreams given to him. The Animais worried that if Sap could not understand his dreams, what chance would the children have with theirs?

Were the dreams proving to be too complex, too terrifying? Were the dreams suited to a different time? Perhaps their dreams needed a different blending of powders to aid interpretation?

Sola dipped a hand in her infiniti, removed the dream powder and rubbed a couple of fingers together. This wasn't the time for reflection, that would come later. While the children were still alive, for the time being at least, she needed haste.

She would give Sap a dream that would stimulate action and, at the end of the sequence, she would add a powder that would stimulate a shock. Yes, that was it. He needed something to get his brain working, to unlock his memory, so that he might help the Sacrum as he'd been entrusted to do.

Sola worked fast, her slender fingers moving like a blur

in her infiniti. In a flash, she was plucking tiny specks of dream powder out of her infiniti and feeding them to the old man as he inhaled. Sola took her time, and, digging deep into her memory of powders, knitted a dream ending with a reminder of a potion that Sap had stored away a long, long time ago.

Sola stared down at the old man. *Maybe this time,* she thought, before inverting into her infiniti and vanishing.

Sap tossed and turned as the dream filled his head. He looked down and found himself wearing a pair of shorts. He was running. He felt young again, the same age as the twins. His skin was smooth and his mind was alert. He had hair! He dragged his hands through it. What a lovely feeling. As he ran, air filled his lungs.

On his feet, he wore a pair of football boots. Red ones, just like Danny's. He looked up. A football was flying towards him, and his immediate reaction was to duck out of the way. But out of the corner of his eye he spotted Anika yelling at him. What was she saying? Pass it? He went towards the ball but it was too fast and it bounced off him straight to an opponent.

This wasn't as easy as it looked.

Anika swore and chivvied him to chase the player.

He took off and was moving at speed. Much to his delight, Sap found himself gaining. He lunged for the ball but tripped the player.

The whistle blew. 'Do that once more and you'll be booked,' the referee said.

Sap caught his breath and brushed the mud off his knees.

Anika was there in an instant. 'What do you think you're playing at?' she said. 'There's hardly any time to go. Don't make stupid fouls like that. We've got to win or we're never playing again.'

The other team lined up a shot and the ball was cruising towards the goal. But Danny danced into the path of the ball and caught it smartly. In a flash, he punted the ball wide.

One of his players passed the ball to him. This time he managed to control it and he slipped a neat pass through to Anika. Anika, now on the halfway line, jinked past one player, and then sped past another, her blonde hair bobbing up and down as she went. Boy, she was quick. He found himself sprinting just to keep up.

A defender forced her wide and she played the ball inside to him. Looking up, he passed it to Olivia on the other flank. He couldn't remember Olivia ever liking football, but she neatly passed it back to him just as she was clattered by an opposition player. He couldn't help laughing at the horrified expression on her face.

Now Anika was screaming for the ball.

Sap found himself running with the ball and it felt brilliant. He did a dummy, just like Anika had, slipping past the player in front of him. He knocked the ball forwards, finding Anika, who held off a challenge and stood with the ball under her foot.

In a flash, she turned on a sixpence, the ball rolling under her other foot. Totally foxing the defender, she headed towards the goal. Sap felt himself sprinting into the area as Anika smashed a shot at the goal.

He held his breath as the ball sped toward the goal. It whacked against the post and rebounded directly into his running path. Out of the corner of his eye, a defender hared towards the ball. He had to get there first, so he sprinted harder, cocked his leg back, and kicked the ball as hard as he could a fraction before the defender got there.

The ball screamed into the roof of the net, tearing a hole, and was still rising just as the defender crunched into his foot.

A heartbeat later, and a lightning bolt smashed out of the sky directly into him. A surge of energy fizzed through his entire body, through every sinew and fibre and particle of his being.

It took his breath away.

When at last the sensation wore off, he peered down to find a bottle of gold liquid on his lap.

Then he woke up, with a start.

The water took her.

Olivia's world went blank. When she came to, her body tingled all over and every nerve and sinew sizzled like a spectacular case of pins and needles.

She coughed, spluttered, and ejected water trapped in her lungs. She gasped as her hands and feet instantly kicked into action, her arms and legs moving faster than she could have ever imagined just to keep her head above water.

She breathed, luxuriating in the intake of air.

Her hand grappled with a shrub branch. She tried to hoist herself up, but it fell away plunging her back under the surface. When she surfaced, visibility zero, she knew she needed to touch down on the cottage side of the river.

Treading water, she did a quick calculation. If the river ran from the moors down into the valley, she had to land on the left bank as it went with the flow. Olivia kicked until she could feel the water pushing against her before twisting with all her strength and swimming at an angle into the current.

Moments later, she touched on something spindly and woody. She pushed her legs down and was relieved to find the water was up to her waist. With her feet on firm ground, she clambered across the bush and kept going until her knees hit on solid ground the other side.

Olivia coughed, spluttered, and retched, as though her insides were coming out. Without hesitating, she continued uphill, searching for the cover of a tree. She found one, leaned in and put her head in her hands.

Now it was exactly like her nightmare, except this time it was for real.

Tears built up and for a moment they rolled freely down her cheeks. Anika! Danny! They'll probably think I'm dead.

She imagined them waiting for her. *Please, please keep going! Every minute spent waiting is a minute wasted.*

She wondered what had happened to Sas. Did she find the boat? In any case, that little boat would fill with water and sink in minutes. The whole thing was hopeless.

Olivia felt herself welling up, but a ripple of water washed against her shins. She had to move. Finding the others was futile now. She'd head uphill from tree to tree and find cover wherever she could.

She had to survive.

'Look at us, boy,' Xinder whispered. 'Well, look at me. Aren't I *magnificent*!'

Xinder studied his body in a tall mirror ringed with dull gemstones. Morning light seeped through a vast window. 'You're here, boy,' he said, as his voice echoed off the walls. 'Right here inside me. That's right; half ash, half man… or boy. Only a fraction ghost.'

Xinder examined his reflection.

His borrowed eyes weren't anything like the proper article, his vision was filtered by a grainy film. But, what a sensation to see anything at all when, for thousands of years, he had tuned into the vibrations and presence of things using his highly developed sixth sense.

He studied his hands and turned them over. He clapped, the noise a muted thud. Ash puffed up and floated quietly through the air.

Oh, the joys of having a body, he thought, *whatever form it took.*

Xinder removed his overcoat, took off his hat, and

returned, naked, to stand in front of the mirror. His figure was the same size as the boy and his torso was covered in layers of flaky ash in every conceivable hue of grey. *How utterly remarkable*, he thought, as he rotated his hips from side to side.

His chest was a boyish replica of the one he remembered. His pectorals and abdomen were not so hard and toned as perhaps they once were, but the sinews and muscles on his thighs, calves and buttocks were pleasingly accentuated by the light.

His feet, he noted, were unusually large. He sprang up on his toes, only to find that a couple of digits simply dropped off. Xinder stared, fascinated, as they instantly regrew.

In the reflection of the mirror, Xinder moved close. His face appeared sallow and partially skeletal, with a flaky grey chin that jutted out more than he cared to see.

He nudged his thick plump lips, prodded his flat nose, and admired his eyebrows. He touched his hair, a mass of ash swept back off his forehead, and admired his eyes that sparkled like polished coals.

Then he noticed a strange cluster at the top of his legs. Wasn't this awfully important? Instinctively, he reached for it, but to his horror – and just as he remembered its purpose – the appendage severed, slipped through his fingers and careered to the ground.

Xinder squealed.

His concerns were short-lived. Moments later it reappeared and he and his organ were reacquainted.

Xinder's mood brightened.

'Thousands of years without one, and instantly it falls to pieces!' he roared.

Xinder realised his new body was a by-product of his incineration all those years ago.

His eyes narrowed.

How could he forget the burning and the eye gouging when his powers were taken away from him?

The verdict from The Council of One Hundred in Genartus, he remembered. *Oh yes, the very bad deal. Part of his original punishment.*

Xinder flexed up and down on his knees. He had movement; real, gravity-based movement, and physical presence. None of this 'floating around' nonsense, none of this walking through walls and doors and people. Although this skill did, from time to time, have its advantages.

Xinder, Frozen Lord of Halaria, is back! He could almost taste the fear of the strange creatures that now populated Halaria. Trolls had moved into the forests close to the silvery sea, a tribe of Neanderthals had swept over the pink mountains that surrounded Halar and some marsh-men had dammed the planet's great river at its mouth. The dragons, snakes, lizards, and reptiles, once controlled by an undefeatable reptilian dragon, had risen in numbers, with many now living on the outskirts of the city of Halar.

Xinder would return from the ashes to free his frozen people, so the rumours said, and bring the frozen domed puddles back to life. Xinder knew that he needed to make the most of his new form, and fast, which was exactly what he intended to do even if it meant that he had to forcibly drag the boy along with him.

First, he would check up on the Sacrum's progress towards their demise, now that their journey through the storm was underway. Perhaps he still had a chance of blending with a Sacrum, instead of this rather cumbersome boy.

Guda's dream-spinners were watching the Sacrum. When the time came, when they were close to deaths door, they would let him know.

Xinder smiled. Everything was slotting into place.

And when the time came, in an instant, he would be there.

14

ANIKA, THURSDAY

Anika shivered, grateful that the rain was not particularly cold. Anika knew, though, that even warm rain quickly chills, and there was just so much of it. She ventured from one side of the path to the other, as far as she dared. She screamed for Olivia, but she knew it was hopeless; she couldn't see and she could hardly hear her own voice.

With every movement, her bones ached and her joints screamed out, as if her energy reserves were on empty. If only she hadn't just played a game of football.

She stamped her feet and jogged up and down. She concentrated hard on the water further down. For a moment, she was sure that she could see, much further down on the river bank, a body climbing out of the water. She shook her head. She must be imagining things, like a mirage in a desert.

She put a hand around Danny and hugged him close. His body warmth was like a hot water bottle. He seemed better, his eyes clearer, and he smiled when she touched his odd hair.

But the shock had rendered him dumb, as though his tongue had been cut out.

What had Danny said earlier? That the storm would follow them until sunset. How did he know? She didn't need him like this, she needed him on full alert, thinking and helping.

Perhaps, she thought, *he needs another shock.*

She slapped him on the cheek as hard as she could.

'Blimey, Anika!' he yelled, rubbing his cheek. 'What did you do that for?'

'Got you back,' she mouthed, kissing his forehead. 'Sorry – necessary.'

'There's no need to hit me,' he yelled.

Anika hugged him tight, and spoke into his ear. 'Aw, but it did the trick. Come on, Dan, we've got to go.'

'What about Olivia?' he cried, waving his arm downstream.

'She's a strong swimmer,' she said. 'She'll be fine. Come on!'

He looked at his watch and shuddered. Only two forty-five. Sunset at what, five fifteen, five thirty? He wished he knew.

Every second of every minute would matter.

MRS PUDDY

Mrs Puddy sat in the kitchen, fretting and fiddling with a bunch of herbs, her hands shaking.

She heard noises in the courtyard. The sounds weren't the sounds of a soccer ball scuffing over the paving slabs, which she associated with Anika and Danny. Nor was it old Sap returning from the cattle. He'd been back a while.

This was more like something being torn in two, and then crashing sounds audible even over the beating rain.

Must be my imagination playing tricks, she thought, as she returned to her task of flavouring a large beef casserole.

She concentrated on lighting the fire, before her ears instinctively pricked up. Those sounds, again.

Opening the front door, she reeled as a wall of water poured like a waterfall over the low, extended roof. Seeing a branch jumping about in the water nearby, she realised that the sounds she'd heard must have been trees crashing down around the house.

A pain, like a stubborn splinter, pierced her. For the first time in years, the long, thick scar beneath the mop of bright orange hair on her forehead throbbed, giving her a pressing headache.

She'd never seen or heard anything like it. Instantly, she recognised the gravity of the children's situation.

The longer it went on, the more she pined, as though the cord that tied her to her children was being ripped apart and pins pressed slowly into her heart. She tried to soldier on and put these feelings behind her. She had to. They would return, she was sure of it. Sap would find them.

But what if they didn't? What if her children were stuck out there?

Tears swam down her cheeks, falling in drops on the wooden surface. Her head pulsed with doubt and sorrow as she cradled it in her hands and wept.

Realisation dawned on her that if this storm continued, and if Sap was to go after them, she might be alone in the world for the very first time.

SAS

'Oh, *ARK*!' Sas exclaimed. 'As in, *"Joan of Arc"*.'

Ryan clapped slowly. 'Blimey. At long last. Remind me never to partner you in a pub quiz. Ever.'

'You mean,' Sas said, 'you've actually been to a pub quiz?'

'Of course, every Friday night with my dad.'

'Really? My parents never do that kind of thing. What's it like?'

Ryan wondered if he should make it sound exciting. 'Well, it's OK. Actually, it's quite nerdy, so you'd probably like it.'

Sas's eyes sparkled. Ryan was full of surprises. *Just goes to show*, she thought, *you really can't tell a book by its cover.* 'So, what subjects are you good at?'

Ryan made his brainiest face, which made him look pretty stupid. 'Particle physics, geography, English history from 1066, current world affairs and, yeah, modern American history.'

'You're joking me!'

'Try me. Go on,' Ryan said, moving even closer.

Sas didn't know what to think. She screwed up her face as though deep in thought and asked: 'Which President of the United States of America wrote the Declaration of Independence?'

Ryan scratched his chin and made lots of quite odd-looking faces. 'Abraham Lincoln—'

'Ha, wrong—'

'Won the Civil War,' Ryan continued, ignoring her. 'Thomas Jefferson was the main author of the Declaration of Independence.' He tried hard not to smile. But he did raise his eyebrows. And they were huge eyebrows.

Sas couldn't believe it. 'Correct,' she said, trying to think of another question. 'Name the English monarch who came after William Rufus.'

'You can do better than that, sexy Sas.' He pulled a serious face. 'William Rufus, heir to William the Conqueror. Shot by an arrow by a noble who thought he was a knob-end. Succeeded by Henry, as in Henry the first, also a son of the Conqueror, who sat on the throne for a middle-age marathon of thirty-five years.'

Sas shrieked. She couldn't believe it. 'Ryan, you're brilliant at this. Why are you such an idiot in class?'

Ryan shrugged. 'Low tolerance to teachers.'

A clunking noise stopped them in their tracks. Ryan raced up to the bow step. 'The Joan of' has hit the roof,' he yelled. 'Here we go.' Ryan ducked his head inside the canopy. 'I hope you're ready for this. Pass me that long bit of wood and sit at the end. And Sas...'

'Yes?'

'Whatever you do, don't scream. It won't help.'

Ryan had never really expected the water to rise quite so high, nor so fast. In fact, he was pretty sure they'd remain in the boathouse, quite safe from the tempest outside. Now, it was different.

He grappled with the piece of wood, eventually holding its base, and thrust it up towards the corrugated sheeting directly above. *Come on, you little beauty. Move.* Nothing happened. He changed his tack, trying to lever the roofing off. *Move, you little tick*, he murmured, as he pushed the wood with all his might.

As he pushed, he became aware that the entire building had begun to move. Ryan stopped hammering on the roof and watched as the shed began to drift off all on its own. He couldn't believe it.

He wondered if, incredibly, the buoyancy of their boat had given buoyancy to the entire building, and now it had gone adrift with them inside it. That, or he was suddenly immensely strong.

The only thing he knew for sure was that the whole unit was moving quickly into the swollen floodwaters. As far as he could tell, they were safe. In fact, he rather suspected they were safer than any place they could otherwise have expected to end up in, so long as 'The Joan of' didn't fall apart.

He ducked down under the canopy to find Sas crying hysterically.

'Everything ship-shape and dandy, Captain,' he said, saluting.

Sas looked confused. 'What's happening, Ryan? I'm scared.'

Ryan shrugged. 'I pushed the roof and the entire shed came away. Funny thing is, I always suspected I had superpowers.'

'Is it safe?'

Ryan looked at her blankly. 'Truthfully?' He shrugged. 'I've no idea, but, so far, so good. Now, how about another brainteaser.' He sat down and put his legs up. 'Can't wait all day.'

Sas peered up at him. She simply couldn't believe his brazen attitude to the disaster unfolding around them. The boat lurched and her eyes widened. But Ryan rubbed his eyes and yawned.

'Ryan Williams,' she said. 'I don't know how you do it.' She took a couple of deep breaths to settle her nerves. 'We're on the verge of plunging into Armageddon and you want another teaser?'

Ryan nodded. 'Yeah. Absolutely.'

'Good Lord.' She took a deep breath. 'OK. Physics question – you said you were good at physics, right?' He nodded. A question popped into her head. 'Where does bad light end up?'

Ryan confidently put his feet on the seat. He was grinning like mad, which Sas later discovered was a sign that his brain was working. 'OK,' he began cagily, 'either it's in an ohm?' Sas giggled but shook her head. 'OR,' and there was quite a long pause. He clicked his fingers, 'In a prism?'

Sas clapped her hands. 'Brilliant! You're a big, strapping genius, aren't you?'

Ryan was bursting with pride. Big, strapping, and genius – in the same sentence – from delicious, sexy Sas. He hardly dared tell her he'd read the answers in a magazine at the dentist. 'One for you,' he said. 'What did the male magnet say to the female magnet?'

Sas burst out laughing. 'I'm seriously attracted to you?' She turned purple on the spot.

Ryan caught her eye. 'Not bad. Want another try?'

Sas shook her head. 'Tell me.'

Ryan looked quite serious. 'From your backside,' he began, 'I thought you were repulsive. However, from the front I find you rather attractive.'

Sas clapped her hands and laughed as Ryan punched the air.

Suddenly, a terrible noise, like the body of a car scraping along a road, stopped both of them in their tracks.

Ryan slipped out the front. Then he dived back in, and dashed toward Sas at the rear. 'Move up front,' he ordered.

Sas shuffled up as Ryan headed out of the canopy at the bow.

Seconds later, he reappeared. Without hesitating, he sat in the middle of the boat and grabbed the oars. He started to row, pushing the oars in the water to go backwards, as fast as he could.

'What's going on?' Sas cried.

'Our time has come. 'The Joan of's moment has arrived.'

With a terrible crunching noise, the back end of the shed levered high into the air, as if the nose had dived headlong into the water. Ryan took a deep breath and, praying that 'The Joan of' held together, rowed with all his might. It sent the little boat backwards, creeping under the raised end, and out into the river. For the first time, the rain whammed into the canopy and the boat rocked in the water.

The sound was deafening.

Sas screamed.

After a couple of minutes, Sas put her head out as far as she dared, and tried to survey the scene. The only things she could see were the faint outlines of cars, wood, and sections of plastic, bobbing along beside them.

She ducked under the canopy, her face ashen.

'Everything alright?' Ryan yelled, noting the distress in her face.

'Olivia, Anika, and Danny are in this, with no protection,' she yelled back. 'They haven't got a hope.'

'They'll be fine,' he yelled back. He looked down. 'Sas,' he hollered. 'Get a bucket NOW and start bailing!'

DANNY

At long last, Anika recognised a boulder at the bottom of the covered tree track.

A mini triumph, Anika thought, as a long booming roll of thunder drummed gruesomely overhead. She covered her ears, wincing, but after only a few paces she realised there was a far bigger problem. She kept close to Danny. 'Mud!' she yelled at Danny. 'Look! Mud and stone, rushing down.'

The lane was so knitted with branches, brambles, and rocks that every step forward was like walking through barbed wire.

Worse still, the canopy of branches, bushes, and creepers above the lane was bowing to the pressure of rain. Branches were falling in. Not just dead twigs, but stems as thick as a man's wrist. Even though they'd only stepped a few metres in, the canopy was clearly close to breaking point.

Danny slipped as a branch whacked into him, the muddy water dragging him down the hill. He dug his fingers into the bank, grabbed a root, and pulled himself to safety.

Anika climbed up onto a large stump on the side of the bank and waited. She looked down the track to see Danny struggling. For every two steps forward, he slipped one back.

'COME ON!' she screamed.

Danny tried to hug the side of the track, but every time the bank collapsed in on him. Not only that, but his ankles were being stripped bare by the mud, stones, and wood.

At last, he made it to Anika's position and climbed up next to her. Gasping for breath, he rubbed his scratched, blood-covered ankles. 'We'll never make it. Not like this.'

'We have to!' Anika yelled into his ear. 'Do you think it'll be any easier out there?'

'But it's a massive ditch,' Danny complained. 'It's become a gigantic storm drain. All the water's cascading down here. It's about as dangerous a place as you could wish.'

'What's your suggestion?' Anika fired back.

'Up the bank and crawl along the top,' he yelled.

'But it's a mile of crawling—'

'I know. One mile of not being swept away. And we can use the cover of the trees. There's no other choice.'

Using the roots of the big oak they were sitting beneath, they climbed up the bank. On hands and knees, they made their way uphill, brushing aside the branches and thorns which willingly tore into them. After several minutes, Anika collapsed under the cover of the next large tree.

She rubbed her legs, pierced by blackthorn and dog rose. 'Great idea, Danny!'

'Look!' he replied.

Through the veil of rain, she could just see a moving

torrent of mud and branches halfway up the bank. It was flushing downhill at great speed.

'OK, OK. *Good* decision.' Anika drew in her breath. 'How far up the track are we?'

'Soon, we'll come to the big oak with the swing rope. We can rest there.' Danny had no idea whether this was true. But he noticed how Anika's eyes kept closing. Giving her a target was probably a good idea.

Another huge boom clapped overhead, followed by a lightning bolt that smashed into the sluicing lane.

They crawled on. Danny led, with Anika closely behind. But, after a short while, when he turned, Anika wasn't there.

He backtracked fast. Hanging halfway down the bank, dangling above the rushing waters, and held only by the thick tendrils of a rose, he found Anika screaming at him.

He grabbed the base of the rose and tried to swing it towards him. But the huge old rose was near to breaking point and sank further, its thorns digging into his hands. He swore.

There had to be a better way. He shuffled to a nearby hedge and noted a small ash tree. He bent down, put his hands around the base of the trunk, and tugged with all his might. The roots slipped their anchors and, with one last effort, it broke free.

In a flash, Danny turned the tree round, ripped off some branches, and lowered it to Anika. She grabbed hold of it and, as the rose tore into her, Danny heaved her out.

They moved under the relative shelter of a nearby oak tree and gasped for breath.

'OK,' Anika yelled between gasps. 'So, we've learnt three things from that. The first is that the bank is collapsing, fast. The second is that I'll be plucking out thorns from my skin for the next decade, and the third is that you've been working out without anyone knowing.'

Taking a wider berth away from the track, they continued on all fours. Every inch of track filled them with dread, the rain pummelling their backs, necks and heads until they were numb.

Eventually, they reached the large oak tree with the rope, which now dangled down from its branch into the running water.

Danny pushed Anika ahead and upwards, her hands gripping the nodules and hand-holds of slippery bark as though her life depended on it.

Where the branch with the rope met the trunk, a huge bough curved over like a mini cave. For the first time in ages, it offered them almost complete protection from the downpour. Danny sat with his back against the trunk and Anika sat in front of him, leaning into him.

They shut their eyes and in no time Anika fell asleep through sheer exhaustion.

Danny didn't mind. He checked his watch. At least an hour until sundown.

The problem with being stationary was the cold, for now the wet had soaked, sponge-like, into every fibre of their bones. Body warmth was crucial.

Danny wrapped his arms around his frozen sister, her body rattling like an old engine. A rest was a good idea, but Danny knew they weren't safe. At some point, they were going to have to keep going.

SAP

Waking up, Sap stared around his room and thumped the air. 'What a blooming goal!' he roared. He stared up at the ceiling, a big smile on his face, his head sizzling as though a rocket had detonated within it. His body tingled. 'What a wonder-apple-tastic dream,' he said out loud to the empty room.

His foot throbbed. 'Ouch!' he said. He looked down and found he'd walloped the end of his bed. Looking a little more closely, he discovered a hole in the wooden sheet that covered the bed-end. He studied it, pulling a few wooden splinters away, chuckling at the absurdity of it all.

Sap wiggled his toes, grateful that he'd lain on his bed with his shoes on. Leaning forward, he heard the rain pounding down and his heart sank. His earlier worries flew back to him. He kicked at the broken piece of wood, as though recreating the goal might lift his spirits. It wasn't the same.

He climbed off his bed and peered out of the window, but the rain was so heavy he saw only grey lines.

His heart filled with heaviness.

Were the children safely tucked away in the school? What if they were outside trying to get home. What could he do?

If something happened, he was responsible.

Sap lay down.

He looked at the hole in the wooden panel. A tiny flicker of light, like a dim torch whose batteries were running low, leeched out from behind it.

Now, wasn't that strange, he thought. *A trick of the light?*

He tried the light switches. None of the house lights were working.

Maybe he should crank up the generator. At least it would give him something to do. He swung his feet off the bed and, as he did so, the flicker from behind the wooden panel intensified for a second or two.

He inspected the hole a little closer and found that there was indeed a faint glow emanating from behind it. He prised it open with his fingers and, feeling more than a little intrigued, began to wrestle with the wooden surround that covered the bed-end.

Sap found a torch, and went to his tool cupboard under the stairs. He selected a crowbar and returned his room.

Sap wedged the metal in behind the panel. He attempted to lever the wood away by leaning on it gently but firmly, as he thought necessary. But whatever angle he tried, the panel would not budge.

He scratched his head and slipped out of the room, returning moments later with a flat head screwdriver and a hammer. Sap thrust the flat head into the tiniest of gaps and gave the end a smart whack with the hammer. The nails securing the panel lifted a fraction.

Placing the crowbar in the newly created gap, he levered it once more. After a few more hits, the panel popped off.

He rubbed his chin. 'Well, I'll be blowed,' he said, as he

ran his fingers over the three panels that now stared back at him. 'What in the apples do we have here?'

In front of him were three beautifully inlaid panels that seemed to glow like three small monitors, rather like the children's computers. The difference was that these were part of the bed, and were surrounded by similar, matching carvings.

He stared at them for a while, his face a picture of confusion and the wrinkles on his forehead deeply etched. Every now and then, images in the panels moved, causing Sap's heart to race.

Was he seeing things?

He noticed that the overlying image was hazy, as though he were looking through water.

Maybe, for some reason, it was mirroring the weather right now.

As he became more accustomed to the panels, the images on them became a little clearer, until he realised there was a figure on each panel.

'Three panels, three figures,' he said out loud. 'And why do they look so familiar?'

He studied the carvings to the sides of the screens.

He touched an ornate arrow icon that faced away from the first panel. To his astonishment, the image moved out, exactly like a zoom on a camera.

He did the same with the next panel, this time pressing on the arrow that turned in. The picture zoomed closer.

The blurry image showed a person in the panel who appeared to be walking, and tripping, as though trying to negotiate a pathway.

He rubbed his hand over another carved icon adjacent to the arrow, which he thought looked rather like a cloud. He pressed it and magically the picture transformed, the layer of rain disappearing from the image.

Old Sap gasped as he stared at the new image. That balance and gait could only belong to one person, and that person was Anika. He pressed the inward arrow a couple of times and saw her in extraordinary detail.

His heartbeat drummed as a thrill passed through him. He was viewing the children, right now, in real time. He realised that if he could determine which buttons to press, he'd be able to see exactly where they were. He did the same to the panel on the right, pressing the cloud and zooming out.

He clapped his hands. Danny! It was definitely Danny, with a kind of spiky hat on his head, sitting right next to Anika. So, where were they?

He zoomed out and saw a large tree.

The oak tree with the swing! It must be. He clenched his fists. He pulled out even further. Apples alive! Look at the track.

Oh deary! NO!

His heart sank. But, at least the twins were together. What about Olivia?

He scoured the left panel and picked out her outline. He honed in on the image, pressing first the cloud icon, and then the outward arrow, in order to try and figure out her position.

She was heading towards a large rock-like object with a sheer face, pushing past bushes and through trees. The only sheer rock he could think of was the cliff underneath the ruin. So, how come she'd separated from the others?

Sap breathed a sigh of relief. They were alive. He looked at his clock. How long was it since he'd been out for a walk? Two hours? He trembled.

That long?

His heart thumped. He needed to find them, fast.

Anika dozed, her head resting on Danny's chest. Her mind swam. She dreamt fleetingly of the cottage, of Sap and their parents. She dreamt of scoring a goal with a sensational bicycle kick and Danny making a flying, fingertip save. The storm could have been a million miles away.

A noise clicked in her brain. It was that same crackling sound, like sizzling bacon. She studied the noise, her eyes shut tight. Then she realised what it was.

'MOVE!' she screamed. 'NOW!'

Danny opened his eyes. 'Eh? What?'

'Incoming. I can hear it. MOVE!'

'Where?' Danny yelled. 'We're on top of a branch!'

The sizzling increased, the noise building miles above them.

'Along it, Dan. GO!'

Danny did what he was told, and shuffled his bottom as fast as he could down the branch, the rain smashing down once more.

'Further,' she screamed. 'As far as you can.' She was skimming along, almost bouncing, when she stopped and wrapped her arms and legs around the thick branch. She hugged her body into the wood and hoped for the best.

Danny continued on his path, oblivious to Anika's action. From out of nowhere, a terrific surge of power smashed into the tree. The branch severed like a beheading and crashed down, bridging the track just above the flowing mud.

Anika convulsed with electricity and her ears smashed with pain. She uncurled her body from the branch as rain crashed over her back and head.

Regaining her composure, she turned around.

Danny?

'Danny!' She called out, barely a croak coming from her. A tear rolled out of her eye and she smacked the bark. Even if she could scream for help, he'd never hear. She scanned the area.

Suddenly, a hand flapped out of the water, and momentarily gripped the end of the branch. Then it fell away, caught in the torrent.

She shrieked and fished into the water, but she felt nothing but twigs, leaves, and debris flashing beneath her.

Anika thumped the branch, tears streaming from her eyes. How much more could she take?

Not much, she realised, now that she was on her own.

DANNY

Danny flew into the air and landed in the middle of the torrent, his body shipped away by the water. He swam with all his might. When he surfaced, a huge branch straddling the track lay directly in front of him.

His lungs burned.

He reached up, but however hard he tried he couldn't get a hand-hold on the bark. After several attempts, he felt his nails starting to detach.

Before long, Danny let go.

The water took him. He needed to keep his head up, but every time he did the rain battered it down. While he searched for buoyancy – a branch or a tree he could grab hold of that might keep him afloat – he thrashed out like a madman, kicking the water beneath him in a last, massive effort to survive.

Something caught around his left leg, rendering him helpless. A root? He succumbed, shattered and beaten. He smiled as he let himself go, Xinder's words coming to him as he floated away: *If it wasn't the thunderbolts and it wasn't the rain, it was the landslides.*

But, to his surprise, he remained bound by the snare around his leg and found the water pushing him towards the bank. He made a grab for a protruding root, twisting his body round while keeping his head up.

He sucked in a mouthful of air and gave his foot a yank. It did not yield.

He tried again, this time while holding the root on the bank with his other hand. It moved! He did it again, and then again. Now there was enough slack to allow him to bend forward and feel his ankle. He pulled his left leg towards him and touched something coarse and thick. Danny's mind worked overtime. Then it struck him. The swinging rope!

He pulled harder and the rope came away a little more. Now there was enough slack for him to try and untie the knot.

It wasn't the trickiest knot he'd ever come across, but the rope was thick and the water pulled him away from his task. The rain beat down, and every time he thought he had untied the knot, the slack tightened and he was back to where he started. He gave the rope an even bigger tug. The whole branch jerked. This time, the rope slipped off his foot and, while holding on to the end, he tied the rope around his waist.

He heard a scream. Even above the roar of the rain and the torrent, it couldn't be mistaken.

It was Anika, screaming.

'INCOMING!'

She's still on the branch!

Danny pulled with all his might and felt the wood slip. He tugged harder, nudging the branch towards him. He gritted his teeth and jogged it, pulling harder, in rhythm.

Suddenly, the branch twisted off the bank and slid just enough to give him encouragement.

There couldn't be much more time. One huge yank was all it needed.

He harnessed the rope around his shoulders and hollered.

The branch broke free and sped forward, just as a thunderbolt crashed into the bank almost exactly where the bough had sat.

Danny wondered if Anika had managed to get out of the way. But, he had no time to think, for now the branch began slipping down the slope, joining the torrent, which was washing everything down the lane.

Danny felt the rope go tense and found himself dragged behind it. Trying to keep himself above the water but gaining speed, he hung on for dear life as the branch hurtled into the main body of the river. As the river levelled out, he pulled himself along the rope, closer to the tree-trunk, and gritted his teeth as he pulled himself up and onto the end of the branch.

He dropped his left leg out, using it as a rudder, and the great branch pitched towards what he hoped was the bank on the left-hand side.

Exhausted, Danny collapsed, his head face down on the wood, with water sluicing over him.

Hearing a noise, Danny lifted his head. Was someone sitting near him on the branch?

'Anika – Ani' he groaned.

'Come with me, Danny Delaux,' the voice said. 'Only I can save you now.'

'Save me,' Danny repeated.

'Say yes, and it will be done.'

Danny's eyelids closed. 'Xinder?'

'Danny, just say the word.'

What did he have to lose, why didn't he just agree?

'You can do the easy thing, boy. Your life is not over by any means.'

Danny's brain swam but all he could think of was his sisters.

Nothing else.

Just Olivia and Anika.

The branch jolted.

Right then, he knew there was no other way. Danny had to move Anika to safety and then find Olivia. Better to die together trying to save the world, than not trying at all.

'I'd rather die with my sisters than join with you,' he called out, weakly.

The voice laughed back, 'I will return, Danny, one more time. You may need me yet. Your dear sister is so very close to her death and, when that happens, you will all have failed.'

15

SAP, THURSDAY

Sap hadn't taken his eyes off the panels. It was impossible. How could children so young survive the tumult out there? *They're only little*, he kept thinking, the tears forming again in his eyes. In a second the panel changed. A huge flash burst onto the screen.

Sap fell back. *Lightning? Sweet apples!* His skin prickled.

Anika lay on the tree branch as it crashed into the bank, but where was Danny? Now Anika hung on for dear life – Danny must have been swept away. What was she doing? Screaming?

He couldn't take his eyes off the scene. Another flash struck directly at Anika. Sap shrieked and felt for his heart. He could hardly bear it. He watched as the entire branch of the tree hurtled down the makeshift drain towards the swollen river.

Danny dragged behind, under the water. Sap yelped and clasped his head in his hands. How did the boy have the strength? Anika lay there, just as she had before. She hadn't moved. The screen flickered, as though faulty.

Sap leaned forward, and gave it a tap in the hope that

that might restore it, but it flickered again. Lines cut through the clear picture as if there was poor reception.

All of a sudden, he figured what this meant.

The colour drained from his face.

'NO, NO, NO!' he yelled out. 'Don't give up, Anika. Whatever you do, littlun, DO NOT *EVER* GIVE UP!'

For every step Olivia took forward, she seemed to slide back two more. When she was out in the open, she found herself pushing blindly through sheets of water with no idea where she was heading.

She extended her hands out in front of her and felt a gentle pull, first one way and then the other. With each step, her feet touched on harder ground. Sometimes, her hands swung her around at right angles, and every so often she had to backtrack. She trusted in it, though, for it was the only hope she had.

The one thing that terrified her was the thunderbolts.

Anika seemed to be able to hear the thunderbolts forming. Every time Anika screamed, they'd run away and a thunderbolt crashed into the spot where, only moments ago, they had been. Now there was no Anika, and Olivia sensed that it was only a matter of time before another thunderbolt would come. She had a deathly feeling in her gut that it would come directly at her out of the blue.

She moved forward, all the while waiting for the crack or the blast. As fast as she went, the trickle of water around her ankles kept swelling. For every surge she made forward out of the water, in no time the level had caught up with her, sometimes to as high as her knees.

A stomach-wrenching fear filled her.

Olivia redoubled her efforts, crawling and scampering over fallen branches and brambles until she bumped into the base of a tree that would offer her decent protection from the rain.

Olivia leaned back and, instinctively, pushed her hands into the air above her head. She forced her palms outwards, her fingers touching.

She channelled every thought, every single ounce of energy she had into protecting herself. She didn't know why, but her hands and her spirit were her last hope.

She closed her eyes and waited.

Just as Olivia thought of putting them down, a thunderbolt sliced out of the sky. A fraction after she heard the distinct crack, Olivia slammed herself towards the space in front of her with everything she had.

An intense burst of heat thumped into her hands, her flesh instantly burning, her body pushed into the ground.

She gritted her teeth and pressed against it harder and harder. The stink of burning skin invaded her, as if rods of molten iron were being welded in the place of her fingers.

As suddenly as it had arrived, it was over.

Olivia slumped to the ground, her hands smoking and her eyes closed, a look of peace fixed on her face.

RYAN

Ryan tried to row with the flow of the water but the current was too strong and, besides, he had no idea where he was going. When he stole a look from under the canopy, he was met by a wall of water sluicing from the sky.

He pulled in the oars, inspected the canopy, and drove a couple of nails into the areas where he sniffed a weakness.

Then he returned to the bench to help Sas bail out water. With the amount coming in, it needed both of them to work flat out.

As 'The Joan of' pitched through the waters, and as the storm smashed down upon their tiny vessel, Sas thought of Olivia, Danny and Anika.

They wouldn't stand a chance out there in this weather, and every time she imagined them trying to soldier on or getting swept away, her spirits sank. Her previous thoughts of rescuing them could never happen.

Every so often, 'The Joan of' would bash into something hard and solid, like a wall or a car, and they would be thrown forward. It was at these moments that both of them knew the strength of the boat would be tested.

All it took was a crack or a small hole, and that would be the end of it.

At other times, 'The Joan of' ground against something, or span around as it diverted off an object, the water pitching the boat one way and then the other.

Several times, Ryan levered the boat away with an oar, lurching back into the swell.

Sas kept her head down, sobbing as he went outside. On returning, Ryan would hold her, and stare reassuringly into eyes which betrayed nothing less than abject terror.

His eyes, she noticed, were wide. Not so much in fear, she thought, but with excitement. To her, Ryan was having the time of his life.

She heard him singing a hearty sea shanty as he tossed the water out with his bucket, his singing grew louder and louder with each movement until it was in direct competition with the rain.

Sas didn't know whether to laugh, cry, or hit him.

For a while, at least, the singing stopped her wallowing about the disaster and about her friends.

XINDER

Xinder wondered how his relationship with Fitzpatrick would work in their combined state. Right now, the boy was slowing him down and there was still so much to do.

Would the boy continue to do as he commanded?

Xinder threw his arms up in the air and clapped his hands as a shower of ash fell over his head.

All of a sudden, a feeling of heaviness overcame him.

Sleep again? Really!

Xinder clenched his fist and found that when his concentration focused on that movement alone, the fingers came together whether the boy liked it or not.

Xinder pressed one foot down, followed by the other. He felt a modicum of resistance, like a badly-fitting drawer that needed to be forced shut.

He willed his leg to move, but the movement felt sluggish and sleepy. Instead, he pulled his leg back and thrust it forward in a loose kicking motion, ash spraying everywhere.

He flailed his arms about, moving them faster and

faster until the boy trapped inside him did exactly as he wished.

'We've places to go, my little friend, and there's not a moment to lose.' Xinder said out loud. He couldn't tell if the boy inside him could hear, though the odd cries he heard told him that the boy wasn't entirely deaf.

'Do my bidding, little friend of Danny Delaux,' he said, 'and everything will work out just fine. We may even get to like one another. Until then, I am going to make you do as I do.'

But as hard as Xinder pushed and cajoled, the boy inside him soon slowed to a standstill.

Where was this child's energy? Wasn't that the point? Or was the boy being deliberately difficult?

A few minutes of rest should do the trick, and then he'd be off.

Perhaps he needed food and water. He'd try Schmerger and see what the elf might come up with. Anything to get the damn boy moving properly.

'In due course, there will be sustenance for you,' he spoke out. 'But for now, boy, I need your energy. Resist, and I will hurt you.'

If the boy was going to be a nuisance, then two could play at that game.

Splashing water woke her up. Olivia opened her eyes, aware that her body was shivering like it did after a swim in the cold North Sea.

The thunderbolt! She'd survived! How long had she been out? Five minutes, or half an hour.

She sat up and inspected her hands. Even in the dim light, she could see that large, black, circular burn marks radiated on her palms. Her body tingled, the electrical charge still fizzing through her like gas in a soda.

How? She thought. *How had she done it?* It didn't make any sense. By rights, she should be frazzled.

She checked her limbs one by one. They worked, even if her body ached like crazy, and her head sizzled as if someone had opened up her skull and given her brain a scrub with wire wool.

'Keep going,' she thought she heard from somewhere. 'Move! Now!'

She looked around.

She heard it again, as if someone was with her, egging her on, boosting her and begging her not to give in.

She forced herself forward and, instantly, fell flat on her face.

Again, she heard the voice, encouraging her on.

She crawled, finding a steady rhythm with her knees, elbows, and hands. Soon she was above the waterline, and she kept on going until she doffed her head on a large, sheer rock.

'BLOODY HELL!' she cried, as she rubbed her forehead, conscious that the rain had now ceased pummelling her.

She must have arrived under a rock shelf, she thought, and, for the first time in ages she felt a thimbleful of comfort.

She sat back, stretched her legs, and cradled her head in her hands. Damn, she was hungry. *But where would the next meal come from?*

That's if she remained alive long enough to eat again.

Olivia pulled herself together and tried to find her bearings.

She inspected a split rock. She wondered if she could narrow down where she was by working out where this type might typically be found on the river bank.

Moments later, there was a terrible explosion of noise, as though two trains were crunching and scraping into one another right above her.

The sound grew closer and closer, until it was right next to her, all around her, and above her.

For a ghastly moment, the noise went right through her.

She curled into a ball, shut her eyes, and covered her head.

Out of the sky, a deadly cascade washed past, careering onto the area from which she had crawled.

Olivia shook uncontrollably. Even above the noise of

the water, the cracking, crushing, and splintering sounds told her that everything in its path had been obliterated.

For several seconds, the cascade rattled on until the landslip had done its bidding and the cacophony ceased. Olivia's heart thumped wildly. She wouldn't have stood a chance.

At length, she ventured out into the rain. Only a couple of metres forward and through the veil of water, she encountered a vast pile of boulders, rocks, mud, and splintered wood, that rose up like a slag heap in front of her.

She slunk back to her sheltered position as a terrible thought began to wash over her.

If she'd found refuge underneath a cliff face, the likelihood was that it was either a landslip off the top of a hill, or - and she thought this to be more likely - a section of the cliff face had simply collapsed. That would explain the boulders.

In her mind, she pictured the geography of the area and, especially, the position of the cliff face. She knew that in front of her probable position was a ledge. Above this, a sheer wall of rock rose up vertically for seventy metres or thereabouts.

Then, like a thought one doesn't want to think about but cannot avoid, she had a terrible realisation that if Danny and Anika had come after her, they would not be alive right now.

The other thing she realised, much to her shock, was that she was completely and utterly trapped.

Seeing Olivia's monitor struck by lightning followed by Anika's monitor crackle spurred the old man into immediate action. What should he take with him?

He turned on the torch and shot off towards the shed. His heart and mind racing, he grabbed a section of rope, a small axe and his hard helmet with a built-in torch on the front. He dashed into his cold room where he stored his huge variety of apples. He selected eight rather small ones from the special box he kept near the door.

In the cloakroom, he found his long, waterproof coat and his walking boots, which he slipped on as fast as he could.

He returned to the bedroom and stared at the screens.

Danny was cradling Anika, he could see that. Tears streamed down his face.

'Oh, you poor things,' Sap cried. 'Keep her warm. Speak to her, little Danny. Don't let her drift off.'

At least they had found somewhere to disembark. It was by a huge pile of rocks, which didn't feel in any way familiar.

Now, where was Olivia?

He furrowed his brow. Blimey, she's in a funny place. Bang next to a rock face and surrounded by a heap of boulders. She's shivering. No wonder. How did she get there? He zoomed out and pressed the cloud button, which cleared away the rain.

'Apples alive!' he exclaimed, bashing his head with his hands. 'They're on opposite sides of the same pile of rocks, and they don't even know it!'

He zoomed out further on Olivia's monitor. 'I know where it is!' he exclaimed, his eyes almost bulging out of his head in excitement. He checked his watch. It was ten minutes before four o'clock or thereabouts. Just over an hour before nightfall. He'd have to hurry.

He darted out of his room, bursting with an energy and purpose he hadn't felt in years, when an idea shot into his head. He turned on his helmet light, and skipped down the cellar stairs.

Now, which door was it? He headed along a musty brick corridor that smelled of old wet rags. He stopped outside a low, thick wooden door laced with metal studs right at the end. Cut into it were the markings "II". Roman numerals for cellar number two.

Now, he thought, *how did the door open?* There wasn't a key, he was sure of that. It was something smarter; keys could be lost or discovered by nosey children or unwanted guests.

He strained his brain trying to work out what it might be. 'Oh, come on!' he cried out. 'Why does my brain always go blank at times like this?'

He thumped his fist on the wall. One of the bricks shifted. His eyes darted up and he groped about, pushing the bricks to see if anything would happen.

Nothing.

He screwed his eyes up. He couldn't even remember the last time he'd been down here. From the corner of his eye he spotted a piece of stone protruding from the wall. *Maybe that was it.* He pushed it.

Again, nothing.

He left his hand there as his head tilted forward, and he tapped the wall with his forehead in frustration. The stone moved! He doffed it further and heard a neat 'click'.

'Ah-ha!'

He twisted the metal ring on the door and the latch clicked open. He was in.

Inside, a smell of moss and dust and linseed oil surprised his senses and, as he brushed past the cobwebs that drooped from the ceiling, he shone his helmet torch to see what he could find.

He smiled. Neatly stacked on slate shelves running around the walls were hundreds of small bottles obscured by layers of dust.

Starting at one end, he picked each bottle up and blew the dust off to reveal the writing which was neatly etched into the glass. Names like Spindle Sap, Ogre Blood, Wood Ox, Willow Potion, and Oak Spit. He hurried on, hoping like mad that when he saw it, he'd know.

A flood of memories rushed in, almost overwhelming him.

These were his bottles. HIS potions! From a time ... well, from a lost time, a time he'd forgotten.

He continued along the row, reading out the names as he went until he spied three bottles with the words 'Resplendix Mix' in bold writing scratched on each.

He pulled one off the shelf and brushed it down. In the torchlight, the colour was like liquid gold, and, as it moved, little diamonds of light danced within it.

Resplendix Mix. This brilliant stuff would help them, he was sure of it.

He shoved a bottle into his pocket and tore out of the room.

Closing the back door, he was instantly set upon by the water, the weight on his hard hat pushing his head into his body.

What was the best way to the bottom of the cliff? he wondered.

The lane was acting like a drain, so the road was impassable.

Maybe he could lower a rope from the ruin and let himself down? He fingered the coils strapped around his torso. But he knew the rope wasn't long enough, and what if he was swept off the top!

No, he would have to go across country, through the woods and then somehow up, along and onto the ledge.

He'd need a lot of luck and he needed to hurry.

XINDER

What a wonder, Xinder thought, rubbing his new eyes. *Sleep. How invigorating! But now I have a strange feeling of emptiness inside me.*

'Food!' he yelled out. 'Schmerger, I think I require food. WHERE IS MY FOOD?'

Lying down, Xinder saw the black pointy beard of his servant stopping at a respectable distance. The little creature bowed. 'Your Lordship?' the bent figure of Schmerger said. 'With respect, Sire, you haven't eaten for a thousand years. Are you yourself today?'

Xinder rose and marched up to the servant. 'I require food, immediately. A feast.'

The servant recoiled. 'You have become ... ASH, Sire.'

'Marvellous, isn't it. I have a human child within me and it requires feeding. Understand?'

'But there is no kitchen,' he replied.

'NO KITCHEN?!' Xinder roared. 'What kind of palace is this?'

Schmerger shook his head. 'May I be bold, Sire, and say

that ever since I was assigned to your Lordship, there has never been a kitchen. Your Lordship banned them.'

Xinder thrust out his arm, picked the man up by the throat and threw him at a table which splintered over the floor. 'Is that so?'

The servant rubbed his neck.

Xinder walked over and pulled the little man up. 'How and where do you eat, Schmerger? Show me.'

The servant bowed and led the ghost down the wide main staircase, down a corridor and through several doors, before entering a small room.

Xinder followed, delighted that for once he could actually see the outline of rooms and his grand bed. Even his dim profile in the mirror was now visible. It was a shame he couldn't see with any detail, but it was a great deal better than nothing at all.

Schmerger picked up a wicker basket. 'From Mrs Schmerger, Sire.'

'Tell me,' Xinder quizzed, 'what is in it?'

'It was my lunch, Sire,' he said. 'There is little remaining.'

'Give it to me!' Xinder said, thrusting his hand into the basket. He pulled out something black and stodgy and, without hesitation, stuffed it in his mouth. For the first time in ages he chewed. Aside from a tingle in his mouth, it tasted like soot. But he hoped the boy inside found it favourable.

Schmerger backed out of the room, trembling, leaving the food for Xinder.

Xinder pulled out another piece and popped it in his mouth. This time, it crunched and splintered. Xinder spat it out. 'Schmerger,' he yelled, 'what is it?'

'It is the leg of a bird,' the servant said from outside the door. 'One does not ordinarily eat the bones.'

Xinder crashed a fist down on the table. 'I need more food. What is there to drink?'

'Nothing but water, Sire,' Schmerger said, bowing. 'Your Majesty has never had a requirement for any.'

'Well, I do now. Bring me some this instant. We have a great thirst.' Xinder marched out of the room a trail of dust behind him. 'Let me see this palace of mine.'

Xinder knelt down and brushed a glass-like puddle, seeing a face smile up at him. 'Let me reacquaint myself with my poor frozen people.' He stood up. 'Let us banquet. Let there be a glorious feast! Bring wine.'

Xinder marched through the doors and found himself at the foot of the grand staircase.

His mood barely less than euphoric. He had an idea.

'Animais, Animais, Animais,' he called out.

Moments later Guda appeared, his infiniti tingling with electrical current. 'You called?'

Xinder smiled. 'Now, my dear ugly Animais, why don't we pay another short visit to find out how the Sacrum are dying? Perhaps I can persuade the boy Danny to join willingly with me one last time, before his poor soul is cast into the wild expanses of space.'

Guda's infiniti opened wide and Xinder, seeing it's outline for the first time so clearly, forced the boy within him to bend down. In one motion, they dived through.

ANIKA

Danny stared at his watch. It had gone four. When was sunset; five, half five? He crawled over to Anika and cradled her in his arms.

'Hey, Ani,' he said, sheltering her face. 'Don't give up on me. There's only a little while to go, you know. And I'm going to keep you alive, if it's the last thing I do.'

He ran his cold hands over her face.

If he was cold, then she was icy.

Softly, he massaged her heart. He didn't know why, but it just seemed the right thing to do. 'Please, Anika, you've got to come back. Don't you dare back out now. I don't know what I'd do without you. If you go, we've all had it. Everyone, not just us.'

Her eyes flickered and the corners of her lips turned up.

Thank goodness, he thought. A spark.

He'd keep talking, and, somehow, he had to keep her listening.

'Right, here's what we're going to do,' he said. 'I'm going to pick you up and start carrying you over these rocks and stuff, OK?'

Very gently, he picked her up and negotiated footholds in the debris. One step followed another, each one swaying, each a desperate act of concentration.

Every so often he studied her face to make sure she was still with him before carrying on. He leapt from one rock to the next, disregarding the rain, disregarding his burden, and worrying only about the next step.

As he climbed, he carried on talking. He spoke about what was going to happen and how safe they were going to be in only a little while. He chattered about anything else he could think of.

When he ran out of things to say, he started singing.

The first song that came into his head was a song their mother had taught them when they were young. With chattering teeth, he sang it as best as he could. When he forgot the words, he hummed it, his voice shaking with cold.

After a few minutes, Anika's eyes flashed open. He looked down at her and smiled, trying to hold back his tears while he continued humming.

He felt her tensing. Her eyes opened wide, telling him something.

What was it?

Her eyes rolled back.

Danny tensed.

NO! NOT ANOTHER ONE!

Instantly, Danny tossed Anika over his shoulder in a fireman's lift. He reached the top of a boulder and tried to see beyond it, but saw only the steady veil of rain.

'Anika!' he cried out, 'I've got to jump and I don't know where we'll end up. If this goes badly, just remember that I love you. You're a cool girl, Sis.'

He had no more time.

Danny sucked in as much air as he could. He closed his eyes, bent his knees, and jumped as high and as far as he possibly could into the dark unknown.

OLIVIA

Shivering, Olivia remembered their last holiday as a family, skiing, high up in the Alps.

Beautifully hot with a bright blue sky, at lunch she had stripped off her jacket, thrown off her hat, and ditched her long johns, giving them all to her mother who crammed them into a rucksack.

They'd jumped on a chairlift and headed up to the top of the mountain. Halfway up, the chair had stopped and swayed in the air. They stayed like that for ages. An hour, maybe more.

Then, the weather had changed.

First, the clouds blew in, followed by an icy, biting wind and horizontal snow.

She sat there, freezing, with nothing but her father's arm around her to protect her. In the seat behind, her mother was holding the bag with her clothes. An hour later, every bone in her body ached, from the top of her head to the tip of her toes.

She remembered how it took two hot chocolates before she could move her jaw open enough to say anything.

What she would give for that hot chocolate now.

What had her father said?

Keep moving, girl. That was it. *And if you can't keep moving, hug someone. Hug them nice and tight.*

A warm feeling filled her as she remembered how Danny thought this was the perfect excuse to go around hugging people. Everyone had thought him rather cute; even, momentarily, Anika.

Olivia tried to smile. Now out of the rain, the cold had begun to creep into her like roots of frost knitting into soil.

She needed to move. Using her hands as a guide, she felt for a jagged, protruding rock so that she might get a decent foothold. She found one, lifted herself up on it and then fingered another further up. She'd done enough climbing to know that planning a route up and making sure one's feet were stable were the keys to success.

The problem was visibility. Combined with the numbness in her fingers, it meant that she couldn't determine if her grip was true. She slipped back and landed with a wet thud on the ground. Olivia shook her hands vigorously out in front of her, and slowly the blood began to return. She jogged on the spot, the wet remains of her trousers sticking to her legs, and rolled her head on her shoulders.

She needed to search further along.

Once again, she followed the face of the rock, guided by her hands, her legs now knee-deep in the water. A little further on, she found the perfect spot; an outcrop of stone concealed by bushes.

Moving them aside, she found two easy steps. She pulled herself up, placing one foot carefully on the first step, then, hugging the rock, she tested her weight slowly on the next. It felt solid, as if purposely carved out of the rocks.

Her arms searched around trying to find another

foothold. She levered herself up and did the same again, noting that the steps curved around the rock face. She climbed until she realised she was on a flat ledge.

With the rain driving at her, she had lost her sense of direction. She sat on the ledge trying to fathom the angle of the steps in relation to the rock face. She crawled on her hands and knees in the direction of the cliff face, scanning for any sudden gaps or boulders. Aside from pebbles, it felt smooth.

She edged on further before she realised the rain was subsiding, then it ceased altogether. She wiped water from her face and leaned into a big, round rock. Olivia felt strangely elated, as if she'd solved a tricky equation.

She examined the boulder, and figured that it sat directly under the cliff face, with the incline protecting her from the rain.

But how would she get out? The logical answer was to head high up to the right, towards Appleside Farm. The light was failing fast, though, and the rain still wasn't letting up. Maybe she'd have to stay put until the morning. At least, she'd be out of the rain.

Anyway, hadn't Danny told them the storm would continue until sunset, or some nonsense like that?

Two lightning bolts suddenly blasted out of the sky. They were directed just beyond the landslide, where she'd come from.

She hardly had a chance to react, only to duck down.

What if those were for...?

In a heartbeat, she dashed forward and threw herself off the ledge, just before a huge charge spat out of the sky and smashed into the exact spot she'd been standing.

Olivia tumbled into the water.

She sank as low as she could go, amazed at how much the water had risen in such a short time. She stayed underneath as long as her lungs could hold her, hugging the cliff face, as splinters of rock and stone punched the pool like deadly shrapnel.

When Olivia surfaced she noticed a big difference in her surroundings. The water level had edged close to the surface of the ledge, so that instead of climbing the stairs, she simply pulled herself out and sat down with her feet dangling in the pool.

She shivered in the near-darkness. Her heart was thumping wildly.

She realised what the difference was. Drizzle! The torrents of rain, the endless pounding, had subsided.

With the quiet came an enormous sense of relief.

She smiled through her chattering teeth.

The remains of her clothes stuck to her like cold, soggy slime, but she still had to survive through the night. The temperature would drop, as it always did at about this time of year, and there was no hope of a warming fire.

In the next breath, her thoughts turned to Anika and Danny. There had been three huge thunderbolts; one each, perhaps, for the three of them. Why this would be she had no idea, but it seemed right to Olivia, even if it was absurdly illogical and absolutely terrifying.

She shuffled along in the darkness.

'Danny. Anika!' she called out. *'Are you there?'*

She listened, but heard only the swishing sounds of the running water beyond.

Again and again she called out, trying to hear a response.

No reply was forthcoming.

16

SAP, THURSDAY

Sap was at the point where he needed to start making his way along the steeper, sharper cliff face. He faced the rock and shuffled along, happier in his step where the mud gave way to stone. As he angled across the cliff face, overhangs gave him welcome relief from the downpour, while other parts showered him with mud and loose rock. He dug his fingers into every tight crevice and small hole. Moving along as quickly and carefully as he dared, he hoped he hadn't started too high.

Presently, he was able to take stock of his position. He rested under a deep overhang where he found a decent foothold. He gulped in huge mouthfuls of air as he leant into the stone.

Should he drive a bolt in to the rock so that he could attach the rope, just in case?

He found a hole, delved into his pocket, and found a quick release bolt. He thrust it in and the metal fastened. He put his weight on it, and it held. Good. He tied the rope to the metal loop, and attached the rest around his body.

As he turned to inspect his next footholds, a huge electrical pulse flashed out of the sky to his left. He looked on in shock. A second bright charge rocketed out of the sky from the same place a millisecond later, almost blinding him. His eardrums seared with pain.

The valley lit up, and he saw everything move like a huge grey beast filled with water. 'Apples-alive,' he muttered under his breath as his heart raced.

He was too high above the ledge.

He felt for a footing, making sure his hold was solid. He tested his grip and bent down, but, in the next moment, a huge thunderbolt smashed out of the sky directly into the cliff face beneath him.

For a second Sap held on for dear life.

There they were!

He could see them all, as clear as day for just one second.

His heart whooped in his chest. He had to get down there fast.

Danny had no idea where he might end up, but a broken leg was preferable to being flash-fried to death.

They splashed in a pool and sank down to the bottom, at the exact moment two lightning bolts smashed into their previous position. Their brutal force displaced shards, pebbles, and larger stones. Everything shook. The water around them fizzed, the currents jabbing at every nerve in their bodies.

Danny stayed down, holding Anika and cradling her head for as long as he dared. Suddenly her eyes opened wide.

Danny thrashed to the surface and winced as the first stone hit him on his shoulder. Another stone whacked him on the head. He let go of Anika and felt his mind begin to drift away.

The pool and the torrential rain were blurring together.

He saw stars spinning.

Anika was accelerating away from him.

With one last effort, he pulled himself up.

His head spun so fast that in no time he felt himself go, his body slipping away to a place of softness and light.

A feeling of warmth enveloped him, like a comfort blanket brimming with love, holding him tight.

WYNN-GARRY

Fifty-seven! Wynn-Garry scrolled down the page of names. He rather hoped that perhaps one hundred people had fled by car, and that many had gone when the lightning started.

Still, that left an awful lot unaccounted for. He hadn't factored in the opposition players, parents, and supporters.

Half the football team were missing; no Sas Smith, no Williams, Fitzpatrick or Allen. The list went on… five of his teachers out there, somewhere, too.

He only had to look at himself to shake with shame.

He'd found the doorway to the tower as much by luck as by design, and was dragged in by Mrs. Rose who'd reached out into the curtain of water and swept him in. Exhausted, he sat on the step catching his breath and waiting anxiously to see if anyone was close by.

Only one other person came in after him. It was a small girl who had felt her way around the exterior walls, inch by inch. Wynn-Garry cried as he helped her up the stairs.

It had made him hope there were more survivors, but no matter how long he stayed, no one else came by.

Looking into the sheet of water flashing from the sky, it was no surprise.

In no time, the water level forced him to move up the stairs, as a pool of water quickly formed beneath the first landing. He insisted the door should be left open, just in case.

The children spread themselves out over the two floors of the library in the tower, cowering together. As the storm smashed overhead, the children sobbed, despite teachers doing their best to keep spirits up. Even the teachers, Wynn-Garry noticed, had anxious eyes as they flicked nervous glances towards one another.

The chef, along with his assistant, fed the group bread buns from a huge sack they'd pulled across the yard moments before it all happened.

Only when the water reached three quarters of the way up the front door did they shut the door. A realisation that the level might get higher and higher dawned on Wynn-Garry and, this time, he was taking no chances.

Wynn-Garry excused himself and headed up to the old library on the sixth floor. It was at the top of the tower, accessible only by ladder. Up there, he removed his jacket and trousers and sank into an old armchair.

Placing his hands over his eyes, he sobbed openly.

He couldn't remember the last time he'd cried. When his father died many years ago, he'd shed a small tear, alone.

Now, tears flowed.

When his grief had subsided, he tried to reflect. Of course, with the benefit of hindsight, he realised that he had been nothing short of a fool. No more, no less. A stubborn fool at that. He hadn't listened.

His brightest pupil had demanded his attention, and he'd refused her.

Worse still, he'd lied to her!

Lied! Dammit!

Wynn-Garry felt his stomach knot. He'd lied to a student who had gone out of her way to prove that something major and remarkable was about to happen.

And he'd shoved her efforts straight back in her face.

He banged his fist down on a dusty table. Wasn't that what headmasters were supposed to be good at, listening? Giving people the benefit of the doubt. Encouraging students in their academic and recreational activities?

All he'd been interested in, he realised now, was his banquet, the glory of his school and his moment in the limelight. And now...

Three times Olivia had tried to tell him. Three times he'd denied her.

All along, it was as if she knew, and Sas knew. He recalled her crazy screaming. Was that part of these strange happenings? Perhaps even Danny knew, the way he let the penalty slide past his foot into the goal.

Wynn-Garry stood up and moved over to the window. On a good day, the view expanded way across the Vale of York in one direction, marked by a green patchwork quilt of fields and woods. In the other direction, the tree line of the Hambleton Hills wiggled around the North York Moors, intersected by cliff faces and shadows.

This was the exact spot, twenty-five years ago - almost to the day - where he'd fallen in love with the glorious scenery, the light, and the big skies, and decided to accept the job at Sutton school.

Now, he stared at death, destruction, and chaos.

He knew that, if and when this rain ceased, the scenery would be a different hue. A new orientation. A landscape made up entirely of water.

'Olivia,' he said. 'Will you ever forgive me for ignoring you? For being such a toady old idiot.'

He sighed and brushed another tear from his eye, knowing that it would be a miracle if the Delaux trio ever made it home.

All that talent, he thought, *gone to waste. And he could have prevented it.*

'I am so terribly sorry.'

OLIVIA

Olivia crawled along the ledge as far as she dared, all the while making sure she kept a firm grip of the surface, calling out for them in turn '*Anika! Danny!*'.

She shivered, her lips quivering involuntarily as she stared out into the darkness. Occasionally she heard a groan, but it was hard to tell if it was the crunching of metal on metal, like cars or sheds being swept down the river and colliding with each other, or whether it was the desperate cry of people or animals.

Tears built as an overwhelming sense of sadness flowed over her. Her feeling of helplessness was almost complete.

As if in response to her cries, a tiny sliver of light appeared on the lip of the horizon and threw a grey light over the water. Olivia peered at it and, for a short while, thought that she must be dreaming. It looked so beautiful, a gentle sparkle of light catching the rim of a silver bracelet. She blinked and shook her head.

The moon? *Moonlight.*

Now, she could distinguish the outlines of boulders and a flat ledge. Looking up, the sheer face of the cliff curved above her like a prison wall. She scoured the valley, observing a dull, ever-changing watery mirror that gently lapped in front of her.

As the moon rose, its brightness lifted her spirits further.

She noticed how the round boulder she had hidden underneath before the lightning struck had been reduced to rubble. Where it once stood, an unnaturally dark hole beckoned her in.

Olivia approached. With every footstep, she grew more curious.

She edged closer, testing the cracked sections that might be unstable, until she found herself peering up at a perfectly symmetrical entrance of a cave.

Without hesitating, she placed one foot ahead of the other and, leaning against the side, she made her way in.

She caught warmth on her face.

Hot air, here?

She took another step, hoping that her eyes would adjust.

It's like a warm hairdryer.

Thermal rocks, here, in Yorkshire? Never!

Olivia was about to take a further step in when she heard a strange cry coming from behind her. Her heart skipped a beat.

Anika? Danny?

She scanned the area but found that the ledge was now only fractionally higher than the river, and it was hard to tell where one stopped and the other started. She heard it again, a groan followed by a cry and a tiny cough.

Her heart raced as she studied the ledge again. She concentrated and pushed her hands out, trusting them.

She ran to the right, urging her eyes to peer deeper into the night.

Nothing.

She walked cautiously to the left.

Nothing.

She repeated her movements.

To her right, all she could discern was a long shape, like a fat, black branch typical of the debris. She walked straight past it but turned when there was a tiny noise.

Olivia was there in a flash.

A body! Face down. Bending down she noticed dirt intermingled with bloody cuts, angry bruises, and ripped clothing.

Someone who never made it, she thought.

Olivia's hopes sank.

As she turned the frame over, the white arms folded limply and splashed helplessly in a puddle.

The eyes were closed.

Olivia screamed as though someone had ripped her heart out.

In front of her lay Anika.

FITZPATRICK

Fitzpatrick felt another long burst of heat on his leg. He grimaced. Reluctantly, he moved his limb and the pain faded.

The Delauxs had to save the world? But they were crazy, nutty kids. Never super-heroes.

Even now, the thought would have made him chuckle, if only he wasn't so filled with pain.

Why wouldn't the ghost leave him alone for just one minute?

When he yelled, Xinder didn't hear him and didn't react. He needed food, water, and rest. How long had it been? Five or six hours constantly moving, constantly burned in little patches from head to toe.

It felt like a week, or a month even. He yawned, and felt his body moving off, his legs clumpy as if made with wet sand. Every time he stopped a surge of intense heat smashed into him and he had no choice but to keep going.

He could see, although not well. The sickly vapours of singed hair and fried flesh caught at the back of his throat.

Every sound was muted, like being underwater. Soon, his thoughts turned to death. If he refused to go on, would he burn to death within Xinder?

S A P

Sap picked his way along as fast as he could, letting the rope out behind him. After several metres, he tightened the rope and started to descend.

The old man sucked in his cheeks and braced himself. Pushing out with his feet, he flew through the air, the rain smashing into his face as he readied himself for the landing.

It was going to hurt, he thought. Rather a lot.

The rope swung out again, this time gaining speed, and all too soon he was back to his starting position like a pendulum. He kicked out, and, as he reached the limit of his arc, he noted that the rain had suddenly stopped.

The shock forced him to hold on, and the moon offered a shadow of light onto the ledge below to help him further.

He swung out one more time.

As he looked down, he saw Olivia directly below him, walking towards a broken rock.

He swung back, grasping onto the rope for dear life. He was wondering how much lower he really ought to be when the bolt disengaged from the rock, and Sap and the rope plummeted down.

Sap lay in a heap, his breath knocked clean out of him, pain searing into his ankle and back.

He watched Olivia walking out and then he heard her scream. Now, muffled cries.

Had she found one of the other children? Anika?

Oh! apples alive, he cursed, *how could he be so hopeless?* He summoned his strength, trying to ignore the pain screaming through his legs.

He urged himself on, but each time he slumped back down.

His eyes watered. He probed the swollen flesh, now like a juicy, purple summer pudding. Was it a tear or a break? He turned his head and his back screamed out as if a knife was stabbing at his vertebrae. Even his hands were hurting, blood pouring from a cut in the middle of his left palm.

What had he been thinking, swinging on ropes at his age? He wasn't a child.

His body was beginning to shut down. It was shock; Sap knew it well. Then it struck him. The Resplendix Mix he'd found in the cellar! Of course, he'd self-medicate!

With his swollen hand, he reached into his pocket. He transferred the bottle to his bleeding left hand and attempted to remove the lid.

Did it twist off, did he have to pull out a cork, or was there some kind of stopper?

Nothing happened, apart from his hand slipping around the rim.

He inspected the bottle.

No lid.

Maybe it needed a sharp pull. He tried, but there was nothing to pull on.

Sap shook his head in frustration. No shaking, twisting, pulling, or yelling would make it open.

He felt his eyelids grow heavy. He thought of smashing the top on a rock, but even this idea slipped away as he fell into unconsciousness.

SOLA

Guda had betrayed them! It was common knowledge now. Sola poked a finger in her infiniti. *In which case,* she thought, *now was the time to add balance to the drama.*

Instantly, Sola was spinning a dream into Sap's mouth.

Good, she thought, *the powders are working fast on the old man. It must be sharp and quick.*

The Animais hovered, waiting.

Sola needed Sap to wake up.

Shortly, the old man yawned and stretched his arms out wide. He howled in pain.

Sola watched as the old man shuffled, his face contorting in surprise as he found the Resplendix Mix. He studied it as he realised exactly what it was.

Now let us see how he does it this time, the Animais thought.

Sola watched as the old man placed the top of the bottle to his lips. He closed his eyes and the seal opened.

Excellent, Sola thought. *It worked.*

Now this will play out to the bitter end.

SAP

Sap gritted his teeth as the Resplendix Mix set to work mending damaged parts. The liquid burned like the white heat of a soldering iron welding him back together.

Shortly, he rolled his head and breathed deeply, the air filling his lungs like bellows. Invigorated, he coiled up the rope and scoured the moonlit ledge.

Now, where were they?

He'd seen Olivia below him from the rope, but the other two? Sap headed out onto the ledge. There was Olivia, bent down over something. A body?

Sap hurried over.

As he neared, he heard a terrible wailing noise. He prepared himself for the worst and coughed as he approached.

'Looks like you could do with a hand,' he said, solemnly.

'Sap!' she said, flinging her arms around him. 'Look! Anika! I think she's, she's…'

Sap bent down and ran a hand over Anika's brow. He felt only coldness. He searched for signs of breathing. Nothing.

'My goodness,' he said examining her, 'you've taken a horrible beating, littlun.' He pulled the Resplendix Mix from his pocket. He noted how her lips were a pale crimson against her white skin.

He felt for a pulse and his heart nearly stopped. He couldn't feel one. If it was there, it had all but gone.

He could sense Olivia staring at him, searching for answers in his face.

'Now, Olivia, there is only one thing I can do.' He showed her the bottle. 'She only needs a couple of drops of this. It's an old remedy of mine for healing and I'll tell you about it another time. Thing is,' he continued, a deep frown filling his forehead, 'the bottle will only open if the potion within can heal the person whose lips it touches.'

Olivia frowned. 'Anything, Sap – hurry!'

Sap lowered the bottle to Anika's mouth and pressed the top against her lips.

'Why don't you just open it?' Olivia growled, mostly in frustration.

'As I said, I can't. The bottle will open itself if it can heal, otherwise I am afraid we have lost her.'

He shook his head.

'What is it?' Olivia cried.

Sap's lips trembled. 'I'm so sorry.' A tear rolled out of his eye and landed on Anika's cheek. He wiped it off, and inspected the top of the bottle, which remained closed. 'I am too late,' he said, his eyes glistening. 'I am so sorry, dear little Anika. So terribly sorry.'

Sap bent over, shaking, tears falling.

Olivia stared numbly at her lifeless sister. Anger of an intensity she'd never experienced before rushed into her. She demanded action.

Directing her hands towards Anika, she closed her eyes and screamed.

'STOP BEING SO STUPID, ANIKA DELAUX. YOU WILL NOT DIE ON ME. IS THAT PERFECTLY CLEAR? I WILL NOT ALLOW IT!'

A strange, pink glow emanated from her hands, cocooning Anika's body.

'YOU WILL NOT GIVE IN NOW,' she roared. 'YOU WILL SURVIVE.'

Anika's eye's flickered.

Olivia reeled.

It worked! What had she done?

She stumbled and fell, exhausted.

Sap, reacted fast.

Placing the bottle to Anika's lips the spout opened.

'Come on, Ani, one drop is all you need.'

Moments later, he noticed a dab of pink in Anika's cheeks and felt the trace of a heartbeat. Euphorically, he scooped her up and carried her into the cave.

Sap shone his torch around the chamber and noticed a circular pit, like an empty, buried paddling-pool. It seemed a good place as any to rest. More importantly, as he stepped inside to inspect it, a soft, sandy, talc-like substance carpeted the bottom. To the touch, it was as smooth as tissue and as soft as thick fur.

He lowered Anika in, making sure her head was propped up. Venturing outside again, he rushed to Olivia's side and placed the Resplendix Mix to her lips. In no time, he'd picked up Olivia, and moved her sleeping body next to her sister into the dugout pit.

Two down, he thought, *one to go.*

At least the girls would be warm and out of danger, while he set about searching for Danny.

DANNY

Danny's mind was a blur, his head whirling. Before long, he found that his body was turning and heading into a spin too.

He steadied and, as he levelled out, he realised he was flying. He soared like a bird, swooping first one way then another before shooting high into the air, twisting as he went, enjoying the sensation of weightlessness. Each gust of wind caressed his body and he cried out at the freedom and the thrill of speed.

Now he was diving, and flying as fast as an arrow. He screwed left and found himself heading, at breakneck speed, towards a rock face as if he himself was a bolt of lightning.

Maybe he was a bolt of lightning.

He couldn't stop, he couldn't turn fast enough and there wasn't enough room for him to manoeuvre. But he wasn't afraid. He would wallop it with his head.

It wouldn't hurt, it couldn't hurt him.

BANG!

The rock shattered into several pieces.

In place of the boulder was the entrance to a cave. He looked inside. Olivia and Anika were there with Sap. They were beck-oning, teasing him to come in and join them. Laughing and smil-ing, they wanted to tell him something.

He raised his foot and carried on through the entrance. But as he did he felt the anger of Xinder smash into him and he fell to the ground. Xinder started kicking him. First in the ribs, then his chest, and finally, his face.

He gasped, struggling for air.

Why would Xinder want to hurt him? They were on the same side, right?

He felt air leaking out of him like a balloon with a small hole, shrivelling quickly.

He gulped, realising he needed to breathe so badly; so badly that it hurt...

Danny surfaced and thrashed the water, desperate to find a hand-hold. His fingers touched on a rock. He pulled himself up and vomited, expelling water from his lungs and gut, retching and hacking until his internal organs threatened to come out as well.

He lay on a flat stone and shivered.

Anika? Olivia? He couldn't see anyone close by. In fact, he couldn't see anything at all.

He crawled further on and curled up like a baby, shaking uncontrollably.

Cold, so cold.

'Help,' he called out, his voice squeaking like a shrew. 'Help me.'

But with Olivia gone, and Anika gone, who was left?

He wanted to yell for his parents, for Sap, for Mrs Puddy. In this cold, inhospitable, broken place, however, he knew there was only one person who could help him.

Xinder.

'*Xinder!*' he yelled. 'XINDER, HELP ME!'

Through the cracks in his eyes, he swore he could see a figure appearing.

'Xinder,' he cried. 'Save me.'

SAS

The rowing boat continued to float freely, bumping into driftwood and other debris being washed out of the river into the North Sea. Occasionally, 'The Joan of' spun and pitched from side to side, but not with the same force as earlier.

Ryan wondered what they were going to eat for supper, before resisting the temptation to demolish a chocolate bar. He headed to the front of the boat where, through the drizzle, he imagined he could see a spark of light in the distance.

When Sas woke, they tucked into a cold pork pie and shared a few pieces of chocolate. Ryan stated, without compromise, that until they had some idea where they were, they needed to conserve every single morsel. Sas complained bitterly, but Ryan made it quite clear that his position was non-negotiable.

By the time they had given each other a few more brain teasers, and told stories about their childhoods, it was midnight. Ryan reluctantly lay down on the planks while Sas kept look-out.

For a long while she hummed little ditties, her thoughts turning to Danny, Anika and Olivia. *What were they doing now*, she wondered, *had they made it? Had anyone survived?*

Once again, Sas wondered why she'd had the premonition of the storm, in addition to the Delauxs. Ryan's comment about her being a twin with Olivia gave her earlier observations about the baby photograph of her and Olivia a firmer foundation than she'd realised, perhaps.

She told Ryan that she'd already decided to investigate further and that she was going to check with the Registrars at the Town Hall. To her joy, he'd agreed to accompany her.

But wouldn't one of the parents have said something?

As she thought it through, she did think how inseparable and similar they were, in so many ways. *But friends do that*, she thought, *don't they?*

At one o'clock, her jaw trembled of its own accord and her fingers reminded her of popsicles. Staring out into the dark night, spat on by the rain as 'The Joan of' bobbed along, her eyelids drooped shut.

Sometime later, her chattering teeth waking her up, she realised that staying awake was a hopeless task.

She climbed under the canopy and instinctively lay down next to Ryan; nestling up to his warm body, rearranging the dust covers, and inhaling the boyish smell of his clothes.

In no time, the gentle rocking of the boat sent her fast asleep.

17

MRS PUDDY, THURSDAY

When she'd seen Sap slipping out of the door, his hard hat on his head and ropes wrapped around his torso, she'd been topped-up with confidence about seeing her children again. After all, Sap had rescued her, so why couldn't he rescue them?

Energised, Mrs Puddy set about keeping busy. She waddled round as fast as her legs would carry her, placing buckets in every grate and under every chimney flue. She mopped water out of each fireplace, rolling up the hearthrugs and adjacent carpets and then emptying buckets of water down the sink.

Round and round the house she went, from the children's bedroom in the attic, to Sap's room, to the parents' room. Downstairs to the kitchen, sitting room and study, then across the courtyard through sheets of rain to her apartment. She repeated this circuit many times, drenched to the bone.

In Sap's room, she noticed five filthy rectangular rugs that sat on the wet floor, each the size of a hearthrug. She folded them up and took them to the back door, giving them a bit of shake under the wide roof trusses. As she did so, flecks of mud and dust flew in every direction.

How revolting, she thought. *Have they ever been cleaned?*

She'd give the old man a good talking to when he returned. If he returned.

As the rain belted down upon them, a black sludge dribbled out, like slurry. Mrs Puddy decided to bring the rugs in, draping them over a wooden clothes-horse under the old porch.

Covering herself in a blanket, quite overwhelmed with tiredness and worry, she nodded off in the rocking chair in the kitchen, next to the warm metal range beneath the thick oak beams.

Later, she woke suddenly and wondered where she was. She yawned and, for a second, thought she could hear tiny, shrill voices. She got up and looked around. No, there was nothing. Just imaginary sounds, like the noises of children playing in the courtyard.

Mrs Puddy shivered.

She struck a match. The bright light extended its reach into the large kitchen before dying back. She added a handful of kindling and two dry logs to the range, hoping she could keep a hot fire going.

Satisfied, she stood up and stretched, feeling the familiar stabbing pain in her shoulder.

Where were they?

Maybe they were safe at school, playing with their friends.

She'd get Danny a whole new uniform when their parents returned. She'd insist on it. No more patched up clothes for Dan.

Then she thought of Olivia and Anika. Funny, pretty Anika with her wavy hair and red cheeks, her keen eyes and her warm smile.

Why, they all had warm smiles, she thought, as a tear rolled down her cheek.

Where were her little ones? Stuck out in that tempest all alone.

She shivered and pulled her woollen blanket tight as she noticed the flames dying again.

How long would they have? What would happen to her if no one returned?

SAP

Sap spied a body at the far end of the ledge.

At first glance, as he hurried towards it, he could have sworn it was Danny's friend. The one who was always so deeply unpleasant to the girls, the boy Danny liked to go fishing with, Fitz-nasty-something-or-other.

As he approached, Sap wondered whether he should check if Danny's friend was alive. But his attention was taken away by a strange groaning noise coming from the flooding. Sap gazed over the water, squinting, searching for Danny.

When his focus returned to the form in front of him, there lay the curled up, shivering figure of Danny. Sap wondered if he was seeing things.

His heart sunk. Danny's mouth foamed, and his eyes flickered in different directions. His body was battered and torn.

Danny called out a name, 'Xinder, Xinder,' over and over.

Who on earth was this 'Xinder', and why did that name strike a chord deep within him that made his hairs prickle?

Sap searched his memory. That name, Xinder, dredged up a confusing mix of love and anger, hope and despair.

Sap sat on the edge of the pit and studied the children who lay sleeping in the strange soft substance in the base. The sound of their gentle breathing was the sweetest music he had ever heard.

He reflected on his fortune; the curious bed panels and the timely rediscovery of his Resplendix Mix potion.

He whistled.

They had survived the torrential rain, the lightning, the mud-slides and the cold. Sap shook his head. How, in all the apples in the world, were they alive?

He lowered himself into the pit and studied them in more detail. The sheer volume of bruises and cuts on their bodies was remarkable. Anika's legs were black and blue, criss-crossed with cuts. Some of these were deep and sharp, like punctures. Other lacerations were longer, where she had been raked by rocks and thorns. Her finger-nails were black, and on her fingers entire nails had become detached leaving red, raw skin. Her shoes had gone and her feet looked as though they had been 'worked on' by a garden strimmer. Her tracksuit bottoms were tattered, and one of her football socks was attached by threads that flapped against her raw shin.

Sap wondered if he should give her some more Resplendix Mix. But this was powerful stuff; and powerful potions, he suspected, needed careful portioning.

His attention moved to Danny. Like Anika, the boy had been battered, beaten, and pulped to within a millimetre of death. But there was one significant alteration to his appearance; Danny's hair, though softer than before, was hard and spiky. It was like brushed strands of metal, exactly as he'd seen in the panels, when he'd presumed Danny was wearing a hat.

He ran his hand across Danny's head and was amazed to feel that his follicles had fused together, as if his hair had been glued.

He inspected Danny's hands, which bore terrible lacerations and bruises. He suspected a broken finger or two by the way his digits were angled. His head and body was marked with blows, as if he'd been sprayed by a rock gun. Some of his cuts seeped, others had already congealed.

Most extraordinary of all, and perhaps even odder than Danny's hair, were Olivia's hands. The markings on her palms looked symmetrical, as if they had been painted on using a circular template and black paint.

Now that he looked carefully, the flesh inside had been burnt through, as though punctured by a red-hot poker. He could see right through them like small peep holes.

Sap sucked in a deep breath and, shaking his head, wondered how he would ever get them home.

They'd be safe enough where they were for a while. He wouldn't attempt to try now, not while they needed to sleep. In the fresh light of morning, he'd address their wounds and give them another drop, but sleep was the best method of recovery as the potion blazed away inside them.

Looking about, he noticed higher ledges; berths he could pop the children on if the waters continued to rise even further.

He climbed out of the pit and headed towards the cave entrance, grateful for the moonlight reflecting off the water just below the stone ledge in front of him.

He pulled himself up onto a higher rock, stretched his arms out, and lay back, trying to envisage how far the water must extend. Two hundred, three hundred metres, or perhaps even a mile towards the Dales? It could be further.

And everything in its path destroyed in the space of a few hours.

18

SAS, FRIDAY

'The Joan of' felt, to Ryan, as if it were climbing up a small hill before skidding down the other side. And the process repeated the rising and falling sensations. Up and down. Up and down.

For a second, Ryan dreamt he might be at a funfair. He yawned, opened his eyes, and found himself looking into Sas's sleeping face.

What a beautiful way to wake up.

He wondered what his breath must be like. Probably gross. Heck.

Trying not to disturb her, he shuffled to the end of the boat.

He yawned, closed his eyes, and stretched his arms out wide, inhaling a huge lungful of fresh air.

He opened one eye, swiftly followed by the other.

After a few seconds, he whistled.

OK, interesting.

He could hear Sas stirring.

'Good morning, first mate,' he quipped, dipping his head under the canopy.

'Oh! Morning, Ryan,' she said, rubbing the sleep out of her eyes while working out what he meant. 'Still floating, still alive?'

'Yep,' he said. 'How was lookout?'

She cringed. 'Thought you needed company. And bodily warmth is very important,' she said, a flicker of naughtiness in the corner of her lips. 'Everything alright?'

He ducked inside and sat down. 'Fine and dandy-ish.'

'I take it that means you have no idea where we are?'

'Ab-so-lute-ly none. Take a look for yourself.'

Sas crept down to the other end. 'Is there anything for breakfast?' she yawned, 'I'm starving.'

She pushed her head out.

Ryan waited, his expectation of a verbal explosion reasonably high.

'Oh, my!' she said, her eyes wide open.

'Oh, my?' Ryan said. 'Is that it?'

'Yes,' she replied, curtly. 'Oh, my!'

Ryan smiled his biggest smile to date. 'We've drifted miles out to sea with no way of knowing where on earth we are and all you have to say is "Oh, my".'

'Yes,' Sas began. 'Oh, my.' She took a deep breath. 'Right, Ryan. I've never sworn at anything or anyone before in my life. But, I've heard my mum do it quite a bit, and I think that now is possibly the perfect time to finally give it a proper go.'

Ryan looked confused. 'Oh?' he said.

'You see, every time she properly swears, it begins with, "Oh, my".'

Ryan raised his bushy eyebrows. 'Really?' he said.

And with that, Sas slipped out from under the canopy. Standing on the back step she took a deep breath and screamed over the wide expanse of sea at the top of her voice:

'OH my $*%@!' &^%*W$!'

FITZPATRICK

Fitzpatrick groaned in agony. Xinder couldn't die. He was nothing more than a spirit who could leave him at any time. But he'd had a chance to say no, and he blew it.

For a brief moment, he'd been peeled out of their union, only to find himself naked on the rocks, instantly set upon by the rain pummelling his skin in place of the slurry of ash.

In front of him had been Danny.

There he lay, battered and broken, his body marked by cuts and bruises and his head bloodied. His body was motionless, pale, and deathly.

Danny was too far gone to make the choice willingly, however, and Xinder knew it.

He thought of Danny's strange hair and managed a wry smile. A classic bad hair moment only Danny could pull-off. Thinking of hair, he wasn't sure that he had any left. All singed. Burnt up.

Fitzpatrick had given himself freely back to Xinder.

Now, he regretted it. He should have refused. If he had

the chance again, he'd subject himself to the violence of the tempest rather than the hell he was now trapped in.

Xinder burned him badly after he went back.

And now, here he was, living in the darkness of a body with no food, no water, and no sleep. Where burns fried his flesh like hot oil.

It was like being trapped in space, he thought, with no one there to hear his cries.

SAP

Sap slept, but fitfully. His mind raced from Danny's shouts about Xinder, to the Fitz-boy with the matted hair, to the terrible injuries of the children. Then his dream flashed to the strange bed panels, and his old cellar, and the pictures on the cave walls, and scoring goals.

A fizzing, gurgling noise woke him. He cursed.

Had he been asleep for hours?

The moon had slipped behind a high cloud and rain was falling as a light spray. He jumped down, his feet splashing into water.

His heart missed a beat. *Water! Here?*

The children! Apples alive!

He sloshed round to the entrance. A sound gurgled from a strange, billowing steam cloud.

Cautiously, he peered in, his eyes wide.

Inside, the cave floor was dry, and water flowed along a neat, straight channel that he presumed led directly into the pit.

Sap's pulse raced.

On hands and knees, he followed the channel through a thick mist. As he crept closer, the colour of the water changed from blue to pink and he could tell it was gently bubbling. He put his damaged hand in. The water tingled on his cut and sent a warm buzz through him.

He leant over the edge of the pit, his heart thumping. Were they alive?

He pulled his hand out and gasped. The wound was healing in front of his eyes.

Then he heard a voice. Or was it laughter?

'Sap, what are you doing?' Anika said, her face appearing in front of him briefly before sinking back into the steam.

Sap reeled.

Anika giggled. 'Hey, why don't you get in?'

Sap felt himself choking up. 'Goodness me. Anika!' he cried. 'Is that you? Is that really you? I can't see you.'

'Yeah, it's me alright. Come on in. It's gorgeous and warm and fantastic,' she replied. 'And it smells delicious, like lavender and pine needles and lemons.'

'Are you alright in there?'

'Yes! We're absolutely fine,' she said. 'Come on in – see for yourself.'

Sap was confused. 'Are ALL of you fine, I mean Olivia and Danny?'

Sap heard a splashing noise. Danny's head popped out. 'Yeah. Fine,' he said.

Sap reeled. 'Apples almighty! It IS you.'

Danny smiled. 'Well, it's good to see you too. How long have you been here?'

'Your head?!' Sap exclaimed.

'Yeah, I know. I think it was a lightning bolt.' He patted his hard hair before drifting back into the steamy waters.

Sap didn't know what to think. Perhaps he was dreaming. 'Olivia?'

'Uh-huh,' she responded lazily.

Sap's heart leapt for joy. It was impossible, a miracle. He had to see it to believe it. 'Right then, you lot, I'm coming in.'

He could hear them laughing.

'There's plenty of room,' Anika said. 'Though watch yourself, Danny might puncture you with his hairdo.'

Sap removed his coat, socks, and boots, and dipped his foot in the water. Then, ever so slowly, he lowered himself into the pool.

The water, like a winning combination of champagne and cream, bubbled up and sparkled around him. He closed his eyes and let himself drift under. Almost immediately, he felt the bubbles caress his aches and pains, targeting each one like mini lasers.

When he resurfaced and opened his eyes, the children were beaming at him.

Sap laughed out loud. 'You did it, you blooming made it! HOW in apples' name...? And, are you better, truly recovered?'

The twins floated over and hugged him.

Sap inspected Danny, looking for the cuts and bruises on his head, hands, and ankles. He did the same with Anika, but the procedure was quick and easy as their skin was smooth and clear, as though the battle through the storm had never happened.

'I can't believe it. I simply can't believe it,' Sap repeated. 'I thought you were, you know, not alive, you twins! Battered to bits you were, and now look at you...'

Sap listened attentively to their stories, noting that each one had survived an almost direct strike from a lightning bolt.

But what was it about the awkwardness in Danny's face, that same expression he'd seen when he'd handed him the strange overcoat? And who was this curious "Xinder" that Danny had called out for?

He remembered the apples and rummaged in his coat pocket. 'You lot must be starving.'

As one they nodded back.

'I took the liberty of bringing you something special. Afterwards, it'd be a good idea to grab some rest. After all, we've still got to find a way out of here.'

'A chocolate brownie,' Danny began, 'with a spoonful of ice cream!'

'Or a plate full of Peking duck pancakes with plum sauce, cucumber, and spring onions,' Anika said.

'Or a huge slice of banoffee pie, with thick cream,' Olivia added, licking her lips.

Sap pulled out the apples.

'Now, before you start complaining, these are my special ones, so make sure you eat the whole thing, understand? Pips and all. They'll fill you right up. Trust me. Don't know how, but they will.'

He tossed an apple at each one, and ravenously the children bit in. They were rewarded as the taste of golden syrup, honey, apple pie, and sweet raspberries flooded their mouths.

The children pulled themselves out of the pit. Their bodies, now devoid of cuts and bruises, dried in the warm air. Using the multicoloured glow of the water, they found four protruding shelves, like stone benches, set into the walls off the floor. It was as though these ledges were individually crafted for each of them.

Anika climbed into the one nearest her and wearily tested it, scrunching her hand in the soft velvety texture, before she lay down.

'This is lovely,' she purred as she sank into it. Before long, little snores filled the void above her.

The others followed, and they too experienced the extraordinary sensation of the warm silky powder, softer than feathers, moulding perfectly around their bodies.

From his bunk higher up on the cave wall, Danny peered through bleary eyes out into the night sky of Yorkshire. Rippling, tiny waves caught the light that flickered over the moving floodwater.

A moonbeam shone into the cave, accentuating what looked like pictures etched onto the walls. He smiled. Strange how there was so much beauty and yet so much destruction in the world.

The thought that someone had been here a long time ago gave him a sense of comfort. They weren't all alone.

He wondered about Fitzpatrick and the ghost. His memory was just a blur, an outline, but he still couldn't work out whether Fitzy had done it to save him, or to deliberately take his place?

Anyway, they'd passed this first test Xinder had told them about. *They didn't have a chance, wasn't that what he said?* His lips turned up at the thought. Then he sighed. His dreams had been right all along. Even Sas had known, and had tried to tell them. *But tell them what, exactly? Was that what she had been yelling on the pitch when he ran over?*

Something to do about finding clues? He couldn't recall. *And something about this Ancient Lady of his dreams that he'd murdered over and over again?* Xinder had to be right about that. *Saving her was the only way ahead, surely?*

Olivia, he thought as he breathed in deeply, *must have known too.* Her frantic efforts to persuade Wynn-Garry to abandon the game now looked like sage advice. What would Wynn-Garry make of it now, if he was still alive?

And poor Mrs Puddy, sitting at home worrying. He could imagine her pacing around, mumbling to herself.

What of all their friends? Had they made it? Would there be anyone left?

He touched his hard hair and wondered if they'd been blessed. He didn't think the others would have been so fortunate, unless they'd run into the tower. Oh well. They'd find out in the morning after they'd found a way out of the cave and climbed their way up through the wreckage and back home.

He yawned and stretched his arms out. And what of that strange creature he'd seen over Anika? Was it a part of this adventure?

His eyes closed.

So long as he didn't get any more nightmares… and what if he really did have the courage of a horse and the strength of a lion…?

A mist of heavy tiredness crept over every part of him.

He could think no more.

Within moments, the Sacrum and Sap were all sound asleep.

To be continued...

<<<<>>>>

REVIEW

Please go and review Xinder Rises right now while it's fresh. Go on. Off you go! I don't mind where!

Your review will spur me on to completing the series.

Thank you for your support.

ACKNOWLEDGMENTS

Thanks to Rebecca Jones for her detailed observations and patience with her edits.

For the cover, from Stuart Bache.

And for everything else:
Sara, Wiz, Cathy, Eddie, Charlie, Robert, Phil,

Most of all, my amazing family - thank you!

ABOUT THE AUTHOR

Restless after schooling, JJ traveled and experienced plenty of adventures. He has been shot at, scaled Pyramids, climbed mountains, been through earthquakes, police detained and even swum with beavers.

JJ specialised in getting lost quite a bit, and has had a series of extraordinary adventures, as well as experiencing hypothermia, dysentery, muggings, altitude sickness, thefts, a broken neck, snapped achilles, desert breakdowns, etc.

He's also had a hatful of careers. From teaching to journalism, gardener to tour guide.

Inadvertently these experiences have set JJ up for a big writing journey. And it's about to get a whole lot bigger.

For More Info:
jjhawken@jericopress.com

9 781910 134191